INTERVENTION

WRAK-ASHWEA: THE AGE OF LIGHT BOOK
THREE

LEIGH ROBERTS

DRAGON WINGS PRESS

Editing by Joy Sephton http://justemagine.biz
Cover design by Cherie Fox http://cheriefox.com

ISBN: 978-1-951528-42-3 (ebook)
ISBN: 978-1-951528-43-0 (paperback)

CONTENTS

Chapter 1   1
Chapter 2   21
Chapter 3   35
Chapter 4   55
Chapter 5   65
Chapter 6   81
Chapter 7   123
Chapter 8   147
Chapter 9   159
Chapter 10   183
Chapter 11   199
Chapter 12   233
Chapter 13   257
Chapter 14   275
Chapter 15   283
Chapter 16   297
Chapter 17   335
Chapter 18   351
Chapter 19   365
Chapter 20   375
Epilogue   383

Interviews   385
Please Read   393
Acknowledgments   397

Dedication

To those wise enough to never underestimate the power of What If?

CHAPTER 1

Standing in front of her, in Etera's morning light, stood An'Kru. Not in the Corridor. Not in the Dream World. Here, in front of her. Flesh and blood. And yet so much more.

His powerful frame towered over her. He was the size of a Sassen, though formed like the People. Adia stared at his chest and forearms and his torso, all covered in the same thick silver-white coat as Pan's, a coat far thicker than that of the other Akassa. His eyes were the Guardians' steel grey, and a soft breeze lifted his flowing silver-white hair.

The powerful aura surrounding him nearly overwhelmed her. She stared at him in wonder, momentarily speechless.

"Hello, Mother," An'Kru said.

"How can this be? You left only recently with Pan —as a young offspring."

"What you remember is a ripple on what you

perceive as the moving river of time, a possibility based on the actions of others. Like all the Great Spirit's creations, I have free will, so I have returned here, at this point in time, to set things right."

"So I am not mistaken; this did happen before? I was here, and the blue bird did visit me?" Adia struggled to try to remember what events had or had not happened at the point when the blue bird appeared. Her hand went to her forehead. "So you are telling me you have the ability to turn back time and change what has happened?"

"Yes, Mother. The prayers of the brokenhearted at Kthama and at Zuenerth and the blood of the innocent crying out from where they fell did not go unnoticed. And just as each Akassa, Sassen, Brother, and other sentient beings have free will, so do I."

"But how? Pan has just taken you to Lulnomia. How can you be back here, now, full-grown? You appeared to me before as an adult, but that was in the Corridor. This is not the Corridor. And a short while ago, I was in the Great Chamber, yet now I am back here reliving something that happened before? I am so confused."

"For me, over twenty years have passed. Over those twenty-some years, I became an adult and obtained my full powers, which I have now used to come back to this point in your time to prevent the atrocities that, without my intervention, will be committed from here forward."

"So—are you then also an offspring at Lulnomia being raised by Pan?" Adia remembered again that Pan had said An'Kru was an Akassa Guardian but also *something more.*

"Yes, my younger self is at Lulnomia, the youngster you said goodbye to and who left his mother just a few short months ago."

As Adia thought about what An'Kru was saying, the tragedy of recent events suddenly came crashing back over her.

"Yes, An'Kru, terrible things have happened. I am struggling so, trying to make peace with it, trying to discover how what has taken place is the best possible outcome as the Order of Functions promises."

"My dear Mother," An'Kru said gently. "The best possible outcome does not necessarily mean the most pleasant. Evil people have free will, just as the good do. And they use their free will to inflict harm, or worse, on others. The Great Spirit will not violate anyone's free will. But the Order of Functions will work to provide a potentially positive outcome out of any tragedy, no matter how devastating, sometimes to open our eyes to something we were unwilling to see. Or to awaken or stir our need for connection with the Great Spirit.

"You have heard it said that the Great Spirit wishes none to perish, which is interpreted as a reference to the death of our physical bodies. Yet, to perish encompasses the utter isolation of the lost souls who do not return from their ways of error and who are on the path to krell. As for the events at Zuenerth, I cannot allow so many to suffer and die at the hands of one so evil. And that is why I am here. I have come to alter the path that is causing you and many others so much pain. A path I cannot allow to come to pass."

An'Kru continued, "At this moment, Khon'Tor, Moart'Tor, and Paldar'Krah have not yet made it to the Mothoc rebel camp of Zuenerth but are close. I will go to them and intervene so there is a different outcome than the one you have just lived through. The blue bird was sent to you as a marker for this moment, so you would remember it. Rest assured that what you know as having happened will not take place. I have come to prevent it. But you alone are permitted to remember what did take place, what you all experienced, so you can help others get through times when it seems the Great Spirit has not heard their cries.

"Many times, harmful events are prevented from happening. Most never know that what was about to happen was thwarted. Altered. Sometimes they are left with a faint echo in the form of a peculiar feeling of familiarity. A quickly fading echo such as you have just experienced, a sense they have done this before or been in that place before. It is a fleeting feeling of *this has happened in the past*, and their attention moves on to something else."

"I hear your words, but I still feel it is my fault, An'Kru." Adia hung her head. "If I had never asked Pan not to leave your side, she could have stopped it from happening."

"And why did you ask her never to leave my side?"

"Because I was afraid. I know, I know. I have seen such miraculous things. And yet," she almost sobbed, "despite everything I have been through, I was afraid."

"Faith is a winding journey through the peaks and valleys of our lives. There are times when our faith is strong and other times when it waivers. When we achieve a level of faith, it is tested again. That is the only way for it to grow. A mother's love is the strongest love; it carries an essence quite similar at its core to what the Great Spirit feels for us. For me to be taken from your care—as young and helpless as I was and to a place beyond your reach—was much to ask of a mother who loves her offspring as you do. You fear the future loss of your loved ones."

"I do, I do. It is my greatest fear. Oh, why did Pan not go to help them in spite of the promise I extracted from her? I would have understood. The needs of the community come before the needs of the individual."

"She gave her word, and if a Guardian's word

cannot be trusted, then what can? But she was also not aware of what was going on. She was not meant to. Each has their own path, their own lessons, and it was Moart'Tor's duty to try to reach his parents and the other rebels. Just as it was also Khon'Tor's and as it was Paldar'Krah's to try to rescue his beloved, Eitel. No, the cause of so many deaths was the evil that lives in others. They and they alone are responsible for the devastation they wrought."

"What happens now?" Adia's voice wavered. Then her gaze was drawn to motion in the thick bushes behind An'Kru. Out stepped her son, Nootau.

"Nootau!" she gasped. Whereas she had been overwhelmed by An'Kru's appearance, she ran immediately to her eldest son and hugged him. "How can this be? Oh, I am so happy to see you as well."

Nootau hugged her back. "So many years have passed, but I am home."

"I am not going to try to grasp right now how that is possible," Adia said, turning first to An'Kru, then back to Nootau. "I am only going to accept that it is."

She stepped forward and took An'Kru's hand. In her memories, Iella had become seeded but lost the offspring because of her trauma over the slaughter at Zuenerth. Adia tried to think back to when she was standing in this same spot that identical time months before. Had Iella already said she was seeded? Yes. Yes, she had. Adia wanted to ask An'Kru if the offspring would be alright. She almost did but then realized Iella should be the one to share her news with Nootau.

"So you are staying now?" She looked at one and then the other. "You will not return to—the future? Your past? Oh, I am so confused."

"It is a difficult concept to understand. In Etera's realm, you think of time as a river. As if you are standing on the banks of the Great River and time is moving past as the waters flow by. Each moment followed by the next, all moving in front of you, passing from the present to the past, like the waters downstream. Upstream is the future. It has not yet arrived, but it is there waiting to float past, and when it gets to you, then it will be the present moment. Now try to imagine a lake with no boundaries, extending in all directions."

Adia smiled, "I cannot. I have never seen such a thing."

"I know. But pretend you can. A lake with no edges, only a still surface. Every point on the surface of that lake exists at the same time. Nothing is passing by as the Great River does. Nothing is moving. If you were big enough, you could touch any part of the surface of the lake because every place on the surface of the lake exists at the same time. That is the true essence of existence. Everything that has ever happened and will ever happen exists at the same time. I simply located the place in time—the part of the lake—I wished to enter, and we stepped into it. That is how we are here with you now."

"But will you return to your future, eventually?"

An'Kru answered, "No. We are here now. Our lives will move forward from this point onward. Even though this is the past to you, it is our present. Nootau is home, as he said. He and Iella will resume their life together."

"Does Pan know you are here, yet also still at Lulnomia?"

"Pan does not know, as she is living in your time-line just as you are," An'Kru explained. "According to what she currently knows, my return to you will not happen for over twenty years. She is still teaching us at Lulnomia. Remember, it has only been a few months since we left the High Rocks with her,"

"It will take me a while to understand this. Or maybe I cannot. Maybe I must surrender and simply accept it," she said. "What happens now, though?"

"Nootau and Iella will reunite. I will speak with Father and his Circle of Counsel, as well as Haan and his. At the right moment, Nootau and I will join Khon'Tor, Paldar'Krah, and Moart'Tor at Zuenerth."

Nootau's eyes widened. "Me? I will be going with you?"

"Yes, brother. Part of your destiny waits for you there."

Adia, An'Kru, and Nootau walked up the path to Kthama. Adia did not know what to do or say. She realized the news of An'Kru and Nootau would spread like wildfire through the community of the High Rocks. She hoped Acaraho would be in the Great Entrance so he would find out first.

She was surprised to discover just that.

Acaraho turned as they walked in and froze. He stared at the three figures for a moment. "Wha—at? How can this be? Nootau, and is that you, An'Kru? You are grown. And Nootau, you are older. My sons, what on Etera is happening?"

Nootau stepped forward and embraced his father. "I have missed you so. Yes, it is really us. We have come back to prevent a travesty. An'Kru can explain it better."

Acaraho released Nootau and stepped over to An'Kru. He felt the energy radiating off his son as they embraced.

"Father, it is good to see you again. The last time we saw each other, I was still just your very young offspring."

Acaraho silently looked An'Kru up and down, waiting for him to continue.

"I have come to stop the events that take place from this moment on."

"Stop them? Stop what? What is going to happen that you need to stop?" Acaraho asked.

An'Kru smiled. "Events that, if allowed to take place, will cause unbearable heartache and loss. Events perpetuated by evil. You must trust me, Father. It is best to explain when all those who need to hear are assembled."

"Before we do that," Nootau interrupted, "I need to find Iella."

"I would like to meet with both the High Rocks and Kht'shWea's Circles of Counsel before you walk through Kthama, Nootau. They must first understand what is going on before they can deal with all the questions your reappearance will create."

"I do not want her to find out in a meeting that I am home, though."

"I know," An'Kru answered. Then he turned to Acaraho. "Father, when both Circles of Counsel are assembled, Nootau and I will join you."

In the next moment, Nootau was standing just outside the Healer's Quarters.

Iella was at the worktable with Nadiwani and Urilla Wuti when Nootau walked in. When she saw him, she dropped the gourd she was holding, and it clattered to the ground, bouncing across the rock floor but not breaking.

She stared at him. 'Is it really you? You are back already?" She hurried across the room to him.

Nootau gently took her face in his hands, "Yes, it is. Yes, I am home, and for good."

Iella searched his face and frowned. "You— You look older."

"That is because I am. I have lived at Lulnomia for twenty years."

"How can that be? You left just a few months ago!" She ran her palm down the side of his face, brushed his lips with her thumb, and stared into his eyes.

"An'Kru has brought us both back to this moment. He will explain when we have the Circles of Counsel of both my father and Haan assembled."

"An'Kru?" she exclaimed.

"An'Kru brought me here with him. He is also older. He is now a grown male with amazing power."

"Where is he?" Urilla Wuti asked.

"He is with my parents." Then Nootau turned to his mate, "You look even more beautiful than I remember."

She clasped both his hands up in hers. "My love, I am seeded," she exclaimed, no longer able to hold it in. "I suspected I was at the time you were leaving but did not know for sure. We are going to have our offspring!"

"What wonderful news. And now, instead of my

returning in the far-off future to find him or her grown, we will raise our offspring together."

Radiant, Iella looked over at Urilla Wuti and Nadiwani, who were watching quietly.

"Truly, we live in an age of miracles," Urilla Wuti said.

While they were waiting for the two Circles of Counsel to be assembled, Adia was left alone with her son.

"You were just seven a few months ago. Now you are grown. I must get to know you as an adult now," Adia said.

"I know it is difficult, Mother. But I am the same son you raised and loved for the first critical years of my life."

"What was it like being raised at Lulnomia?" She looked up into his steel grey eyes. The eyes of her son.

"Lulnomia is much bigger than Kthama but otherwise very similar. The Mothoc, Pan's people, are huge. I had to get used to being the smallest one there, and it helped to have Nootau with me. There were many who were especially kind to us. Pan's mate, Rohm'Mok, took us both under his wing. In time, both Nootau and I adjusted. Nootau found a place there telling the other Mothoc about the

Akassa and Sassen they left behind and answering an unending string of questions about what life is like for them in their various communities now. The Ancients did not want to leave either the Sassen or us. It deeply grieved them to do so. But they did it so we might become masters of our own fate instead of leaning on them for everything. They never forgot us or the Sassen, so they deeply appreciated Nootau's stories of what life is like for everyone now."

"Iella is seeded," Adia shared. "I am sure she will tell Nootau at the earliest moment."

"I am very happy for them both. Nootau will make a great father. After all, he had the best—and the best mother!"

"I am so grateful. You are here now. Despite whatever is going on, I am thrilled that you are back. I thought I would be waiting for a long time before seeing you again, and if you can keep that future from happening, I am even more grateful."

"Yes, and to help them understand that whenever possible, the Order of Functions spares us suffering. Ultimately the goal is for the rebels to awaken from their misconceptions and distortions so they may fulfill their purpose on Etera and return to the path home. I will do my best to make sense of it for everyone." His eyes were filled with love.

"I have a question," Adia said. "Did you send the blue bird that landed in the tree next to me? The blue bird that made this moment stick in my memory."

"It was not I who sent the blue bird, Mother, but someone else who also loves you very much."

The Circles of Counsel were called.

Many of Kthama's members saw Haan's Sassen walking through the passageways of the High Rocks. It was an impressive sight, and it did not take long for word to spread that the two Circles of Counsel were meeting.

From the High Rocks were Acaraho, Adia, High Protector Awan, Mapiya as head female, Nadiwani, and First Guard Thetis. Haan's Circle of Counsel consisted of his mate Haaka, who was due to deliver soon, High Protector Qirrik, Healer Artadel, and Sastak, representing the females. Overseer Urilla Wuti made it twelve in all.

Once everyone was seated comfortably in the meeting room Acaraho had selected, An'Kru and Nootau walked in with Iella in tow. The powerful, energetic wave emanating from An'Kru washed over them all. In reverence of the moment, some touched their foreheads, while others placed their palms on their hearts. Many exchanged glances, overwhelmed by what they were feeling. After only a few months, An'Kru and Nootau were standing in front of them.

"Greetings," An'Kru said. "I know you are filled with questions, and I will do my best to explain. Nootau and I have returned to you here, at this point in time, to stop terrible and unjust events that will take place without our intervention. If allowed to unfold as they could, irreparable damage will be done to the future of Etera."

"You are wondering how it is possible for me to return from what would be your future. And to bring Nootau with me, both of us grown males. But I have the power to achieve that, as evidenced by our standing here. Please, each of you, try to suspend your mind's need to understand. In the many years that followed my going to Lulnomia with the Guardian Pan, my abilities grew under the tutelage of her and another Guardian, Wrollonan'Tor."

"Wrollonan'Tor? How can this be?" Haan was incredulous. "Wrollonan'Tor was Guardian before Moc'Tor. It was upon his death that Moc'Tor assumed Guardianship of Etera."

An'Kru explained. "The Mothoc people believed there could only be one Guardian of Etera for any length of time. So, when Wrollonan'Tor no longer appeared to them, the Mothoc assumed he had died. But he did not die. He only left so Moc'Tor could take his place as Guardian."

Those in attendance glanced at each other, sharing in their confusion.

An'Kru continued, "In the events which are about

to take place, there will be great losses. Unrecoverable losses. But there is more than what is about to take place at Zuenerth. In the years during which Nootau and I have been at Lulnomia with the Guardian Pan, the Waschini devastated the Brothers' communities. In carrying out their plan to remove the Brothers from their land and relocate them to other, less desirable areas, they decimated the Brothers' population.

"When I would ordinarily have returned to fulfill my destiny, there would no longer be enough of them to turn the Waschini from their path of destruction. So, for several reasons, I am here now."

Nadiwani pulled her courage together, swallowed, and asked, "But, please, An'Kru, everyone involved has free will. Whatever took place—or is about to take place, no matter how devastating you say it will be—is that not a result of their free will? Have you then been sent by the Great Spirit to override their free will?"

"The Great Spirit will never violate anyone's free will, Nadiwani. It was a gift freely given to each of us. But I also have free will. I have just as much right as anyone else to use my free will and abilities to affect the events that are waiting to unfold. And since I have abilities others do not, such as to return here to you from what you consider your future, I am able to intervene with my free will to prevent terrible wrongs from being committed."

An'Kru watched them looking one at another and realized more explanation was necessary.

"The laws of this realm are set in place by the Great Spirit and never violated. The Order of Functions is always in action, providing the best possible outcome for all involved. But by best, I do not mean necessarily the most enjoyable or pleasant. Our purpose in this lifetime is to come into a closer relationship with the Great Spirit. And there are many steps along the path toward reunion with the One-Who-Is-Three. Unfortunately, there are those in Etera for whom it is only through suffering that their hearts become open to a different way."

Sastak, head of the female Sassen, asked hesitantly, "So the Great Spirit causes suffering to get us to turn to him?"

"A brave question, Sastak. But the answer is no. The Great Spirit does not cause suffering. It is people's alienation from him and their resultant acts that cause suffering. But it is a self-correcting cycle. For most, when someone's suffering becomes unbearable, the shell of what they are sure they believe is fractured. The very mistaken set of beliefs causing their suffering is finally broken open enough for other possibilities to enter. Then they become teachable. But for many, it takes a tremendous amount of suffering for them to let go of their self-defeating beliefs, and it is only when their lives become unbearable that they become willing to examine themselves and discover their own hand, even if it be small, in their unhappiness."

"Him? He?" Nadiwani asked.

"It is simply a way to refer to the Great Spirit. You may use *she* if you prefer."

"The Healers pray to the Great Mother, the receptive, creative, feminine aspect—*she*. I think I understand."

Silence now filled the room as they took in all that An'Kru had explained.

An'Kru turned to the Overseer. "Urilla Wuti, when I have accomplished the tasks that lie immediately ahead of me, I will ask you to call together the Brotherhood. The rest of what I need to say must be heard by as many as possible."

Adia said, "Are you going to the rebel camp? Where Khon'Tor, Moart'Tor, and Paldar'Krah are headed?"

"Yes. Though there is something I must do first."

It was late evening, and the family fires were burning brightly in the dark spring night. Chief Is'Taqa was sitting with his family, enjoying a quiet moment at day's end.

In the midst of the darkness, in the center of their village, a light began to glow. One by one, each person's attention was drawn to the growing manifestation until finally, the burly figure of An'Kru stood among them.

Chief Is'Taqa rose to greet him.

"Chief Is'Taqa, it is me, An'Kru. Son of Acaraho, Adik'Tar of the High Rocks, and of the Healer, Adia."

No one present, including the Chief, questioned that he was who he said he was. There was no need to question one who radiated such power.

"How can we help you, An'Kru?" the Chief asked.

"I have need of your help, Chief Is'Taqa, and I can promise no harm will come to you because of it. I need you to go with me to the rebel Mothoc camp, the one to which Khon'Tor, the Mothoc, Moart'Tor, and the Sassen, Paldar'Krah, are approaching."

Then An'Kru turned to speak to Chief Is'Taqa's people.

"Have no fear. I come to do no harm. Some of you know me only as a youngster who recently left with the Guardian Pan for the Mothoc community of Lulnomia. Yet here I stand, a grown male. Trust that in time all will be explained. Until then, rest in the love and guidance of the Great Spirit and prepare yourselves for the service to him that will be asked of you."

CHAPTER 2

Eitel dreaded the rebel Leader's visits. They were becoming more and more frequent. Each day Kaisak came, he escalated his intentions toward her. What had started out as visits to deliver gifts were now visits to deliver gifts, followed by physical advances forced on her. He would stand behind her and press himself too close, whispering into her ear, or, if he caught her on her sleeping mat, would lie behind her, rubbing himself between her legs. So far, he had not penetrated her, saying he enjoyed teasing himself leading up to the moment. But she knew it was not long before he would finish what he intended.

While Iria, the Healer and Dak'Tor's mate, visited her as much as she could, Eitel spent most of her days either sleeping, daydreaming, or praying. When nightfall came, her stomach would start twisting. Was this a night on which Kaisak would arrive?

She wondered if anyone knew. Until after the community had turned in, either Gard or one of Kaisak's other males was always stationed outside the entrance to where she was being kept. And Kaisak would come so late that no one would still be out there. So, each night, it was hard to sleep as she struggled not to think about it.

One morning, Eitel was delighted to see a beautiful little blue bird at the tiny opening in the outside wall of her quarters—her makeshift window. She was still lying on her sleeping mat and wanted to sit up to see more clearly but was afraid it would fly away. Backlit by the rising sun, it turned its little head left and right, and then she made out something dropping from its beak to the sill before the bird flew away. She threw back the sleeping cover and went to look. A deep red jasper.

Eitel gasped. Was this a sign from her beloved? Or the Great Spirit? Was it intended to shore up her faith?

She picked it up, turning it carefully over and over in her hand. It was shaped a bit like a blade. Was this a message that help was on its way? After she had admired it for a moment, fearing someone might come by even this early, she pawed out a little cavity in the floor right beneath the head of her sleeping mat and tucked it safely into the hole. Then she replaced her sleeping mat. What a treasure and what a gift.

"Thank you, Great Spirit, for the message of hope. Thank you for not forgetting about me."

It wasn't long afterward that she heard a lot of commotion. Voices were raised, but she could barely make them out. The first was Kaisak's mate, Visha. She thought she heard the name of Visha's lost son, Moart'Tor.

Was it possible Moart'Tor had come to rescue her? Eitel could feel her heart beating against her chest.

The voices came closer and became clearer.

"You are home!" Visha called out, her voice ringing with excitement.

Eitel listened closely as she identified Mothoc, Akassa, and Sassen voices. She recognized Moart'-Tor's voice, and she heard him introduce his companions. Her beloved, Paldar'Krah, had come to save her. And Khon'Tor, one of the Akassa Leaders. However, she had to fight down anxiety; their coming to Zuenerth had put them in grave danger. To quell her rising fear, she dug up the red jasper and clutched it to her chest.

Eitel heard her beloved ask about her, and she wanted to rush out and run to them. But she decided to wait and listen a while longer. She knew if she did as she wanted and if she was not stopped on her way, all the other conversations would come to an abrupt end before she could learn what was going on.

A moment later, however, Visha entered and

grabbed Eitel by the hand. "Come on, hurry! Your beloved has come to rescue you. I know Kaisak will not allow it and most surely will kill him and those with him, but you have a right at least to see him before he dies."

They ran out, hand in hand. Visha pushed through the crowd that had gathered and, once they were clear of the crush of long-haired bodies who had gathered to watch the spectacle, let go of Eitel's hand.

"Paldar'Krah!" Eitel called out and ran to him. She jumped into his embrace, wrapping her arms around his neck.

"Saraste'," he cried out. "Oh, thank the Great Spirit, you are alive."

Kaisak motioned, and his guards surrounded the four of them. He glared at Visha, his eyes narrow slits. Then he looked back at Eitel and Paldar'Krah and sneered, "Enjoy your reunion. It will be brief."

Just then, Dak'Tor and several of his followers emerged from the crowd. He introduced himself. "I am also the brother of the Guardian Pan."

"We know her well," Khon'Tor said. "I am a direct descendant of your father, Moc'Tor. It is recorded on the Wall of Records housed deep within what was known as Kthama Minor."

Eitel could not tell how many, but a large number of voices rose, apparently partly in disbelief and partly in astonishment at hearing that the Great Spirit had entrusted such treasures and ancient secrets to the Akassa and the Sassen.

Dak'Tor looked surprised. "Kthama Minor has been opened?"

"Many years ago," Khon'Tor answered. "It is a long story."

"Who lives there now?" Dak'Tor asked.

Paldar'Krah answered. "We Sassen live at Kthama Minor, which is now known as Kht'shWea."

"New beginning," Dak'Tor said, translating the name. "And you?" He turned back to Khon'Tor.

"The Akassa still live at Kthama, which was Kthama Major. We have a peaceful co-existence. There is also a brotherhood that includes those you knew as the Others. We live in service to the Great Spirit, and we offer you a chance to join us."

"It is blasphemy!" Kaisak said, pointing to Khon'Tor and turning to address the crowd. "It is blasphemy for an abomination to speak of service to the Great Spirit."

Just then, Eitel saw Iria step forward and try to intervene, asking Kaisak at least to hear the visitors out.

The Leader scowled and said to Khon'Tor, "Since you are answering questions, how many of you are there living at Kthama and this Kht'shWea?"

"No doubt you know by now that your kind no

longer live among us. So the answer to your question is, not enough to thwart an attack should you move against us," Khon'Tor answered.

Many of the Mothoc gasped.

"You admit we could destroy you?" Kaisak laughed.

"It seems obvious looking at your numbers here. I am not saying we would not defend ourselves or that there would not be casualties on your side, but ultimately, you would prevail."

"So you come here begging for mercy?" the rebel Leader scoffed, leaning closer to Khon'Tor.

Eitel knew the Mothoc were large, but seeing how much larger they were than the Akassa made her stomach twist.

"We come here, as I said, in service to the Great Spirit."

"And what service is that?" Kaisak challenged him.

Eitel listened as Khon'Tor gave an impassioned invitation for Kaisak and the people of Zuenerth to join the Brotherhood. That there was no need for them to be at odds with each other.

He explained the risk to Etera if the division between them continued. How Etera needed every drop of Mothoc, Sassen, and Akassa blood.

It did not surprise Eitel that Kaisak rejected outright everything Khon'Tor said. Her heart was pounding more rapidly. *They are all going to die.* She had no doubt that Kaisak would slaughter them all. She clung even tighter to her beloved.

"Father," Moart'Tor spoke up. "I have lived among the Sassen. They are no different than us. They love their families. They worship the Great Spirit as we do. They wish us no ill; they want only to live in peace."

Eitel cringed as Kaisak shouted back, "It is clear that living with them has poisoned your mind. You come here defending them? You are a traitor to your own kind!"

Just then, Visha flew at Kaisak, her arms flailing. "How dare you call our son a traitor! He has come back to us, and we should be rejoicing, not attacking him."

Eitel saw Dak'Tor motion at a large group standing not far from him. The males there stepped forward, and the females started leaving with the offling.

Khon'Tor then appealed to Kaisak's responsibilities as Leader, saying surely he wanted what was best for his community? Again explaining how the Sassen and Akassa were no different from them.

Kaisak stepped through the circle of guards surrounding the four and lowered his face to Khon'-Tor's. "Do not preach to me of my own history! What do you know of it?" he bellowed.

Eitel closed her eyes and buried her head in Paldar'Krah's chest. She prayed in silence for help.

Kaisak raised his voice even louder, "Moc'Tor and Straf'Tor betrayed the Others, the very ones who were ours to protect."

Paldar'Krah responded. "You are mistaken. Khon'Tor knows much of our past and yours. The entire history of Wrak-Wavara is recorded on the Wall of Records, buried deep within Kht'shWea. Not far from the chamber entombing the bodies of Moc'-Tor, Straf'Tor, and E'ranale."

Kaisak left the circle of guards and shouted at the crowd. "Enough. Do not listen to their lies!"

Eitel could see Dak'Tor was studying the Akassa closely. From the coloring, it seemed Khon'Tor must be his descendant, and she wondered if that meant anything to Dak'Tor.

Moart'Tor raised his hand into the air and pleaded for the crowd's attention. "Listen to Khon'-Tor. Nothing created by the Great Spirit can be an abomination. Abomination comes from the evil we harbor in our hearts and the actions we take. The evil we do is the abomination. If you could know them as I do, you would understand there is no reason for the Great Spirit to want the Akassa destroyed. If you believe, as my father says, that Moc'Tor and Straf'Tor betrayed their wards, the Others, then you would be doing the same thing by harming the Sassen and the Akassa—because the

Others' blood flows in their veins. They have come here offering peace. To offer you the same brother-hood they share among themselves and with the Others. Yet my father says they all deserve to die?"

Kaisak motioned to his guards, who raised their spears and pointed them at the four standing together. "I have heard enough of their lies. I will hear no more talk of how the Akassa and Sassen are just like us. But all this talk *has* opened my eyes further. It is not enough to cleanse Etera of the Akassa and the Sassen; the Others must be killed too. That way, there will never be the temptation to breed with them again."

"Father!" Morvar'Nul now spoke out. "Do not say that. I have seen the Others. Both my brother and I have. They are not a threat. We should be protecting them, watching over them. You go too far!"

"Even you turn against me, even though you are my son?"

The rebel Leader next turned to Moart'Tor. "As for you, it is time to demonstrate how I treat traitors. You will be executed alongside the Akassa and Sassen abominations you have brought here."

"You cannot!" Visha grabbed her mate's shoulders and forced him to look at her. "You would murder our son? The one who, from the time you started pursuing me, you promised to love as your own. How can you say you will have him killed?"

"Well, he is not my son, now is he?"

It was as if Kaisak had physically struck Visha. She stumbled backward, and her sons Morvar'Nul and Nofire'Nul caught her before she could fall.

Eitel saw a terrible viciousness rise in Kaisak's eyes. Viciousness she had feared all along was possible.

Visha's youngest son Vollen'Nul came running over to stand next to his mother.

Dak'Tor pointed at Kaisak. "I will not stand by and let you slaughter innocent people because of your own hatred and prejudice." Then he pointed to the captives. "Look at them. The Akassa and Sassen. How different are they really? The Sassen look much like smaller versions of us. The Akassa are larger and darker versions of the Others—the very ones we were sworn to protect, as *my* son Moart'Tor said!"

By now, nearly all the females and offling had cleared the common area. Eitel saw Dak'Tor looking around and thought he had also noticed.

"People of Zuenerth," Dak'Tor continued. "How long have I lived among you? Worked beside you? Hear my words. If Kaisak can do this to Moart'Tor, whom he promised to raise and love as his own, what reason do you have to believe he would not do this to any of you or your offling if you also opposed him. I thought Kaisak would be different from his predecessor, Laborn. But he is the same. He is a tyrant and a monster who would murder his own son. Who will stand with me against such hatred?"

Eitel was shocked at how many voices rose in his support.

"Enough, Kaisak," Dak'Tor countered. "Enough of your hatred. What has it brought any of us except unhappiness and struggle? We are tired of hearing about your desire to kill the Sassen and Akassa. We can see they are no different than us! We need a new Adik'Tar!"

Nearly all the voices of Zuenerth rose, chanting in unison, "Dak'Tor! Dak'Tor!"

Kaisak was furious. "You are all traitors! Guards, where are my guards?"

Then Moart'Tor shouted above the din, which quietened down. "Please listen to me. You do not have to live like this, struggling to find resources, with no joy in your lives other than that which you can scratch out day to day. There is a thriving community of Mothoc living in a place called Lulnomia. All the Mothoc except you live there with their offling, and theirs, and theirs. I have been living there for a while now, and the Guardian Pan has declared that you are welcome. You are welcome to live out your lives in peace, surrounded by your own kind. Friends, perhaps even family, the eldest of you left behind at the time of the Great Division. Your offling would grow up to find mates and have families of their own."

Dak'Tor raised his voice. "Moart'Tor, you are speaking of Lulnomia. My sister, the Guardian Pan, talked about it before I left Kthama. It was to Lulnomia our kind went in their thousands when they left the Akassa and Sassen."

As those in the crowd heard there were thousands of other Mothoc existing elsewhere, they began to whisper among themselves.

"The Guardian Pan offers you a new life," Khon'Tor said. "A chance to live in peace among your own kind."

"You heard them!" Dak'Tor shouted. "The community led by my sister is waiting for us. Waiting to welcome us. Who will leave this life of toil and hardship and join me at Lulnomia?"

A nearly deafening chorus of voices rose up, proclaiming that they wanted to go with Moart'Tor and Dak'Tor to Lulnomia.

"Yes, take us with you. There is no future here," one voice called out, and soon, others joined in. Only Kaisak's guards remained unmoved.

A male shouted, "Not all of us believe the Akassa and Sassen are abominations. I and my family will be glad to leave here and never look back."

More and more added their agreement until a cacophony of voices were all joined in rebellion against their Leader.

"You have lost, Kaisak," Dak'Tor said. "All your years of spewing hatred and malice cannot prevail against the truth. Your people have had enough of your lies."

"No one leaves!" Kaisak bellowed. He grabbed the huge spear from the hands of a nearby guard and charged at Dak'Tor. Overhead a hawk let out a piercing cry.

CHAPTER 3

A crack of thunder tore through the silent air, startling them all. Then a piercing flash of light appeared. Kaisak shielded his face, stumbled, and fell, the spear in his hand flying to the ground. When he opened his eyes, a huge figure stood between him and Dak'Tor.

The crowd gasped and splintered away.

Even Moart'Tor was taken aback, and just as at the High Rocks, everyone there immediately felt the power of An'Kru's presence.

An'Kru stared down at the rebel Leader. Kaisak turned on his hands and knees and crawled away as fast as he could, lugging the spear with him. Pulling himself to his feet, he stood staring slack-jawed at the newcomer.

"I am An'Kru. The Promised One."

Voices rose, one louder than the others. "The

Promised One is real? But you are some type of Sassen."

"Shut up!" another cried. "Do you even have to ask? Can you not feel his power?"

"I am Akassa. I am An'Kru'Tor."

Though he towered over Khon'Tor and had a thicker coat, An'Kru did not look like the Sassen. Many simply could not imagine the Promised One would not be Mothoc.

Kaisak found his voice, "Blasphemy! The Promised One could not be an Akassa!"

Visha shouted at her estranged mate Kaisak, "Open your eyes. How can you deny it? He appears as if out of nowhere with the sounds of the heavens announcing him, and you doubt he is who he says he is? I can feel his presence, can you not? The Guardian Pan told us the day of the Promised One would come."

An'Kru stepped forward, revealing someone standing behind him. Nootau. Another gasp rose from the overwhelmed crowd.

Khon'Tor called out to him, and Nootau joined Khon'Tor and the others inside the circle of guards, which had automatically parted to let him in.

"How is this possible?" Khon'Tor asked.

"I will explain when we are back at the High Rocks," Nootau assured him.

"This is nothing but trickery," Kaisak bellowed.

"Death to the Akassa! Starting with you!" Kaisak tilted his spear and, once more, lunged toward Khon'Tor, who was now standing behind Nootau.

Khon'Tor shoved his son out of the way as Kaisak's spear closed in.

"Nooooo!" Nootau rushed into the path of the spear, and just as the blade was about to pierce his core, he twisted his torso down and around, bringing his leg up and kicking the spear from Kaisak's grasp.

To everyone's surprise, Gard and two of his most loyal males rushed over and wrestled Kaisak to the ground.

Once Kaisak was subdued, Gard shouted at him, "Enough! Enough of your hatred and killing. Moart'Tor has offered us a new way of life, one that is not based on hatred and vengeance, and we are leaving with him."

At a nod from Gard, the two males picked Kaisak up by the arms and dragged him off to the side. They trained their spears on him as he finally surrendered.

"Who will join Moart'Tor at Lulnomia?" An'Kru asked calmly and stepped into the crowd.

As he did, the group divided again. The majority stood where they were, almost welcoming his approach, while others unconsciously stepped closer. A few moved further away as if being repelled by his presence.

Iria had returned, and Dak'Tor clasped her

hands in his. "It is what you always wanted. To live peacefully among our own kind."

Iria's eyes were sparkling. "It is a dream come true. Yes, let us go with them. And you can be reunited with your sister."

Dak'Tor fell silent. "I have much to apologize to her for."

"Shortly," An'Kru announced, "you will gather your most precious belongings, your Keeping Stones, and those items that carry good memories. Everything else will be provided for you at Lulnomia. Return here when you are ready. Do not worry about food or water for the journey. In one moment, you will be here; in the next, you will be at your new home."

Eitel glanced up at Paldar'Krah, then turned to An'Kru. "What of us? What will become of us?"

An'Kru smiled kindly. "I will return you to your loved ones, as I will also do for Khon'Tor and Nootau."

Visha approached him. "Please, what of my sons? Will you take them with you? With us?"

"That is not up to me, Visha," he answered.

Visha looked surprised that he knew her name.

"Whoever in their hearts has turned from their desire to annihilate the Akassa and Sassen will be taken with me when I go. Those who have not, who only pretend to have repented, will be left here to live out the rest of their days with their hatred."

She went back to Morvar'Nul, Nofire'Nul, and her youngest Vollen'Nul. "Have you had enough of this? Are you strong enough to leave behind everything you have known? To open your hearts to a different way of living? I pray that you are. But if not, as much as I love you, I will be leaving with Moart'-Tor. I cannot live with hatred in my heart any longer."

Her sons were silent. In desperation, she turned back to An'Kru. "Please. I will go with you, but is there nothing you can do to open my sons' eyes?"

An'Kru stepped aside and suddenly, as if from out of nowhere, stood one of the Brothers.

Everyone in the crowd gasped, including Khon'Tor and the others.

"This is Chief Is'Taqa," An'Kru explained. "He is the Leader of one of the Brothers' villages. The Mothoc knew them as the Others. These are those whom the Great Spirit handed into your care and protection."

Chief Is'Taqa stood still, letting them have a good look at him.

Only the eldest of the Mothoc had any direct knowledge of the Others, and then very little. The Ancients had been the Others' protectors but had seldom interacted with any of them. They took in his face, his hair, his brown eyes, and the tone of his skin. They trailed their gazes over his frame, noting his manner of dress. Of all of them there, he was the puniest, the most fragile, yet the future of Etera rested on his kind, just as it had once before, eons ago.

Chief Is'Taqa stood proudly, fearlessly, and unfailingly met each gaze.

After a few moments, An'Kru looked over at Eitel and gestured for her to come to him. She looked up at her beloved, then walked across.

Then the Promised One looked directly at Iria, beckoning for her also to join him. He placed both females to the left of Chief Is'Taqa.

"Introduce yourselves to each other, please," he said to them.

Iria turned tentatively to Eitel and said, "I am Iria of the House of 'Del."

"I am Eitel of the House of 'Del," Eitel answered.

Both females were from the same House. The resemblance was suddenly remarkable. Only the rebel's hatred and prejudice had kept them from seeing it before. Eitel was, for the most part, just a smaller version of Iria. The same beautiful dark coloring, the nearly black eyes. Eitel's nose was not as flat nor broad as Iria's, her canines not as pronounced, her coat not quite as thick, but there was no mistaking that they were related.

An'Kru gave a moment for the truth to sink in before continuing. "You reject the Sassen and the Akassa because their blood is not pure Mothoc. You have seen them as abominations, yet standing before you now are not abominations but the lifeblood of Etera. It is as Moart'Tor tried to tell you; within the veins of the Akassa and the Sassen flows the blood of the Mothoc as well as that of the Others. How can they be abominations?"

An'Kru had given them one last chance to open their eyes and their hearts.

Tears came to Visha's eyes as her son, Vollen'Nul, spoke first. "I will go with you, Mother."

"So will I," said Nofire'Nul.

Visha looked over at An'Kru and said, "Thank you!" Her eyes searched for Morvar'Nul, who was keeping to the back.

"All who will go to Lulnomia," An'Kru announced, "go now and collect your things."

Except for a handful, everyone scattered to do An'Kru's bidding, and before long, the crowd had reassembled, arms holding baskets, little hands clutching favorite strips of hide. An'Kru stood before them with Khon'Tor, Nootau, Paldar'Krah, Eitel, and Moart'Tor next to him.

Dak'Tor, Iria, and their family were at the front of the crowd, and Dak'Tor stepped toward An'Kru. He had a small, hide-wrapped parcel in his hand.

"This belongs to you, I believe." He held it out for An'Kru to take.

"The crystal from the 'Tor Leader's Staff," An'Kru said.

"Yes, Promised One. I have committed terrible

wrongs, but I hid and protected the crystal all this time."

An'Kru reached down and placed his hand on Dak'Tor's shoulder. "You have done well."

It was time. An'Kru picked up a nearby stick. He leaned forward and drew a long line in front of the crowd standing in front of him. Everyone waited to see what would happen next.

"Those who would live in peace and harmony, shaking off your desire for vengeance and extinguishing the hatred in your hearts, come with me now." Then he stepped back just a little way from the line and waited. Khon'Tor and the others immediately followed him, careful to step over the line and not on it.

Dak'Tor and his family were the first from Zuenerth to cross the line. Visha, Nofire'Nul, and her youngest, Vollen'Nul, were next. Then Gard, followed by nearly all the rest. Everyone lifted their feet high as they stepped across the threshold An'Kru had drawn, as if expecting it to do something to them.

Visha had not lost track of Morvar'Nul standing on the other side of the line, seemingly avoiding her gaze. She reached out her hand in his direction. "My son, come on."

"I cannot cross."

"Why not?" she took a few steps back toward the line.

"I cannot. I tried."

An'Kru stood watching.

Morvar'Nul dropped to his knees. "Oh, Promised One, please let me cross. Please do not leave me behind. I am sorry. I do not know how to quell the hatred in my heart. I have been taught all my life to despite the Akassa and the Sassen. I do not want to feel this way, but I am powerless to extinguish this prejudice against them."

Visha looked pleadingly at An'Kru.

Morvar'Nul then prayed aloud, "Great Spirit, please remove the hatred from my heart. Please do that which I cannot seem to do. I do not want to live like this any longer. I ask for your mercy and help." He remained kneeling.

An'Kru walked back over the line and stood over him. He reached out a hand to help Morvar'Nul up and said, "Come. Come with us now."

Morvar'Nul looked up at hearing An'Kru's voice and stumbled to his feet. An'Kru led him to the threshold.

The Mothoc slowly walked forward. He held his breath and lifted his foot over the line.

Visha ran to embrace her son.

Dak'Tor turned to An'Kru, "Promised One, you said only those whose hearts had released their hatred could go with us."

"The path to harmony with the Great Spirit is

often a long one. It begins with the first step, which is the intention to walk that road. Though Morvar'Nul has not yet achieved the peace he seeks, his intention is pure. That is sufficient. The Great Spirit does not demand perfection, only the willingness to follow."

Soon nearly everyone was on the other side of the line except for Kaisak and several of his guards. An'Kru turned his back on those left and walked away with the crowd following him.

"'*Rok* this!" one of the remaining Mothoc exclaimed. "I am not staying here to starve to death with no females, just you and your pitiful handful of followers." He threw down his spear and hurried toward the line.

He was about to step over it, but suddenly he could not. Something was making it impossible for him to keep going. Confused, he turned and looked back at the others behind him.

"What are you doing, you fool?" Kaisak bellowed, pulling himself to his feet. He hurried over to where the male was standing in front of the line.

Kaisak found he could also not cross. He walked to the right and tried again at another spot. The same. He simply could not cross over An'Kru's line drawn across the ground.

"Look!" one of the remaining males exclaimed. In the distance, the crowd following An'Kru seemed to be slowly disappearing, as if walking into a fog that wasn't there. In a moment, they were gone from sight.

A strong breeze came up, becoming a large whirlwind. Those remaining covered their faces with their hands and arms against the onslaught of twigs, leaves, and dirt carried up into the air. Then, as quickly as it came, it was gone. When they looked again, the line An'Kru had drawn in the ground was erased.

One moment Moart'Tor and the others were following An'Kru, and the next, they were standing outside a place Moart'Tor recognized. Turning to the others, he gestured. "This is Lulnomia!" He pointed to the entrance partway up the mountain that housed what would be their new home.

"Lead them there, Moart'Tor," An'Kru said. "Explain to the Guardian Pan what happened—that I came to bring you home. Take your people and move forward into the future of your own making."

"You are not coming inside?"

An'Kru chuckled. "No, I am already there. But tell Pan I will see her soon."

Moart'Tor frowned but then motioned for the others to follow him. They made their way up the snow-covered path to home.

Khon'Tor and the others were following An'Kru, and then suddenly, they were standing with him outside the entrance to the High Rocks.

"You have brought us directly to Kthama?" Khon'Tor asked. "Yet the Guardian Pan said there was not enough of the Aezaitera in our blood to allow that?"

"My powers surpass those of the Guardian Pan," An'Kru answered.

"Where is Chief Is'Taqa?" Khon'Tor asked, looking around.

"I returned him to his village."

An'Kru turned to Eitel and Paldar'Krah. He extended the crystal to them. "Take this and give it to Haan. Ask him to keep it somewhere safe until I have need of it."

Eitel and Paldar'Krah looked at each other, "He will know what this is?" Eitel asked An'Kru.

"He will understand it is of great value to Etera's future."

Neither of them moved to take the crystal, so An'Kru reached out, took Eitel's hand, and placed it in her palm. "Your families are waiting for you."

"What do we tell them?" Paldar'Krah asked.

"The truth." An'Kru's eyes, though stormy grey, twinkled with kindness.

Khon'Tor said, "I need to return to the Far High Hills. My mate—"

"Of course. Please allow me to return you to your beloved."

CHAPTER 4

I n the next moment, Khon'Tor was standing outside the Far High Hills. There had been no motion, no feeling of displacement or movement. Just as before, within the space of a breath, he had been in one place and was now in another.

He ran up the path and inside, looking around quickly for anyone to announce his return to. Finding High Protector Dreth, Khon'Tor asked him to tell Harak'Sar he had returned, then he unceremoniously hurried down the tunnels and hallways toward his quarters.

"Tehya!" he called out as he approached their open doorway. "Saraste'!" He rounded the turn and was quickly inside their quarters.

His mate had been resting on their sleeping mat, but on hearing his voice, Tehya jumped to her feet and flew across the room into his waiting embrace.

"Oh, my love!" she cried out. "Adoeete! You have

returned. You are safe." Tears came to her eyes, and he cradled her against his chest.

"I am home. I am safe. And, oh, I have such a story to tell you, but first, I must apologize for leaving you as I did. I know I caused you distress."

"I understood." Her voice was muffled against him, and she curled her fingers into his chest hair, as was her habit. "You are who you must be. I will never ask you to be less. But not giving up hope of seeing you again was one of the hardest things I have ever had to do."

Khon'Tor held her a while longer. "Where are Arismae and Bracht'Tor?"

"With my parents."

"For how long, Saraste'?" he asked.

"Long enough," she replied and raised her face for his kiss.

Khon'Tor swept her small frame into his arms and carried her back to the sleeping mat. He gently laid her down on her back and stretched out next to her. He smoothed her hair from the side of her face and gently brushed the tears from her cheeks. "My beloved. By the grace of the Great Spirit, I have returned safely to your arms. And I wish never to leave you again."

She lifted her lips to his, and he breathed deep her familiar scent. He kissed her sweetly, then buried his face in her neck, enjoying the softness of her hair. He felt her reach down and begin to stroke him, beckoning him to take her and reaffirm their love for each other. He welcomed her invitation and braced himself over her on his elbows. He was home, their gentle joining not to be rushed but savored. They moved together in the familiar rhythm, having learned over the years how to please each other and bring each to the sweet release of the splendor. There was no rush, just a lingering expression of their love for each other. When they had finished, he lay on his side and pulled her up against him, cupping her body with his.

"I do not dare fall asleep," she whispered.

"It is alright, Saraste'. I will still be here when you wake. It is not a dream; I am truly home."

A round of gasps, followed by happy exclamations, broke out when Paldar'Krah and Eitel came into sight. Word traveled quickly, and soon both sets of parents were standing with them.

Hola threw her arms around her daughter as Eitel's father, Arpan, waited his turn. Paldar'Krah's parents both embraced him.

Eitel gasped when she saw her beloved brother, Naahb, slowly approaching with support from his mate.

"Oh, are you limping?" she cried.

"The Healer Artadel said it would take time for

me to completely heal. I was lucky I survived," her brother answered.

"He suffered a serious head injury," Hola explained. "There are some—lingering effects."

Tears welled in Eitel's eyes. Her brother was maimed as a result of Morvar'Nul's attack. If he never fully recovered and was not able to provide for his family, she knew the community would take care of them. But still. No male wanted to be dependent on others.

"Oh, do not look so sad, sister," Naahb said. "You have returned safely, and that is what matters!"

Eitel stepped forward and gently took her brother's hand and pressed it to her cheek. "My dearest brother, I cannot bear it that you were hurt."

"I may well recover yet. But if not, my encumbrance is a small burden compared to what you have endured. We are all safely reunited. You are home now, and you and Paldar'Krah can continue with your pairing. Let us place all thoughts of this behind us. We should be rejoicing."

Eitel released his hand and leaned in, resting her head against her brother's shoulder as he hugged her.

"Naahb is right; this is a time of celebration," Arpan announced. "Let us get you something to eat, then perhaps at the evening fire, you can share what you wish of your story with the rest of our community."

"We have a pairing to plan, yes?" Hola asked.

"Hopefully to take place soon," agreed Paldar'Krah.

Just as Eitel and Paldar'Krah were reveling in their return home and safe reunion with their loved ones, so were Nootau and Iella grateful for their good fortune in being back together.

After their lovemating, Nootau leaned back so Iella could rest comfortably against him. He placed his hand on her belly and told her what had taken place at Zuenerth, but it wasn't long before the conversation turned to his time at Lulnomia.

"Maturity looks good on you, my love," Iella said as she toyed with a lock of his long hair. "Please tell me about Lulnomia and your time there."

"There is so much to tell; I am not sure where to start. It is very cold there, perfect for the Mothoc with their heavy coats, but difficult for An'Kru and me. We often had to wear heavy wraps even inside Lulnomia. Physically, it is much like our own cave systems, only on a much larger scale. The system extends far into the mountainside that houses it. It stretches so far that, in all this time, the Mothoc have never fully explored it. They simply gave up as there was no need, though before I left, it sounded like that viewpoint was shifting. Perhaps they will once again send scouts down to see just how far it goes and where it might surface. But it would be a long journey because of the extent of what they have already discovered to be its reach."

Iella examined his hair. "Is this a strand of grey?" she teased him.

"I am not old enough for that, and you know it," he exclaimed.

"At first, I was not sure why I was there. I knew I left here in order to take care of An'Kru, to be his big brother and support him in any way I could. Later, I found I had another purpose, and that was to help ease the Mothoc's pain over having left our people and Haan's. Many of them carried guilt over it, even after all these thousands of years. They are very old; did I tell you that?"

"How old?" she asked.

"They live thousands and thousands of years. Some of them, the oldest, were alive when Moc'Tor walked Kthama's halls. My father told me that when Haan first arrived from Kayerm, he said the Sassen had lived at the High Rocks and that the parents of his parents were part of the exodus that ended up at Kayerm and elsewhere. Those parents were the Mothoc. The Leaders of that time, Moc'Tor, Straf'-Tor, E'ranale, and the Mothoc who lived before them are referred to as the Ancients."

"And the Guardians live longer than that," Iella mused.

"They are practically immortal, though I have realized that is not the blessing it appears to be at first."

Nootau went on to tell her of those who had befriended him, in particular, Pan's mate, Rohm'Mok, and Clah of the white Sassen Guardians. He also explained who Wrollonan'Tor was and told her about the ancient Guardian's interest in him, and explanation that Nootau was not just there to watch over An'Kru.

"He said I was also there to learn. And I did. I learned so much I do not know if I can explain it all. And my abilities were increased. Before, I would occasionally be given information about something, much as happens to Haan, only now, it happens more frequently. And also, sometimes I know about what is going to take place just before it does."

"Really?" she propped herself up on one elbow.

"Yes. For example, while we were at the rebel camp, I knew the Leader, Kaisak, was going to try to spear Khon'Tor. I was able to get between them before he could do it. Then Khon'Tor pushed me out of the way, but I knew he was going to do that, and I was able to twist around and kick the spear out of Kaisak's hands. Things like that."

"Do you know if our offspring will be a male or a female?"

"No, that I do not know." He smiled and started gently rubbing her belly.

"The concentration of the Aezaitera flowing into our realm through the Mothoc," he continued, "is the lifeblood of Etera. That is why it was so important that the rebels be brought back into alignment with the Great Spirit's will. Etera cannot spare a drop of Mothoc blood. The rebels had reached a point where there were no more safe breeding choices. Now, their bloodlines will be revived in the larger community at Lulnomia."

"Is Etera safe now the rebel Mothoc have been reunited with the rest of their kind?"

"I wish that were true. But there is still the Waschini negativity, which continues to spread."

"When the rebel Leader, Kaisak, tried to attack Khon'Tor, An'Kru must have been close by. Why did he not stop it?"

"I thought about that myself, but maybe An'Kru knew I was going to intervene; I truly do not know. But I think my saving his life perhaps showed Khon'Tor I do not hate him."

"We can hope it did. Do you know what your brother is going to do?"

"What lies ahead of us immediately, no, but ultimately his destiny is the only hope for the lost to rediscover the path home to the Great Spirit. An'Kru will make a way for them to find their way back. However, ultimately it will be their choice."

"What will happen if whatever he is going to do fails?"

A shudder passed through Nootau. "I do not know. We will find out together, I guess. The most important thing I have learned is how powerful each of us is. We have the power to bring good or bad into our realm by our will, our intentions, our actions. We each create positivity or negativity. We do not stop and think how powerful we are, how our actions affect others. We have the power to manifest love, compassion, kindness. And it is not just our actions but the intentions behind our actions. Intentions are the movement of our soul toward good or evil."

"Can you give me an example?"

"Take two situations; in each of which someone dies. In one, it is a case of self-defense. Say someone tries to harm you, and the only way I can prevent it is to kill the assailant. In another situation, I kill someone out of revenge or malice. In each instance, someone has died by my hand. But in the first one, my act was not driven by darkness. In the other, it was. Vengeance, bitterness, and hatred all bring darkness into our realm. Intention matters."

Nootau looked down at her slightly swollen belly. "The fruit of our love grows within you, Saraste'."

"At last."

"I missed you so. I prayed every night for your safety."

"I understand why you had to go."

"I know you do. But as the years passed, I worried more and more about my leaving's effect on you. And yet, here I am back after what is to you only a short time. That in itself is a miracle, though I will always carry the memory of our years apart."

"In my own selfish way, I am grateful I was spared all those years alone," Iella said. "I cannot quite understand how, in your lifetime, I lived through all those years without you. And yet, now I will not need to."

At that moment, Nootau swore to himself that he would never tell her anything of the life that had unfolded for her while he was away. There was no need for her to know.

"With the Mothoc reunited at Lulnomia," she asked, "what will happen next?"

"When the Brotherhood is assembled, An'Kru will explain what lies ahead."

CHAPTER 5

Grace tended to the children and waited for her husband, Newell, to return home from his office in town. Though she had wanted to wait to have them, life had other plans. The last six years seemed like one long string of pregnancies, and her swollen belly promised delivery of their fourth soon enough.

Newell's business had expanded, and he was as well established now as he previously was at Millgrove. Wilde Edge had grown into a decent-sized town due to its convenient location on the now more heavily traveled trails running east and west.

They were both happy, Newell with his clients and Grace raising their family. Their oldest son, Nathan, was just getting to where he could be of some help to his mother. They had animals to care for and a modest garden to tend. The sale of the Morgan horses had given her parents, Matthew and

Nora Webb, a nice cushion over and above what the Morgan trust provided. The Baxter boys who had been helping with the Webbs' farm were old enough that most of them had moved on to building their own lives, but Newell had found help elsewhere to take care of the things Matthew couldn't do because of his back injury, so many years ago now.

Though Grace's brother, Ned, had tried to return every spring, he had not been home for some time, and all of them were anxious for his return. He had married but, due to the political climate, had elected so far not to bring his wife to Wilde Edge. It saddened Grace and her mother that they were unlikely ever to meet the children he and his wife would have—if they did not already have some.

Newell walked in and placed his hat on the wall hook and found her in the kitchen preparing dinner, her little dog Pippy lying in his bed not far from the cookstove's warmth. Newell lifted one of the pot lids and nearly burned his fingers. He instantly let it go, but luckily it landed right back in place on the pot instead of clanging to the floor.

Grace unsuccessfully tried to frown at him.

"I know, I know," Newell laughed, putting his singed fingers in his mouth.

"It's your favorite, beans. The cornbread's in the oven—which is also hot," she teased.

He put his arm around her waist and drew her close for a kiss. "How did your day go?"

"Busy as yours, no doubt, just a different kind. Fortunately, the boys have been entertaining themselves, pretending to hunt pheasants. Tommy likes to be the pheasant!"

"Instead of helping you?" he frowned.

Grace chuckled, "I'll send them to work with you tomorrow, and you can see just how much help they can be. Luckily, Nat does help by occupying his younger brothers."

Newell walked over to the kitchen window to watch his sons playing. "A born leader," he mused, referring to their oldest, Nathan, who went by Nat.

He turned back to Grace. "The garden is looking good."

"It is. But our family has grown, and I think we need to expand it. It was fine years ago for just you and me, but I think it's time."

"We have never had any problems. My business is flourishing, and most people pay with barter anyway. Keep letting me know whatever you need, and I'll get it for you."

"I know you will," Grace untied her apron from behind and draped it over one of the high-backed chairs. She leaned back to stretch. "I would just feel better if we were more self-sufficient."

"How is she doing?" he asked, looking at Grace's belly.

"You're so sure it's a girl."

"After three boys, it's gotta be."

"Is that so?" she smiled. "I'm not quite sure it works that way. But it would be nice to have a daughter."

"As much as we all want Ned to come home soon, I would love for him not to come until his niece is born, so he can meet her."

"You're not giving up on a girl, are you?"

Her husband winked at her, "No. It's definitely a girl."

As if anyone needed any more commotion at either the High Rocks or Kht'shWea, Haaka was almost ready to deliver. Haan had sworn he would not be nervous, but he was. There was no true risk to the offling, as there had been when his Akassa mate, Hakani, was seeded by him, but he still waited impatiently for news that he or she had been safely born.

Finally, Haan's Healer and friend, Artadel, emerged from Kht'shWea's entrance and walked over to the Leader, who was fiddling with the evening fire.

Haan looked up, and his heart stopped when he saw Artadel. He dropped the stick he had been nudging the fire with and stood up.

Artadel put both palms up, "It is fine, Haan; Haaka and your son are fine."

"Son? I have a son?"

"Yes. Very healthy. Unfortunately, he looks as if he is going to take after you."

It was one of the few times Haan had ever heard Artadel make a joke. But it broke the tension, and he laughed before hurrying off to see his mate and son. Artadel went to tell Eitel, who was watching Haan and Haaka's offling, Kalli and Del'Cein.

Haan hurried down the tunnel to their quarters but tried to quell his excitement and enter as quietly as possible. Haaka was relaxing on their sleeping mat, propped up against the wall, a bundle snuggled safely in her arms.

He knelt down next to her and kissed her softly on the lips. "I believe we have a son."

"You have been so patient, Haan, and through so much. First, with losing Kesta, then Akar'Tor's birth, and the heartache of losing him. Almost losing both Hakani and Kalli when Hakani gave birth. Then, when Hakani took her own life. And waiting for me to have Del'Cein before having an offling with you."

"All true, but, oh, look at him," Haan said. The little offling yawned and turned his head to his mother's warm breast.

"You have many waiting to see you. I will come back later." He kissed her again, took another look at his son, and left her to receive her other visitors.

"May we come in?" Eitel asked from the doorway. She was carrying Del'Cein, Haaka's daughter seeded by an Akassa. Kalli, Haan's daughter born of Hakani, walked hand in hand with Eitel.

"Of course." Haaka shifted her position to sit up more so they could see the offling and addressed her daughters, "You have a brother now."

Kalli looked at the little face.

Silence. Then, "He looks like you and Papa. Not like us." She looked up at her sister, who was on Eitel's hip.

"We are a family. It does not matter who looks like who," Haaka said. Kalli turned to hide her face in Eitel's coat, and Haaka looked up at her friend.

Eitel set Del'Cein down, then knelt down to comfort Kalli. "Your brother looks different, but he is still your brother. Look at me; my coat is nearly black, others are brown, and the Guardians' are even silver. We all look different."

"But Del'Cein and I don't have any of those coats. We are both different from all of you."

Haaka exclaimed, "Oh, no, no."

As if on cue, Eitel released Kalli and took the little one, freeing Haaka to hold out her arms. Kalli ran into them.

The day Haaka feared had come, the day when Kalli realized she and her younger sister were different.

"No, no, please do not think that." Haaka held her daughter until she stopped crying,

After wiping her nose and eyes on her arm, Kalli

stared at her mother, who braced herself for what was coming.

Kalli lightly touched Haaka's face, running her fingers over her mother's chin, her nose, her eyebrows. Then she did the same with her own. Finally, she turned and looked at Del'Cein.

"I do not look like you. Or Papa. Or anyone here except Del'Cein."

Haaka watched her daughter's little lower lip quiver. She had expected this from Kalli long ago and was surprised it was just coming up now, but she realized it was the birth of her son that had triggered this realization of how different Kalli looked from the rest of Kht'shWea.

Del'Cein was just watching, not really understanding the weight of what was being said.

"We have talked about this," Haaka said, pulling Kalli down to sit next to her on the sleeping mat. "Your father had a mate before me, your blood mother. She was an Akassa. Your mother was like those at Kthama. And your sister's blood father is also an Akassa. That is why you both look more like them and each other. But we are still your parents. Just as we are to your new brother."

"It is not true. The others told me I was different, and I did not want to listen to them," Kalli said. "He gets to be both of yours. But I am only Papa's, and Del'Cein is only Mama's."

Haaka thought her heart would break. She guessed that by the others, Kalli meant her friends.

Just then, the new offling started to cry.

Kalli looked over at her brother in Eitel's arms. "Can I stay here with you for a while?" she asked.

"Of course. I would love that. Lie here next to me while I feed your brother."

Eitel said, "I'll take Del'Cein with me. You have some time together, and I will check back later."

Kalli snuggled up next to her mother and wrapped her little arm around Haaka as far as she could reach.

Haaka let her son nurse, and then a thought came to her. "Would you like to help me name him?" she asked.

"The mama is supposed to name the offling."

"I know. But you will be a mama someday, and this will be good practice. We can name him together."

Kalli sat up and peered into the face of her brother, who was still contentedly nursing.

"How do we figure out what his name should be?"

"Well, we do not really figure it out. It just sort of comes to you."

"What about Del'Cein? Should she help too?" Kalli asked.

"She is a little young for this yet, I think. Let the two of us come up with a name."

"What if Papa does not approve?"

"Ah, that is a good question. But since it is through our bodies that the Great Spirit delivers the gift of a new life, we have the honor of naming the offling. If our mates do not approve, they pretty much have to just go along with it."

"Is that fair?" Kalli asked.

"When you are older and understand more, I think you will feel that it is pretty fair after all."

The offling finished nursing and burped, which made Kalli laugh.

"He is cute. I hope he will not be a pest," she said.

"You are his oldest sister, and I will need your help with him. Will you help me?"

Kalli didn't answer and continued to stare at the offling propped up over Haaka's shoulder.

"How about Srakkah?"

Haaka thought a moment. "Srakkah. Meaning one of honor. I think it is a good name. Your father will be pleased."

"When do we tell him?"

"The next time he comes home. We'll tell him then."

Kalli was quiet for another moment, then said. "I will help you with him, Mama."

Moart'Tor's mind flew back to when he had first stood with the Guardian Pan at the entrance to Lulnomia. Despite her assurances that he would be accepted, he had been unsure what to expect. Now the hundreds of Zuenerth Mothoc were no doubt feeling the same as he had. Before he led them inside, he silently thanked the Great Spirit. The day he had hoped for had arrived.

He wondered if somehow Pan knew what had happened. Even after all the time the Mothoc had been at Lulnomia, it seemed no one truly understood the extent of her abilities. And certainly not those of Wrollonan'Tor.

He stepped inside and turned to beckon them in. Slowly the huge group entered, looking up and around just as he once had. They took in the high ceilings bridging the enormous walls of the Great Entrance and, off in the distance, the many tunnels branching out in multiple directions. The room echoed with the shuffling of their feet as they poured into the massive chamber.

Moart'Tor saw heads turning and looked ahead to see the Guardian Pan and her mate, Rohm'Mok, walking toward them.

"Welcome home, Moart'Tor," Pan said, extending her hand to him. Then, looking around at the faces staring at her, she said louder, "Welcome to Lulnomia, everyone." As she continued to glance around, she saw a face she had feared she would never see again. He was much older, but it was him.

Her brother, Dak'Tor.

"Brother!" she could not stop herself from exclaiming.

She saw Dak'Tor hesitate, then break from the group and approach her. He knelt in front of her and took one of her hands in both of his, and bowed his head. "Pan. Oh, Pan, I know I do not deserve it, for my crimes were many, and there was no justification for them, but I pray you will find a way to forgive me."

Pan knelt down in front of him. "Dak'Tor, all these years, I was afraid to know more than that that you were alive and that you were well. My joy at seeing you again is boundless. Welcome home!" She put her arms around him and held him against her.

Rohm'Mok came over when she and Dak'Tor had stood up. "Your sister is glad to see you, and so am I." Rohm'Mok reached out and rested his hand on one of Dak'Tor's shoulders.

"There is something you must know," Dak'Tor said. "The crystal I took from the 'Tor Leader's Staff, I protected it all these years. And I never revealed its existence. I gave it to An'Kru when he came to Zuenerth to free us."

Pan wasn't sure what to react to, that the crystal was safe, or that An'Kru had appeared at Zuenerth. *He has this power as a young offling?"*

"An'Kru appeared at Zuenerth?" she repeated.

"Yes. Along with an Akassa named Nootau. An'Kru showed up at just the right time to avert what would have been a deadly fight, and I gave the crystal to him."

"I need to hear this story as soon as possible, but not right now," Pan answered.

She saw Dak'Tor frown; clearly, there was something that didn't make sense to him. And there was much that didn't make sense to her either. Could An'Kru already possess such powers? Yet he was rarely out of anyone's sight.

"Of course, sister." Dak'Tor thanked Rohm'Mok and then turned to find his family. He motioned for Iria, their offling, and her parents to join him.

After quick introductions, Pan returned to her role as Guardian of Etera to further address the group.

"People of Zuenerth, the people of Lulnomia are waiting to welcome you. Here, you will find peace, and life as it is meant to be lived, among family, among friends, and in service to the Great Spirit."

"Guardian," Moart'Tor spoke up. "May I go and find my mate and our son. She is not here and most likely does not know of my safe return."

Pan nodded her permission.

By then, others had heard the commotion in the entrance, and as the word spread of what had happened, more and more poured into the chamber.

Rohm'Mok had to make arrangements to hold back the flow lest the newcomers be overwhelmed.

"We were unaware you were coming," he announced, "so if you would bear with us for a while, we will prepare living arrangements for you all. They will be temporary, as we do not yet know you or how your families are divided. We can make adjustments as it seems fit to do so."

Word had reached Moart'Tor's mate, Naha, and she was on her way to find him. When they met, they embraced heartily.

"I was so worried," Naha said. "I came the moment I heard."

"There is much to tell you, but later. Right now, I need to help my mother and brothers get settled, and then all I want is to be with you and our son, Akoth'Tor."

"He is with my mother. Yes, I understand. Go and take care of your family. Oh, I do not know if I have had a happier moment than hearing you have returned. And Eitel? At least tell me before you go; is she safe?"

"She is safe. There was a battle and a few losses, but it is a long story that deserves the time and setting to tell it properly."

When Moart'Tor returned to the Great Entrance, members of Lulnomia were still trying to determine which would be the best temporary living areas for the Mothoc of Zuenerth.

"Mother," he said to Visha, "I know this will be a big adjustment. But in time, it will begin to feel like home, as it did for me. Later, I will introduce you to my mate and our offling."

"I am looking forward to meeting them, and so are your brothers. I hope you will now be able to speak freely of your experiences from the time you left us."

"There is much to tell, but it is a long story that deserves the right time and setting to tell it properly."

Rohm'Mok had overheard the end of the conversation. "Many will be interested in your story, Moart'Tor.

"As they will in yours and that of the others from your community," he said to Visha.

Moart'Tor's brother, Morvar'Nul, joined in. "I am also anxious to learn more about the Akassa and the Sassen. How and when our people left their communities, what happened, and why."

"All in due time," Rohm'Mok answered. "There is much to tell and learn. For now, we need to get you settled and established in Lulnomia. The sooner it starts to feel like home to you, the happier you will all be."

Dak'Tor stood with his mate, Iria, and their offling, waiting for direction. From time to time, he would scan the people coming and going. He knew who he was looking for. He just didn't know if he wanted to get it over with or put it off as long as possible. He had amends to make.

CHAPTER 6

Lulnomia was brimming with excitement at the arrival of the Zuenerth Mothoc. It took the rest of the day to get the newcomers settled and explain the layout and routines.

In her station as Guardian, Pan helped with getting everyone settled, but she was distracted and anxious to find Wrollonan'Tor. She hoped he would be able to explain how An'Kru could have gone to Zuenerth—if even he understood how it had been possible.

Finally, she was able to slip away to find Wrollonan'Tor.

After making sure An'Kru was not present, Pan began the story. "A miracle has happened. Moart'Tor has returned to Lulnomia and brought most of the rebels from Zuenerth, including my brother, Dak'Tor. I believe only a handful remained. I do not know any details except Dak'Tor said An'Kru came to help them avert violence that otherwise might have been disastrous. An'Kru. Has An'Kru attained such abilities already?"

"I know what took place, Pan. And why. But only because it was explained to me. Sit down."

Wrollonan'Tor explained to Pan what would have taken place had the adult An'Kru not intervened. When he was done, she sat there a while in silence.

"An'Kru used his free will to change the direction of the Order of Functions?"

"No. He used his free will and his abilities to prevent the murder and suffering of many, from the Mothoc trapped at Zuenerth to the future decimation of the Brothers at the hands of the Waschini. You know the Order of Functions is continuously adjusting to the free will of others to provide the most beneficial outcome. An'Kru not only has free will, but he also has the ability to move through what we call time. Only, as he is now, an offling in our present time, he has no knowledge of this, and neither does Nootau. I do not know what effect it might have if they were to learn of it. It is important that his training continue uninterrupted."

"Then I must ask the people of Zuenerth not to speak of An'Kru? It seems that would be impossible to achieve."

"No, we must explain what happened as minimally as we can. They will find out soon enough that the Promised One is but a young offling and not the grown adult who appeared to them and brought them here."

"You have not yet told me how you know of this, Wrollonan'Tor," Pan said solemnly.

"An'Kru told me of it."

Pan stood and threw up her hands. "I should not be surprised by any of this, yet I am. And confused. You said An'Kru does not know of this, of what he will do in the future, and yet you say it is he who told you what happened. Would happen."

"He told me in the Corridor," explained Wrollonan'Tor. "You know the Corridor is not governed by Etera's time, that it is outside of time."

"But the young An'Kru who is with us now does not know of the Corridor. How are we to explain his training to him without changing the future from here—so he does return and free those at Zuenerth? So he still prevents those many travesties from taking place, including, you said, the devastation of the Brothers' communities."

"It is enough for him to know he will eventually have the power to return to that point in time to help Moart'Tor free those at Zuenerth and bring them here. He does not need to know what would take place without that intervention. In addition, because he has changed the future, in the new timeline that now lies ahead, he may not need to return."

Pan sighed. "I will leave it to you to explain to him until my understanding is more solid."

"To the extent that each needs to know, I will explain it not only to him and Nootau but to all of Lulnomia. We must meet with An'Kru and Nootau as soon as possible, and only after that should we introduce An'Kru to our newcomers."

All the Mothoc were assembled outside in an expansive meadow not far from Lulnomia.

Some of the Zuenerth Mothoc had already reconnected with relatives, and the air was filled with excitement and gratitude.

When it was time to start, Pan addressed the group.

"Once again, we are grateful for the return of our lost friends and relatives from Zuenerth. And let us remember to pray for those remaining there whose hearts are still hardened against our cousins, the Akassa and the Sassen. No doubt many of you have heard the story of how An'Kru helped Moart'Tor bring his people here. And no doubt you have questions."

Just then, the ancient Guardian appeared. Those from Zuenerth, who did not know of him, stood in shock.

"I am Wrollonan'Tor," his voice boomed across the open, white landscape. "Yes, I know it was believed I had died, but as you can see, that is not true. I am sure those of you from Zuenerth have questions, yet my existence is not what is important here. What is important is that our people are nearly all reunited. And for that, we must rejoice."

The crowd complied with cheers and shouts.

"You have no doubt heard that it was An'Kru who helped Moart'Tor bring his family and community members here. And I am sure you are wondering how this could be possible, so I will explain, but let me first introduce him to those of you from Zuenerth." Wrollonan'Tor stepped aside to reveal An'Kru standing behind him, heavily bundled in wraps against the chill winter winds.

A murmur rose up from those from Zuenerth. "That is the Promised One? But he is not grown. The An'Kru who appeared to us was a full-grown male."

Wrollonan'Tor spoke over the crowd's voices. "This is indeed An'Kru, the Promised One. Yes, he is not yet grown, but when he is, he will use his abilities to return to you as an adult, to help free you from your Leader's grasp and your misconceptions."

Young An'Kru stepped forward and looked at the crowd but said nothing.

"How is it possible?" a voice asked.

Another from the crowd answered them, "Well, it is. Do you not remember how he appeared, with the peal of thunder as if out of nowhere? He is indeed the Promised One, and this is just further proof, without any doubt."

Many voices were raised in agreement.

Then Pan spoke. "So set your confusion aside and release your mind's need to understand. You have seen it with your own eyes; let that be enough, and turn your hearts and minds to your new life here as members of Lulnomia."

"But there was another with him!" This time it was Morvar'Nul speaking up. "Where is he? An Akassa!"

Pan turned to Nootau and motioned for him to come forward.

Once again, the crowd murmured among themselves. Whatever small doubt might have remained that An'Kru was not the Promised One had just been eliminated.

Dak'Tor still had not found the one he knew he needed to speak with. His first mate, Ei'Tol. He wondered if perhaps something had happened to her, yet it was more likely they had simply not yet crossed paths as Lulnomia was huge. He thought by now she must have heard of his return. Did she perhaps resist meeting up with him?

He discovered that the daughter of Rohm'Mok and Pan, Tala, was the Leader of the Mothoc from Kthama. She had taken over the leadership from Pan's sister, Vel, a while back.

"I would like to speak with her, please," he said to Rohm'Mok, "because I need to address all of the Mothoc from Kthama."

After listening to Dak'Tor, Tala agreed to call the Kthama community at Lulnomia together. But not until after he had spoken with his first mate, Ei'Tol.

Accordingly, Tala arranged for Dak'Tor and Ei'Tol to meet the next day.

Ei'Tol knew Dak'Tor had returned and that he had a mate and offling. She was relieved he had survived but had mixed feelings about meeting up with him, although, like him, she knew it needed to happen. Their daughter, Diza, remembered nothing about her father. If Diza had once carried any resentment against him, she had hidden it from Ei'Tol.

"Everyone is surprised to see you, Dak'Tor," Ei'Tol said. "No one expected you were still alive." She briefly looked him up and down, noting he had only become more handsome with age.

"It was only by the grace of the Great Spirit that I am. Life was difficult at the rebel camp as the Leader needed me but hated me. It is a long story and not why I wanted to see you. I have had a very long time to think about how we parted, and I want you to know that I understand how I failed you completely as a mate and Diza as a father. You had every right to ask for our pairing to be set aside. "

"You paired again," Ei'Tol said.

"Yes. We have three offling, and we thought we would never get away, so I am exceedingly happy we will live out the rest of our lives in peace, especially for Naha's sake. Hopefully, our offling will find mates here; there was no future for them at Zuenerth. What about you? You must have paired again. You deserve to be happy, and I always hoped you were. I expect it was with Jhotin."

"I know you did not get along with him, but Jhotin was never anything more than a friend."

"In retrospect, I can see he was trying to make me be the mate and father I should have been all along. I was in the wrong, not him. So where is he?"

"He is still a Healer's Helper. He paired not long after we came to Lulnomia. As for me, yes, I am paired. A male from the Deep Valley community, though he came to live with us here at Kthama so as not to uproot Diza. He helped me raise her."

"How is she?"

"She is remarkable. So bright. She has no memory of you, though."

"I did not expect she would. I am sorry I treated you so poorly; you deserved better, and I am glad you found love."

"Thank you, Dak'Tor. I appreciate your seeking me out. That was brave of you, I think."

"That is another thing; I am no longer a coward. All the hardships I endured only served to make me a better person. It was a rough road, but it was what it had to be to change me."

Dak'Tor was now ready to address the Mothoc of Kthama.

When all had gathered, Tala announced, "You know why I have asked you to assemble. Standing next to me is Dak'Tor, brother to the mother of my blood, the Guardian Pan. He has asked to speak with you."

"Thank you for coming," Dak'Tor started. "I have much to say; mostly, I have much to apologize for. But first, I am so happy to know that you live here at Lulnomia and that, as painful as it was to leave the Akassa and Sassen, you have made new lives here. I hope to do the same.

"Those of you who remember me know I committed a grievous crime. Not only did I betray my father's wishes about who was to take over the leadership of Kthama, but I also betrayed my sister, Pan. I manipulated circumstances so she would have to become Leader of the High Rocks, a burden she did not want but a duty she did not shirk. I, on the other hand, was a coward and ran from every challenge and every obstacle I faced.

"Some of you also remember I had a first mate, Ei'tol, and a daughter. I failed them, as well as the Mothoc of Kthama. I was not a good mate, and I was an absent father. They both deserved better, far better than I gave them.

"After my crime was discovered, I fled before the High Council could banish me. I knew it was coming. Though the result would have been the same, somehow, leaving on my own felt better than staying around for them to enforce it. Eventually, I was discovered by members of the rebel camp, Zuenerth, and I have lived there ever since. During that time, I paired, and we had our own offling.

"Though I do not deserve it, I hope you can forgive me. At least give me a chance to prove myself to you. If not, I understand, but I do beg you, please, not to punish my family for what I did. My mate, Iria, and our offling have done nothing wrong. The fact that I found happiness at all at Zuenerth to me speaks only of the Great Spirit's mercy. My family has known nothing but hardship, and I pray they may find a life of happiness and inclusion here at Lulnomia." He looked around, trying to read the faces staring back at him. In some, he saw acceptance. In others, he saw scrutiny, and some, he could not read at all.

Just as he was ready to stand down, to his surprise, Ei'Tol came to the front.

"Dak'Tor spoke with me yesterday and asked for

my forgiveness. I believe he is sincere. He is not the male who abandoned my daughter and me, nor the one who betrayed Pan. We all make mistakes and hurt others, but only the wisest of us know it. I hope you will forgive him and accept him and his family into our community."

Visha walked back to Lulnomia with her sons, Morvar'Nul and Nofire'Nul. The younger of the two, Nofire'Nul, put his arm around his mother's shoulder as they walked. "I wonder what will become of Father. If only he could see this place. If only he could have let go of his vendetta against the Sassen and the Akassa."

"Can he, in time? I wonder," said Morvar'Nul. "And would it make any difference? Would he still be allowed to join us here if he could soften his heart and admit he was wrong?"

"I suppose the only one who knows is An'Kru, who came to us there," Visha replied. "But he will not exist for several years. By then, who knows what will have become of the few who stayed behind."

The winter cold had set in hard, and Kaisak and his handful of guards at Zuenerth were struggling. All the females were gone. There were none left to be their companions and none to have their offling, even if it had been allowed. There would be no future Zuenerth.

After An'Kru had left with the others and the whirlwind erased the line he had drawn in the snow, those remaining quickly turned on each other.

"Where are they? Where did they go?" shouted Drall, one of the original rebels who had left Kayerm with Ridg'Sor so long ago.

"How do I know?" Kaisak bellowed back.

"Well, you seemed to have all the answers a day ago? And now what?" Drall snarked.

"And now what? Now you want to fight with me? Is it not enough that we are left here to die? If we fight among ourselves, we will surely die sooner. We must stop and think and make a plan to provide for ourselves."

"Bah!" Drall spat on the ground in front of Kaisak's feet. "You have led us to our destruction. Your arrogance caused us to lose everything. Everyone is gone, and all we have now is to wait for death. You are an even worse failure than Laborn!"

Kaisak threw himself at Drall and knocked him to the ground. "Is this who I am left with? A helpless weakling who cries like a female and blames her mistakes on others? You had as much of a chance to go with them as did anyone."

"You are wrong!" Drall pushed Kaisak off of

himself and rolled away. "I tried to cross the line on the ground, but I could not. None of us could. Because of you. Because of how you have filled us with hatred and vengeance and made us unfit to go with the others. You were our Leader, as Laborn was before you. And both of you wasted all our lives with thoughts of murdering the Akassa and the Sassen. We threw our lives away, following you!"

Other voices joined in, and soon a fight broke out between the remaining six guards and Kaisak. When it ended, Kaisak was lying on the ground, bloodied and writhing in great pain. As the others walked by, they sneered at him. Some kicked snow in his face.

Kaisak lay there for some time, partly from exhaustion and partly from the pain he was in. He knew he should get up, as even with his heavy coat, he was in no condition to stay there on the frozen ground any longer. He rolled over onto his side and realized his left arm must be broken. The ground under him was tinged with red from where the others' attack had penetrated his heavy winter coat and cut open his skin.

He dragged himself up to his knees, his free hand cradling his broken arm to his chest. He slowly made it to his feet and headed in the direction of the living quarters he had shared with Visha, believing it would have more provisions in it than the one he was now living in.

Kaisak stumbled down the dark tunnel and into

what had been his and Visha's living area. He eased himself down on the sleeping mat, grateful for its insulation from the cold ground. The winds howled outside, but the thick rock walls kept the draft from him. He could smell Visha's familiar scent in the bedding, and he was suddenly overcome with emotion. He clutched the branches and animal hide to his face, and for the first time he could remember, he was afraid.

From a distance, Drall and the other remaining guards watched their Leader rise and stumble off.

"What do we do now?" Drub asked.

"The others could not have taken everything with them. There has to be food in the other living areas. Let us collect what we can. It will not last forever, but it will sustain us for a while until we can come up with a plan."

"What kind of plan?" Org asked.

"One that will keep us alive."

The pairing day had come—and quickly. Haan, as Adik'Tar, was ready to announce Ashwea Awhidi over Eitel and Paldar'Krah. Family and friends were gathered in the sacred meadow above Kthama. Since the Sassen had moved into Kht'shWea, their customs were being influenced by those of the Akassa, and the Akassa's by theirs. The culture divided by the closing of Kthama Minor and the ancient Rah-hora would someday become one again.

Acaraho and his Circle of Counsel were also present. Everyone was smiling and filled with happiness for the young couple. The families of Eitel and Paldar'Krah were the happiest of all. Well, not quite as happy as Eitel and Paldar'Krah, of course.

As was the Sassen custom, the pair stood facing each other, the circle of their well-wishers surrounding them. The males formed an arc around Paldar'Krah, and the females formed one around Eitel. Then the Sassen began the pairing chant, their deep voices filling the air. This time the Akassa joined in with them. The ancient words had their usual, almost hypnotic effect, and everyone was put into a deeply relaxing state.

Paldar'Krah gently placed his hand on Eitel's head. He gazed into her eyes and declared, "I, Paldar of the House of 'Krah, choose you over all others."

Eitel looked lovingly at her beloved and said, "I, Eitel, daughter of the House of 'Del, choose you over all others."

Then in the combining of rituals, as Haan had asked, the Overseer, Urilla Wuti, stepped forward, and Eitel and Paldar'Krah turned to face her. She grasped a hand of each in hers, then joined their hands together. The couple turned to face each other again, and at that moment, she raised their hands in hers and pronounced loudly, "Ashwea Awhidi!"

Kah-Sol 'Rin. It was done. Eitel and Paldar'Krah were now paired for life. Their journey together as one lay before them.

They returned to their new quarters, which had been decorated as was custom. For the rest of the day, they would get to know each other as male and female, sharing the physical pleasures and joys to which they were now entitled.

"You are beautiful," Paldar'Krah whispered as he lay next to his beloved. "I cannot believe you are mine. The most beautiful female of all Etera and the greatest gift I have ever received from the Great Spirit."

"We would not be here if you had not come for me. You are my champion and my beloved."

Long into the night, they professed their love and devotion to each other. After their physical desire had been quenched, they fell into a deep sleep, intertwined in each other's arms.

An'Kru was meeting with the Overseer. "I need you to call the Brotherhood together. I must address everyone at once. I must tell them of the changes to come and what they must do to prepare for them in these final days."

"Final days?" Urilla Wuti asked.

"I will tell you what is to happen as you need to know. Everyone else will hear about it once the Brotherhood is assembled."

"It will take time to send messengers to all the communities and then for them to travel here to the High Rocks. Maybe Iella can send the most powerful birds of the air to carry messages telling them of the time they are to assemble here. That will cut the waiting time nearly in half.

An'Kru agreed, "We must not tarry, for time is now of the essence."

Iella did as the Promised One and the Overseer asked. In no time, the appropriate symbols had been drawn, and the hide notes secured and sent out to the far reaches of the Akassa communities. As for the Brothers, their messages were simpler because Ned and Awantia had taught almost all of them the Waschini methods of speaking and writing.

If things went to plan, all would be gathered together at the next full moon.

Before the meeting of the Brotherhood, there remained two more people for An'Kru to speak with.

Acaraho and Adia were with their son. They knew of the calling together of the Brotherhood but did not know to what end. They were about to find out.

When An'Kru finished, they both sat there still as stone.

"There is no other way?" Acaraho asked.

"At present, no. But the Order of Functions is always shifting and adjusting. Just as the flocks of birds in the air and the clusters of fish in the lakes move as one at some unknown command, so the Order of Functions is orchestrating everything to produce the best outcome possible. I am also governed by the Order of Functions, so it *is* possible that what I believe has to happen may not come to pass after all."

"Even you, An'Kru?" Adia said. "Even you do not know for certain what must be?"

"Mother, I feel your struggle. I only know what I must do. The outcome always rests in the wisdom and will of the Great Spirit."

"I *am* struggling. It seems my life has been one long struggle trying to keep my faith. A faith that continues to be tested and which I have to fight to re-

establish. But this, this may be more than I can bear."
She hung her head.

"I assure you it is not," An'Kru said softly. Then,
rising from his seat, he sat next to her, reaching out
and covering one of her hands with his.

"Mama."

Adia's head jerked up, and she stared at him. In
all his life, he had never called her mama. It had
always been mother.

"Do not fear for me," An'Kru said. "Or for my
future. We have spoken of this before in the Corridor.
What is given to me to do, I bear gladly, just as you
have borne the trials and burdens of your own life."

He turned to Acaraho. "And you, Papa. I feel your
strength and your conviction, just as I always did
growing up here. You have taken Straf'Tor's words to
heart; you have accepted that you are a Leader in
your own right, never to be in anyone's shadow. You
both have all you need to carry you through this."

"How long before this must take place?" Acaraho
asked.

"After I speak with the Brotherhood, everyone
will have four full seasons to prepare. A year."

The Brotherhood was assembled, and Kthama was
filled almost to breaking point. Every living space
was occupied; some of the People of the High Rocks

had even moved in with friends to make room for their guests. Many who had not in a long time seen their relatives from the High Red Rocks, the Great Pines, and the Far Flats were reunited and spent whatever time they could exchanging stories of their lives. No one remembered the last time anyone from the Far Flats had attended an assembly of any kind, so there were many introductions taking place. To fill in the gaps in their knowledge of what had taken place over the past few decades, Acaraho had arranged preliminary meetings for those who had not attended any prior gatherings.

Every Chief from every known community of the Brothers was there, along with some of their Elders and their Medicine Men and Women. Chief Is'Taqa sat with his family, now grown quite large, with Oh'Dar and Acise and their children and Pajackok and Snana with theirs. The Chief's life-walker, Honovi, was on one side of him, and his son, Noshoba, on the other.

Only Oh'Dar's grandparents were absent, both now too frail to attend.

Adia was standing off to the right with Acaraho, her hand clasped in his. She calmed herself and took in the comfort of his presence. Her protector, her beloved, her mate. She felt him give her hand a squeeze and knew it was time to begin.

Acaraho stepped forward to address the crowd. "Welcome and greetings. I hope you find your accommodation comfortable. We here at Kthama recognize the long distances many of you have traveled, especially those of you from the Great Pines, the High Red Rocks, and the Far Flats. It has taken much on your part to get here. Please trust that the invitation was not given lightly, and soon you will understand the great importance of our coming together at this time."

Acaraho motioned for Urilla Wuti to step forward.

"I am Urilla Wuti, the People's High Council Overseer. I ask that you quiet yourselves now and prepare your minds and hearts to receive the message the Promised One has come to deliver."

Despite Urilla Wuti's request for quiet, when An'Kru stepped out of the shadows into the speaking area, gasps and talk broke out throughout the Great Chamber.

He waited for the clamor to die down. When it finally did, he spoke.

"I am An'Kru, the Promised One prophesied by the ancestors of the People. I have come to usher in the Wrak-Ashwea, the Age of Light. I understand the confusion of many of you, as a season ago, I was still a young male in my parents' care. Please try to release your need to understand and accept that what I am about to tell you is true."

"Many of you no doubt were expecting the Guardian Pan to appear, but she is busy with my training, for in truth, I am here and also with her, still the young offspring who left here so recently. How is it possible for me to stand here before you as an adult and yet be there as an offspring? You must only accept that it is true. You have seen other wonders already, for example, the messengers sent by the Healer Iella to carry the request for you to join us here. As for my presence here now, I have come in answer to the prayers and pleas of the faithful and to set in motion the birth of the Age of Light.

"I bring positive news. Thanks to the efforts of a few, all but a handful of the rebel Mothoc have changed their hearts and been reunited with the others in a community established by the Guardian Pan thousands of years ago. But though the threat of negativity presented by the rebel Mothoc has been vastly reduced, Etera is not out of danger. If I do not call into existence the Age of Light, the growing negativity of those such as the Waschini, and others lost in their fear and distortion, will expand to such proportions that, by itself, could destroy all of Etera."

The crowd rustled and stirred.

"You have many questions, I know. I had to return because, during the coming years of my training, the Waschini will devastate the Brothers' communities until there are so few of you left that any hope of turning anyone back to the path of the Great Spirit will be lost."

Adia was watching the crowd and could see the

struggle on their faces. She understood their confusion, yet she also knew they would have to accept what he was telling them rather than get lost in trying to understand it. This was a time of surrendering in faith to the truth that was evidenced before them.

"The numbers of the lost will only continue to increase until there are more of them than you can imagine. If their path is not thwarted, in a relatively short while, they will develop weapons capable of destroying all of Etera, making it uninhabitable for any of her creatures, including all of us—and themselves. One of the People's Healers, Apricoria, has seen the culmination of this path herself and spoke to you of her vision at our last assembly."

"But that would be madness," someone from the crowd spoke out.

"Separation from the Great Spirit is a form of madness. Because without connection to the Great Spirit, the Shissu—what the Waschini call the soul—loses its way."

"But the Shissu are those who have already returned to the Great Spirit." It was Nadiwani this time.

"Ahhhhh, yes, that is how the term has been used. But the Shissu is who you are, your essence. Your body will, at some point in time, perish, but you will continue to exist. The question is only whether your Shissu will move toward further communion with the Great Spirit or toward further isolation from him."

"Krell," Adia said absentmindedly, then realized she had said it out loud, and the others were now looking at her expectantly. "The journey into krell is a descent toward further and further isolation from the Great Spirit. It is a journey of becoming more and more lost. I experienced it once, as a Healer, while trying to help others escape from it. In krell, there is no shared experience. There is only isolation, separation, and the dark, black unending night. It is a place of ultimate despair and hopelessness."

Urilla Wuti looked for Apricoria, the Healer who had the gift of seeing the future. She had traveled to the High Rocks for this assembly. At the Overseer's beckoning, the young Healer approached the front.

"For those of you who were not here at the prior assembly of the Brotherhood, it is true I have seen the future that awaits us if the Waschini and the others like them are allowed to continue in the direction they are going."

Apricoria then addressed the Brothers, "In the coming years, the Waschini will decimate your communities."

She returned her attention to all gathered. "Then, many of the Waschini and their kind will use their gifts of inventiveness, coupled with their greed and self-centeredness, to discover great power within Etera. They will unknowingly use it to isolate themselves and their future generations further and further from the voice of the Great Spirit. In time, this same inventiveness will allow their kind to develop tremendously destructive weapons such as can obliterate all life on Etera."

An'Kru spoke again. "The future is only a projection of the individual and collective paths created by those who inhabit Etera. Each of us has free will. We have been given the power to change the future by what we do in the present. This power is available to us in each and every moment. It is our choice to bring love, compassion, and joy to ourselves and others through our actions and intentions of whatever magnitude, or like the Waschini and their kind, create separation, competition, fear, and lack. Every part of Etera gives of itself except those who are lost. They take and take beyond their share, giving little in return and leaving behind decimation and scarcity."

An'Kru next directed his remarks directly to the Brothers. "The Guardian Pan explained it will fall to you to help turn the lost from their path. But, as yet, those in control, in power, are unteachable. They will influence the rest of their kind, over time, to become more and more alienated from the voice of the Great Spirit, living in such a way that the quiet needed to hear the Great Spirit's voice will be almost entirely out of their reach. Their minds will be so occupied by distractions and addictions that they become deaf to his voice. And as those distractions become more and more their way of life, the chance for them to be reached decreases almost to impossibility. And by then, you, the Brothers, will be all but annihilated. Those who do survive will be allocated to communities that isolate them, and the Waschini will be beyond your ability to influence. That must not come to pass."

Silence filled the chamber. The next words An'Kru spoke sent a chill through each and every member there.

"Time is running out for the Waschini and their kind to find their own way back to the Great Spirit. The destruction of Etera is approaching."

It had been a long morning. The crowd was silenced and filled with apprehension by An'Kru's words, and they needed a break. Acaraho glanced at his son, who seemed to have read his mind and nodded.

"You are weary," Acaraho said. "We are weary. Our minds are racing. Let us convene after mid-meal. Rest, replenish, and we will reconvene when the Call to Assembly Horn sounds."

As the others were leaving, Oh'Dar approached those still at the front: his parents and An'Kru. "I am going to spend the break with my grandparents. They have lately not been well."

"Allow me to go with you, brother."

So, together, An'Kru and Oh'Dar left the Great Chamber.

Ben and Miss Vivian were in bed, for warmth, lying closely side by side. They were holding hands in a deep, peaceful slumber.

"Perhaps we should not wake them," Oh'Dar said. But just then, his grandmother's eyes fluttered open.

"Grayson," Miss Vivian said in a voice much weaker than it had been before. "Please come and sit." She tried to make room for him but did not have the strength.

"I will stand; it is fine," Oh'Dar said as he stepped close and took her free hand in his. "How are you feeling?"

"I am tired beyond belief."

Just then, Miss Vivian noticed An'Kru. She nudged Ben awake. "Try to sit up, dear. We have company."

Ben groaned and slowly came around. "Was I dreaming? I was in the most beautiful place." Then his eyes widened as he saw the figure with Oh'Dar.

"An'Kru. Is that you?" Ben asked. "I was with you in the most wonderful place. You're grown up, exactly as you were there."

"I am grown, and I have come to help you on

your way home. It is time to say goodbye to your life here on Etera."

Oh'Dar looked up at An'Kru in horror.

"Goodbye? No!" he exclaimed.

Miss Vivian patted her grandson's hand. "Hush, Grayson, An'Kru is right. It is time for us to go. We have known for some time this day was coming, and so have you. I am ready."

"So am I," Ben said weakly.

"I am not ready." Oh'Dar's voice broke.

"No one is ever ready to say goodbye to their loved ones. I know this will be hard on you, dear Grayson," Miss Vivian managed to say. "But we are ready, and it is time."

She laid back down in exhaustion, releasing Oh'Dar's hand.

"What your grandmother is saying is true, son," Ben whispered. "We are ready to go, but we will love you forever. Thank you for bringing us here and letting us share this adventure with you—" Ben's voice drifted off, and he slumped back down on the thick mattress.

An'Kru asked Oh'Dar if he would like to say anything else. When he shook his head, An'Kru moved to stand across from him at their bed.

"Release all fear and concerns," he said. Then he reached down and gently placed a palm on each forehead. A great peace fell over the room, with only the ticking of the clock in the background to break the silence.

Both Miss Vivian and Ben smiled, and each let out a long sigh. Miss Vivian roused the tiniest bit and said as if in greeting, "Rachel! Morgan!" Then both were silent as all tension left their frail frames.

An'Kru said softly, "*Kah-Sol 'Rin*," and stepped back. Oh'Dar slumped forward across their now still bodies.

After walking over to the sideboard Oh'Dar had bought, An'Kru opened the round glass door of Miss Vivian's treasured mantle clock and stopped the hands. The room was now utterly silent except for Oh'Dar's quiet sobs.

An'Kru patiently waited until Oh'Dar had risen, smoothed his grandmother's hair, and arranged the covers.

"They have served well, and they are at peace now, brother. They are reunited with their loved ones in the Corridor, the first step in their return to the Great Spirit. You will see them again, I promise."

"Thank you; I believe your coming here has made this easier for me," said Oh'Dar. "For now, we know miracles are afoot and that the Great Spirit hears our prayers. I believe you when you tell me I will see them again. I know they are at peace."

"In the meantime, until you join them, you must see to it that your grandmother's task of documenting the People's journey is continued. In time, I'Layah will take up that mantle."

Oh'Dar looked stricken. "I'Layah, Tsonakwa, and Ashova. They didn't get to say goodbye."

"They knew this was coming. I took time to meet with them all a short while ago to prepare them," An'Kru reassured him.

Oh'Dar took a deep breath and, after straightening his wraps, brushed his hair back in place. "I must go and tell them. And the others."

After they left the room, An'Kru closed the wooden door and effortlessly placed the huge stone door across the entrance. The same stone door that had stood out of the way since Miss Vivian and Ben first came to the High Rocks to live.

Oh'Dar assembled his family. "My grandmother and Ben are gone. An'Kru and I were with them, and their last moments were peaceful, even joyful."

Acise pulled the children close to her and her parents, and they joined hands. Adia and Acaraho pulled Oh'Dar into their circle along with Nelairi and Aponi.

"I would like to have them put to rest in the meadow where my father and mother were buried after you found them," Oh'Dar told Adia.

"It is fitting and appropriate," Chief Is'Taqa said.

"And," Oh'Dar added, "at least for a while thereafter, I would like their room to remain sealed off."

Acise spoke. "Oh'Dar! I'Layah, Tsonakwa, and Ashoka have not said goodbye."

"It is alright, Momma," I'Layah said. "We all understand. Closing the room is a matter of respect. We know they are no longer there; An'Kru showed us."

"He showed you?" Oh'Dar released himself from his parents' comforting circle.

"Yes," I'Layah said, looking at her grandmother, Adia, for help. "He took us to the Corridor. Death is a birth, a passageway. We know that now."

Then she turned to Acise. "Momma, I am not afraid of anything anymore. And I do not think I ever will be."

With a pleading look at Adia, Acise reached for her daughter and kissed the top of her head.

As soon as everyone was silent, Acaraho announced the peaceful passing of Ben and Miss Vivian.

"They have been a welcome part of our community. It is because of them that so many of us have learned the Waschini language. And Ben's help with the research of Bidzel and Yuma'qia into our most viable pairing combinations has been noteworthy and much appreciated. They have also helped to draw our Brotherhood closer together. Let us have a moment of silence to honor their lives and the blessings they bestowed on all of us by their presence."

After a few moments had passed, Acaraho added, "At the wish of their grandson, Oh'Dar, they will be buried next to his parents, near the Brothers' village, and in accordance with the Waschini custom."

Voices murmured their condolences to Oh'Dar and his family. After a respectful period of time, An'Kru stepped forward to speak again.

"Oh'Dar's grandparents are proof we can live in harmony with each other. All of Etera can—but only if the intention to do so lives within each of us."

Then he addressed the Brothers directly. "The time has come for you to finalize your preparations. My father told you to begin shoring up your stores to prepare for hard times ahead. It will befall you to help provide for the Waschini when the time comes, as they will not all be able to provide for themselves. But this is just another way in which you will soften their hearts and teach them about kindness and forgiveness.

"Thanks to the efforts of Ned and Awantia, nearly all of you are now able to speak and write the Waschini language. All of this has been part of preparing you for what is to come. But as has been said before, not all the Waschini are evil. Many of them will also rise to help their fellow people through what is to come."

"What is to come, An'Kru?" someone called out. "What is going to happen; tell us, please!"

"When the time comes," An'Kru answered, "the Sassen Guardians and I will join together in the sacred circle in the meadow above Kthama to release the power of the vortex. In this event, all the Waschini's inventions, including their weapons, will be destroyed. Nearly all their structures, too. But none of their people and none of Etera's other creatures will come to harm, making them realize something supernatural has occurred. When everything they depended on is removed, they will be forced to turn to the Brothers for help. We must pray that, in humility, they will listen and learn. It is the last hope for them."

"Destroyed? How is destroying everything part of the Great Spirit's will?"

"Destruction is part of the creative process. The trees lose their leaves, and the grasses die off, only for new birth to come in the spring. Old forms that no longer serve our journey must be broken down so new ways can take their place. So it is with us, too. But even with this humbling experience, it will be for each individual to decide whether they will turn to the path of reunion with the Great Spirit. Their minds will be turned to survival instead of furthering their own selfish ways and persecuting the Brothers. And you, our Brothers, must step in and offer to help them survive. In this way, if they accept your guidance, their eyes can be opened."

Nadiwani spoke up again. "How will we know when it is time for this to happen?"

"When the winds begin to roar and night turns to day, you will know the time is upon you. But I will return to you before that final time. Before that, there will be three warnings at measured intervals. You have four seasons to prepare until the final moment comes. But help will be given to you. Two of the Healers here, Eralato and Taipa, have extraordinary abilities to help produce abundant crops both in the coming year and in the times to follow. I ask that they team up with Ned Webb and Awantia to revisit the Brothers' villages and use their abilities to fill all the storerooms."

Adia watched as the crowd came alive. Ned, sitting with his mate Awantia, seemed particularly agitated.

"Remember," An'Kru added, "those Waschini who are already aligned with the Great Spirit will help the others cope with what happens. The Brothers cannot be everywhere. Together, they will all lead the Waschini to a new future.

"I will leave you now to your preparations. Listen to your hearts. Accept that this is what must be. Were it any other way, that way would have been provided. It may yet be, but you must prepare, regardless."

With that, An'Kru left the front, and the crowd

turned their attention toward each other, avidly discussing what had just been shared.

Ned turned to Awantia. "This can't be right. What about my family, who are already serving the Great Spirit? How is this fair to them? I must warn them; I must do something. My parents. My sister—"

He hurried away to find Oh'Dar. "You, of all people, must understand. What about my family? Why should they have to suffer through this? You brought your grandparents here; why can I not be allowed to bring my family here?"

"You must speak to my father, Ned," Oh'Dar answered him. "And to the Overseer. Make your case to them. Because, yes, I do understand."

Ned pushed through the crowd to find Acaraho. "May I have a word?" he asked.

"My family. My parents are older. My father is not able to provide for them. They are dependent on others to raise their crops and care for their animals. My sister and her family have only a modest vegetable garden. Please, may I not return to them and bring them here where they will be safe?"

Acaraho looked over to his mate, who was occupied with Nootau and Iella. "I understand your concern. It is not as simple as that, Ned. Think of the adjustment you went through in learning not only of our existence but that of the Sassen. Will they be able to handle it?"

"My sister's husband, Newell Storis, knows all of

this. He knows that Oh'Dar's grandparents came here to live. He was with me when we rode with your son, Oh'Dar, to rescue the Brothers from the Waschini soldiers. He will help them understand. He will help prepare them."

Acaraho let out a long breath. "It is not my decision alone to make. This should involve the High Council. I will ask the Overseer to call together a High Council of only the People. All the members are here, so it will not take long."

With the High Council assembled in a smaller meeting room, Acaraho explained Ned's request and then let him plead his own case. When he was finished, Harak'Sar asked when he would leave, considering the Promised One had said he should start taking the Healers around to the villages.

"I would want to leave right away," Ned answered. "I don't expect I will convince them on my first visit. And, yes, An'Kru asked us to start taking the two young Healers around to the villages to help create bumper crops. So time is of the essence."

There were very few questions for Ned. Finally, the Overseer put it to the usual vote, and the majority asked that the Overseer make the decision.

Having listened carefully to Ned's petition, she placed her hand over her heart and reflected. Finally, she spoke. "I am old, but with that burden comes wisdom and understanding. We cannot protect all the Waschini from what is to come, but we can do this much. If you can convince them to come here, Ned Webb, Acaraho and I will make sure they are welcomed and helped as much as possible to adjust to life here. A life in a world they cannot possibly imagine exists."

A flood of relief passed through Ned. He impulsively reached out and took Urilla Wuti's hand. "Thank you. Thank you." Then he turned to Acaraho and the others. "And thank you to you all."

"I understand the great trust you have placed in me," he added. "And I will clearly explain that this is not to be shared with anyone else—neither the existence of the People and the Sassen nor any of what is to come."

"That is all anyone can do. We pray you are successful," Urilla Wuti said.

After Ned left the room, Urilla Wuti turned to the group. "We have other business to discuss. Ned's request only moved up the time of our coming together. Because I was not part of the High Council when this next topic came up, I have asked Harak'Sar and Khon'Tor to lead the discussion."

Harak'Sar from the Far High Hills came to the front. "Much time has passed since the Overseer Kurak'Kahn stood before the High Council and spoke of the challenge facing our people. Many of you were part of that conversation, except perhaps my son Brondin'Sar, who has more recently assumed leadership of the Far High Hills. At that time, Kurak'Kahn introduced Bidzel and Yuma'qia, who explained that without some type of intervention, our People would no longer have safe pairing options after seven generations. In the time since that announcement, the next generation has reached pairing age."

Harak'Sar nodded to Bidzel, beckoning him to speak. "At that time, Yuma'qia and I had only limited combinations to work with, as our records went back only so many generations. With the discovery of the Wall of Records within Kht'shWea, of course, that all changed. However, despite the wealth of information recorded on those chamber walls, we are in no better shape than we were. We are still faced with running out of pairing combinations."

Khon'Tor spoke next. "Though we committed ourselves to finding a solution, none has been found. It was even suggested at that time that we consider breeding with the Waschini, much as the Ancients bred with the Brothers. But it was such an abhorrent idea that it was dismissed from consideration. At that time, we, in our own prejudice, believed they were all heartless creatures who took what they wanted without regard for anything or anyone else; that all they were capable of was brutality and sacrilege. I was one of the worst and pronounced them barbarians. How small-minded that now seems, after what we have since experienced. Our own experience with Oh'Dar and his grandparents, Ben and Miss Vivian, has proven those beliefs wrong. And, if Ned Webb brings his family here to live among us, their presence will only convince others of the same—that not all Waschini are bad.

"Yet, as An'Kru said," Khon'Tor continued, "in time, the Waschini will develop weapons capable of tremendous destruction. Some of you may remember a demonstration I once performed with a Waschini weapon brought here by Oh'Dar. And one of the Sassen was killed by a Waschini using a similar weapon. Yet these are nothing compared to the power of those they have yet to invent. Can we guarantee they will never discover our communities? Because if they do, there are those who would surely annihilate us, given a chance."

The room was silent.

Khon'Tor picked up his original thread of thought: "We also spoke of the Sassen, whom we called the Sarnonn. We pondered whether they still existed, whether we might be able to connect with them. We sent out scouting parties from our own communities, hoping to make contact, with no success. Little did we know they were honoring an ancient Rah-hora to avoid all contact with us. It was only when their Leader, Haan, found the High Rocks, breaking the Rah-hora in order to save his mate. Through Haan, we learned the true story of our history and the secret of Kthama Minor. We learned about the Ancients, whom the Sassen call The Fathers-Of-Us-All. So much has happened, too much to enumerate. But through it all, despite the discovery of another pocket of Sassen who were joined with Haan's community through the Guardian Pan, we have not resolved the threat of inbreeding. Not for ourselves or for Haan and his people."

Adia spoke up, "Within Haan's community are two offspring, both females. One was born to Hakani, seeded by Haan. The other was born to Haaka, seeded by an Akassa. Most of us from Kthama know of this."

"So, the challenge still remains," Urilla Wuti took over. "What path will we choose? Breeding with the Waschini? I know that seems an impossibility, but we have seen the impossible happen before. Inter-breeding with the Waschini would take us further in the same physical direction as had breeding with the Brothers. We would lose physical strength, probably the ability to navigate using Etera's magnetic currents but gain in dexterity, possibly inventiveness. Or, there is breeding with the Sassen. As Adia explained, that has already taken place, so we know it is feasible."

"Must we do this at all?" Gatin'Rar, Leader of the Little River, asked. "Is there no other choice?"

"There is another choice," Urilla Wuti answered. "We can stop having offspring. When we have reached the seventh generation, then all pairing will be forbidden. If that is what we decide, we will have the right and the authority to bind our future offspring to this decision, but then we must accept that the People will perish from Etera. Perhaps our time is meant to come to a close. Nothing lasts forever. As somber as it sounds, it may be time for the People to pass into history. It is a viable choice."

The room fell totally silent as each member considered that alternative. No more offspring running through the halls of their communities. No more watching them grow, pair, and establish their own families. No more looking at the next generation coming up and finding solace that as each faces their own death, the joys they have known will be discovered and cherished by those coming next. No more lovemating. No passing on of the joys of life. The halls of the High Rocks and the other communities, all silent. The culture of the People, of peace, of harmony with the Great Spirit, passing downstream on the river of time and being washed away forever.

Change was hard for the People. Yet, in order to survive, change they must.

Ned hurried back to Awantia and explained. "I must immediately leave for Wilde Edge. I wish you could go with me, but we both understand the many reasons you cannot."

"Be careful, my life-walker. Be careful and be mindful that your message may not be received as you are hoping it will be."

"I will only stay away as long as I must, and I hope you are wrong. Newell already knows this is all true. He can help my parents and Grace understand. He can help prepare them all, including his and Grace's children."

Then he pulled his mate close, "Please do not worry. But pray that they receive my message."

"While you are gone, I will speak with those here about where they would live. How many are you thinking of?"

"My parents and my sister and her family, seven in all. Oh, and the dogs, Buster and Pippy. We cannot leave them behind."

"The People accepted Oh'Dar's wolf, Kweeuu, and apparently all the other small wild animals that followed An'Kru inside Kthama over his young years. I doubt a small dog would be a problem."

CHAPTER 7

The graves had been prepared for Miss Vivian and Ben, just as Oh'Dar had asked, right next to his father and his mother, Grayson Stone Morgan II, and Rachel Morgan. The spring flowers were just beginning to push their bright green shoots out of the ground, reminding everyone of the promise of spring's return and An'Kru's words about rebirth.

Acaraho carefully lowered first Miss Vivian's wrapped body, and then Ben's down into the prepared space. Soft greens and mosses cradled their remains. Oh'Dar had foregone wooden boxes, wanting them to be nestled in Etera's arms.

When Oh'Dar signaled that he was ready, Acaraho spoke.

"We come to bid good journey to two members of our family who have returned to the Great Spirit. Oh'Dar's grandmother, and her mate Ben, the

Waschini great-grandparents of I'Layah, Tsonakwa, and Ashova. Their time with us was too short, yet what of it there was did bless us all."

Oh'Dar nodded and gently tossed a handful of loose soil down into the graves. Acise came up and released a few of the earliest spring blossoms, which fluttered down and rested upon their forms. Then each of their children followed suit.

Acaraho said to Oh'Dar and his family, "Go on your way if you wish. I will make sure the rest is completed in accordance with your instructions."

Oh'Dar turned to Acise. "I would like a moment alone."

She nodded and motioned to the children to walk ahead with her.

Alone, Oh'Dar knelt down between the two open graves. "Thank you both for loving me. Thank you, Grandmother, for taking me in and accepting me, and showing me how to live in your world. I know I caused you pain and heartache, though not intentionally, but you lost your son Louis because I showed up. I know that grieved you terribly. I am so happy you got to know Acise and see your great-grandchildren born. And Ben, you became another father to me. You looked after me at Shadow Ridge. You thwarted Louis' plan to kill me. You both gave up your comfortable lives there, lives of ease and privilege, to live here with me. I believe you were happy. I am sure you were. But I want to acknowledge how great a sacrifice that was for you both, even if, in the end, you thought it worthwhile."

He got up and stood there a moment. He squeezed his eyes tightly shut. "I will think about you every day. Talk to you and believe that you hear me. I loved you both so much. My world is emptier now that you are gone but so much fuller because you were in it."

Adia had walked over to stand with her mate. "What a long journey this has been. From the day I rescued Oh'Dar and incurred Khon'Tor's wrath, through the time Oh'Dar left us to find his Waschini family to the time he asked permission to bring them here. And now to this, a farewell."

"Only a temporary farewell," Acaraho said.

"Did you seal their living quarters?"

"Yes, just as Oh'Dar asked, until he is ready for me to open them again. Though I'Layah did ask for a moment alone in there before I did it."

As I'Layah walked back with her family, she spoke to her great-grandmother in the stillness of her thoughts. *I won't forget, Great-grandmother, I will continue your legacy of documenting the People's story. When Papa turns*

the task over to me, I will not let you down. And I did as you asked me to do when you died—I removed your personal journal and gave it to Adia. She said she would keep it safe for me until I am ready to read it.

With the ceremony over, Ned and Awantia went to Chief Is'Taqa's village, from where Ned would leave to return to Wilde Edge. After they said their good-byes, Ned snapped the reins and was off to see his family.

Nora Webb heard a knock on her door and opened it to see her son standing on the front porch.

"Ned!"

"I am home only for a short while, Mama. I am sorry it has been so long since I was last here."

"Your father, Grace, Newell; they will be thrilled you are here. So will the children!"

"I wish I knew the children better, but perhaps circumstances will give me the opportunity to do just that."

Nora ignored her son's cryptic remark, having learned long before to let such things go. When he was ready, he would tell her what that was all about.

"I am going to put something special on for dinner. Wash up if you need to, and then go and surprise Grace. She will be so happy to see you!" Nora smiled to herself, knowing that the surprise would also be on Ned, as he had no idea Grace was pregnant again.

"Ned! Oh, Ned!" Grace exclaimed. She threw her arms around his neck, as she always did.

"Whoa, whoa, wait, what is this?" He stepped back to look at her protruding belly. "Oh, my goodness. It looks like you are almost due!'

"I am. Oh, you could not have come at a better time. I was praying you would get here before she was born."

"She?"

Grace laughed, "Newell swears it is a girl this time."

"Well, whichever it is, I am happy for both of you."

"I keep hoping you will bring Awantia."

"I know. But the climate of feeling against the Locals keeps me from doing just that. And it seems to be getting worse with time."

"It is. We used to seldom hear about any of the Locals being taken from their villages. Now it seems to be happening nearly all the time. It is very sad. And it is so wrong."

"Where is Newell? At his office, I assume?"

"Yes, his business continues to flourish. He usually makes it home before dinner, though."

"Mama said she is going to prepare something special for us all. Have you started making your meal yet?"

"Only the day's bread is made. I was running late. I'm having a little trouble with back pain at this point."

"Then, good," Ned said and led Grace to the sofa. "You can sit here and relax with me until Newell gets home. But where's Pippy?"

As if on cue, Pippy came bouncing around the corner, followed by three puppies.

"Wait. I thought Pippy was a boy?"

"He is. But he has–or had—a romance. Unfortunately, her owners weren't happy about it and said they didn't want to keep the puppies. They found homes for a few except these last three. They said they were going to drown them."

"Oh, no! How horrible!"

"Yes, I know. Hence, here they are!" Grace smiled as the circle of puppies romped and played with each other in front of the sofa.

"You're going to have your hands full in a little while."

"I know."

Brother and sister sat and talked for some time until the wooden front door opened, and Newell stepped inside.

"Grace, whose horse is that outside? It almost looks— Ned!"

Ned jumped up and gave Newell a brotherly embrace.

"You're just in time," the lawyer exclaimed.

"Grace told me. And dinner is at our parents' house tonight."

Matthew said a blessing, and then the chatter began, virtually non-stop, while hands reached across and passed warm, creamy mashed potatoes and steaming hot biscuits. They had as many questions for Ned as ever, and he patiently answered each one as best he could. Then he listened to Newell talk about the escalated persecution of the Locals, which Grace had already mentioned. Buddy kept his place under the table, no doubt hoping for something to fall.

"What is frightening about this," Ned said, "and if it has not occurred to you yet, it should, is if they can do this to the Locals, what would keep them from doing it to any other group of people they took a dislike to, or who was in the way of *progress*."

"Ned," Newell said, "for reasons you know I

understand, you have a dim view of our people. But I am not sure it is fully warranted."

Ned felt the sting of Newell's words but said nothing. However, the words surprised him, as Newell had been with him when they rescued Chief Kotori's village from the hands of the military outpost commander. He had seen the condition the Brothers were in, how they had been treated. Nearly starved to death, freezing, the elderly sick and dying.

"Tell us about your wife," Nora suggested.

"She is well. We have finished our travels to the neighboring villages. We have taught many to read and write English, and it can only serve us all in the future. I think it also helped the Brothers to understand that not all of our kind are bad."

"Hopefully, you can both now have some quiet time. Perhaps, someday, you will have a child?"

Ned put down his fork and wiped his mouth with his napkin. "I hope so. But we are happy, regardless!"

"I am sure it will happen in time. But I am glad you have found happiness among the Locals. The Brothers."

"It has been incredibly rewarding, and I would not have missed it for the world. So much better than becoming an animal doctor, as I had set out to do. Life presents some amazing opportunities if we are brave enough to reach out and grab them."

Ned then noticed Grace eyeing him. She knew

him well, and no doubt realized he was trying to plant some type of seed.

When dinner was done, the dishes washed, and the remaining food all put away, Grace asked Ned to go out with her and see their parents' garden.

"It looks to be off to a good start," Ned said, staring across at the neatly plowed rows and freshly tilled soil. He inhaled deeply, "Nothing smells as good as newly prepared ground."

"You say that about everything. About newly cut wood, burning wood, fresh hay, the night air, freshly fallen snow, puppies. If I didn't know better, I would think Awantia made her way into your heart through your nose!"

Ned chuckled. "What you say is true. Just trying to appreciate life, I guess. It can turn so quickly, can't it?"

"What is the matter? Please tell me."

"I did not want to mention it at dinner time, but Grayson's grandparents died."

"What? Oh no. Both of them?"

"Yes. Essentially, at the same time. It seems it was very sweet, though. They died smiling and holding hands, I am told."

"Oh, poor Grayson. And his children. It's all gone now. Shadow Ridge, Ben, Miss Vivian."

"They have strong beliefs about where our souls go after death. Their entire culture is very spiritually oriented."

"I know there is something you are not telling me. I mean, besides the grandparents' passing."

Ned looked up into the sparkling night sky as if looking for help.

"There is no way for me to say this that will not be a shock. Come back with me. All of you. Mama, Papa, you, Newell, the boys. Buddy. Pippy and the puppies!"

"Come back with you?"

"Yes. All of you. Come back and live with Awantia and me."

Grace stared at him. "Oh, Ned. That— That doesn't make any sense. We can't just uproot our lives like that. Newell's business is doing extremely well now, and the children, they need a proper education. It's too much to ask, and as much as we all miss you, I'm sorry; how could we possibly? And why?"

"I wouldn't ask if it were not important. It is more than important; it is imperative."

"Imperative? But why? The Locals aren't a threat to us if that is what you are worried about? About their rebelling?"

"No. Oh, there's no way for me to explain this without sounding like a madman."

Grace stood quietly, waiting for him to continue.

"There is trouble coming. Something on a scale you can't imagine. It won't be safe for you to be here. Any of you. The way of life you know is going to disappear. Overnight. Everything will become a struggle. But if you all come with me, yes, it will be a big adjustment, more than I can explain, but you will be safe and protected."

"I have never known you to lie, and you know I trust you. But this is hard to accept. I am not saying I don't believe you; it's just—"

"I know. It sounds far-fetched, and that I could be wrong about what is coming." He took one of her hands in his. "But Grace, I'm not. I'm just not."

She let out a long breath. "If I am having trouble with this, Mama and Papa are going to have more. And Newell."

"Newell should have the least trouble understanding it—at least, the kind of lifestyle change I'm talking about. It takes adjustment, but it is not as difficult as it sounds. And there will be lots of help."

Ned let her hand go and sat down on a nearby bench. "Oh, maybe I am asking too much. There isn't any way for you to accept this, I know. And if I try to explain further, it's just going to make it worse. As if I *have* lost my mind."

Grace sat down next to him and put her arm around his shoulder. "Can you at least tell me *how* you know this? Is it some military secret you have discovered? Are they planning on something worse for the Brothers? Not relocating them but perhaps massacring them?"

"It's too complex to explain. I just need you to trust me."

"I think you need to talk to all of us at once. If you say Newell understands something of what you are talking about, maybe he can help you explain it more clearly."

Ned's stomach was twisting. The impossibility of what he was asking was hitting him. There was no way they were going to believe him, even if they said they did. It was too fantastic. And on his word alone, they should believe this horrible devastation was going to happen? But he had to try. He had to try.

Ned spent the next day collecting his thoughts. He walked out to one of the fields and paced back and forth, pitching his story. The crows on the fence posts cocked their heads as if listening, trying to figure out what this creature was all about as he moved through the tall grasses chattering away to himself. Ned was trying to hear it from his family's viewpoint, and no matter how he put it, it seemed impossible to believe.

Finally, he stopped and did what he had learned was the best way to approach a problem; he prayed. "Please, please give me the words to say. Please prepare their hearts and minds to hear me. Please don't let me fail them."

That evening, Ned asked everyone to stay at the table after dinner as he had something important to talk to them about. Nora and Grace quickly cleared the dishes and sat back down with the men.

"What I am about to say is going to sound crazy; I know that, and I am braced for your reaction. But I am hoping you will realize you know me well enough to understand I am not crazy and that I would not risk this suggestion if it were not critically important for you to believe me. Just please listen before you say anything."

All faces were turned to his. Even Buddy kept his eyes on Ned while settling down in his little bed by the warm hearth.

"There is going to be a widespread catastrophe. I can't tell you how I know, but I know. And there is no question it is going to take place. When it does, the life you know now will no longer exist. Every convenience that people enjoy will be taken away. Most of the buildings will be damaged, if not destroyed. Life will return to what we would call a primitive state for quite a while."

He saw them look at each other. Grace reached over and laid her hand on Newell's as if to reassure him Ned was telling the truth. Matthew tilted his chair on its back legs as he was wont to do when thinking.

"Ned—"

"Father, please; I know it's hard, but you have to believe me. It is going to happen."

"When?" his father asked.

"In about a year, so there isn't much time."

"Much time to what? Prepare?" Newell had raised his voice. "Are you going to tell us how to prepare? Though, if everything is going to be destroyed, it doesn't seem there is much we can do to prepare."

"There must be a reason you're telling us this, Ned. What is it?" his mother asked.

"I want you to come back with me. All of you. And anything we can manage to bring. Chickens, goats, horses. Corn seed. Clothing."

Matthew's eyebrows rose, and he gave his wife a look.

"I know, I know. It sounds like nonsense. But it's not. It's not."

"You are saying we should leave everything here and go live with you. Where?" Newell asked. Ned knew what he was asking. What about the People and the Sassen? How did they factor into this?

"With Awantia and me at first. At her village. Then, eventually, we would find other places."

"Other places," Newell repeated.

"Yes, other places. But that doesn't matter now. At least you would all be safe, and the Brothers—and I —would help you get established."

"And what about this place?" Matthew asked. "We just walk away from it? From everything I've worked for to provide for you and your mother? And Newell? Must he just up and sell a lucrative business?"

"There isn't going to be any business; that's what I'm saying. Nothing is going to remain of what your lives look like now. You have to believe me!" Ned could feel he was beginning to sound crazy or desperate, or both.

"I don't know how to say this without sounding like I don't believe you," Matthew said. "But it is too much, son. It is too much to do without—"

"Without some proof?" Ned said. "Oh, I am not offended. If I were in your shoes, I would no doubt be saying the same thing. It is too hard to believe, and only on my say so, no matter if I am your son."

"Well, is there any other way for us to know this is going to happen?" his mother asked.

Ned thought for a moment. "There will be three signs before it happens."

"Signs?"

"Yes. I don't know what they are, but they will be unusual enough that you will notice them."

Ned's father lowered his chair to all four of its legs. "All I can say is that I will think about it. And if these signs come, then that will help me think."

"Thank you for listening and not shutting me down. You are going to think about it; that's all I can ask. But you would all have to come, and before too long. Trust me, if some of you stay behind, when it happens, I'm concerned I won't be able to come back and help you."

Ned dropped the subject, and the rest of the evening ended early. Upstairs in his childhood bed, with Buster curled up next to him, he reflected on how it had gone.

He hadn't expected them all to accept what he was saying at first blush. He knew that was too much to ask. And if he had to gauge how they were each feeling, he would say his father and Newell were the most skeptical—not that anyone was ready to pack up. But Newell, that surprised him. Newell, more than anyone, knew the odds were high that Ned was telling the truth. Then why had he fought so much? Ned knew he must talk to Newell alone.

After they had settled down in bed, Nora asked, "What do you think of all this, Matthew?"

"I don't know what to think. He's always been a level-headed boy. Never gave us any trouble. Never had outlandish ideas or made up any stories. Never even had that much of an imagination, really, not like some kids. And he's a full-grown man now, with a wife and responsibilities. There isn't any way he's making this up. He believes what he is telling us; I have no doubt of that."

"So the question is, where did it come from, and do we believe it or not?"

"My goodness, Nora. To pack up and leave everything behind? And then, even though he obviously believes it, what if he is wrong? We can't just come back. We'd have sold the farm. Newell's business would be gone. We'd have to start all over from scratch."

"But what if he's right?"

"Well, that's the rub, isn't it. What if he is right? If it was anyone but Ned, I would say they were crazy. But it's Ned. That's what makes it so difficult."

"What do you think Newell is thinking?"

"Newell is a lawyer, a businessman. He would never agree to do this. I could see it on his face."

"And he knows more about Ned's lifestyle than any of us. Do you think that's why? He knows how hard it would be?"

"Maybe. Something like that. But whatever he knows, it isn't swaying him toward doing this, that's for sure."

Across town, Grace and Newell were having a similar discussion in front of the fire in their sitting room.

"Newell, you have been quiet ever since we left my parents. I know you're thinking about what my brother said."

"I have thought of nothing else."

"Please talk to me. What are you thinking?"

"Grace, it's impossible. What he is asking is impossible. We are finally established here, we have children, and you are about to deliver our daughter. That would make her less than a year old when we would leave."

"Well, it would have to be before then. We couldn't wait until the last minute; that wouldn't seem wise."

"Don't tell me you would even consider this." He turned to face her.

"It's Ned. You know he doesn't make things up. He wouldn't tell us this if it wasn't true; he knows we might think he'd lost his mind."

"Just because he believes it's true doesn't mean it is true. People have often thought the world was coming to an end, and none of them has been right so far."

"So why would it be someone like Ned who was finally right? Is that what you are saying?"

Newell released her hand and stood up. "I don't know what I am saying. Yes. No. Maybe."

"Can you find any possibility that you would even consider he is right?"

Newell got very quiet. He knew so much more than anyone else did about where Ned was living and about the People and the Sassen, and that was what bothered him the most about it—that there was a chance it could be true. Because he had learned that fantastical things can be real. And this might just be another of those.

He sat down again. "Yes, there is a part of me that thinks this could be true, but it is a small part. And my mind is fighting even considering it. I am not ready to accept it, and I am not ready to start turning our lives upside down merely on the chance that he is right."

"I think my father feels the same way. I don't know about Mama."

"Honey, our children. They would grow up never knowing a proper life. Where would they find wives? And our daughter—"

"Maybe we wouldn't be the only ones. Maybe others would be there too. We don't know. And look at Ned. He and Awantia are very happy. I know you're not prejudiced, Newell—"

"No, I'm not. I just want everything to stay the same. I want to have a normal life." He leaned back. "Here is what we will do. I'll talk to your father. Maybe we can come to an agreement that if these signs do happen, then we will seriously consider it. The way Ned talked, there won't be any mistake that something unusual is happening. How is that?"

"That's fair. Thank you. I don't want to uproot our family, either. I also want us and our children to live a normal life, but if what he says is going to happen does come about, there won't be any normal life. At least, presumably, for a long time."

The next day, Ned looked up Newell at his office in town.

"I was expecting you," Newell said. "Close the door and sit down."

"You know why I'm here."

"Yes. You want to know why I wasn't more supportive of what you were saying."

"Exactly. You know there are things that seem impossible yet are true. You've seen them with your own eyes."

"I know. But it doesn't change how I feel. I want my children growing up with their own kind."

"They don't have to know about the People. Or the Sassen."

"I wasn't talking about them."

Ned's jaw dropped.

"You mean the Brothers? I can't believe you are saying that."

"Look, Ned. I'm not prejudiced. Really I'm not. It's just that—"

"Well, it certainly sounds as if you are. And if so, you had better get over it because the Brothers are going to be the only hope for our kind, the Waschini, to survive."

"People have survived on their own for a long time, Ned. It's only those of us who are a little more dependent on the small towns who might be in trouble."

"You weren't listening. Buildings, implements, and weapons are going to be destroyed. The normal way of life won't exist. It's going to be a struggle to survive. And what do you think is going to happen? That everyone will pull together and help each other? That works when not everyone is affected. But I am talking about wide-scale devastation. There isn't going to be anyone to rescue you. Everyone will be on their own."

"Well, that's your opinion. I guess I think a little more highly of us *Waschini* than you do."

Ned let out a long breath. "Newell. The buildings. That doesn't just mean houses and storefronts. Prisons, Newell. And what do you think all those criminals are going to do when this happens? Just go up to the least ravaged farmhouse and knock politely on the door and ask for a meal? No. They'll be desperate and afraid, and they'll kill everyone inside and take what is there for themselves. Think of the likes of Snide Tucker. Wake up, Newell. It's going to happen, and I am fighting for your lives."

"And who told you all this? Who?"

Ned shook his head. "You don't believe what I have told you already, even with what you have witnessed with your own eyes. How would you believe anything else? You'd have to see him to understand.'

"Him? So there's a *him*. What is this, some spiritual leader? Someone the Brothers all follow?"

"Something like that."

"And you believe him."

"You would too if you saw him. If you met him."

"That, probably, is what it would take." Newell pushed his chair back from his desk, the legs scraping loudly on the old wooden floor, and stood up.

Ned knew the meeting was over, and he stood too. "You know I'm right. You just don't want to admit it."

"I don't know if you're right. I know you believe you're right. There's a big difference."

"I am right. And I'm going to do everything I can to convince my family, which includes my sister and her children, to come with me."

"*Our* children. They are my children as well, and I determine what happens to them. Not you. Not Grace." Newell opened the door and motioned for Ned to get out.

Ned walked down the steps out into the dirt street. He had seen a side of Newell he hadn't known existed. Perhaps what they had gone through together had proven too much for him, after all, and had rattled his view of reality. But Ned had done his best. Now it would depend on the three events, whatever they might be, to convince his family to come with him. *I just hope they are what An'Kru said they will be.* Something unmistakable. Something not even Newell could deny. And that whenever they happened, there would still be time to save his family.

As much as he wanted to stay for the birth of Grace's fourth child, Ned was relieved to be leaving. He had to get back to the village to do An'Kru's bidding, and he also had much to think about. Mostly how unnerved he was by Newell's reaction.

CHAPTER 8

Adia finally had some time alone with Acise, who began by saying, "I know you have spoken of the Corridor, and now An'Kru supposedly took my children there, all three of them."

"I have as many questions as you do. And though we may not know the reason, we have to trust it is only for their welfare."

"Why is it important for them to be shown the proof that we continue after death? What did they talk about? Is something coming that is so devastating that they, above all others, needed to be shown this?"

"We do not know who has been shown the Corridor," Adia gently pointed out. "Perhaps this happens frequently. Maybe it is to prepare them for what is to come, or maybe it is to prepare them for their paths."

"Either way," Acise said, "it worries me. Either

way, it sounds as if the challenges in their lives will be great, that they need such assurance in order to prepare them to get through what is to come."

Adia took Acise's hand. "We can ask An'Kru. That is the only way to know."

"Will he tell us?"

"There is only one way to find out."

An'Kru listened to the two mothers.

"I am not surprised by your questions; I expected them, but what the youngsters and I spoke of is between them and myself. I assure you that it was only for their benefit."

"Please, they are my children," put in Acise. "I do not wish to live in fear of what the future holds for them."

"Nothing will be asked of them but what they are capable of bearing or achieving. The future is not written, and the events they are being prepared for may not take place."

He turned to Adia. "You of all people should know this, Mother."

"This is the last stronghold," Adia said. "My fear for my loved ones. For you, An'Kru, and your siblings, and for I'Layah, Tsonakwa, and Ashova. I know we cannot protect them from life, yet my heart still longs to."

Acise took a moment to reflect before speaking.

"I know what you are saying is true, An'Kru. I will work on my faith." She glanced at each of them and smiled bravely. "Now, I will leave you to spend some time together."

Once Acise had gone, An'Kru turned his attention back to his mother, "I know you understand that we continue to live on in the Corridor and beyond, that you only wish for them not to suffer." His voice became gentle. "You have had this conversation before with E'ranale, have you not?"

"Yes," Adia answered.

"Perhaps it is time you hear it from another."

In the next moment, Adia and An'Kru were standing in the meadow she had come to know so well. The familiar richness of everything filled her senses. She had almost forgotten how much more real this existence in the Corridor was than the one she experienced on Etera.

A meadow lay before them, filled with blooms of colors so rich she could feel each one, and through it, a lone figure approached. It was a female about Adia's age, but no one she recognized. The female wore a shimmering greenish-blue wrap of a material unknown to Adia, and the flowers seemed to make way for her, closing their ranks after she had passed.

Her face was kind, and Adia could see love shining through her eyes.

"Do I know you?" Adia asked.

"We only met once, briefly, a long time ago, but you know of me, Adia; I am your mother."

"Mother?" Adia was overcome with emotion. "You are my mother?"

The figure stepped forward and embraced her. In that instant, Adia's every longing to be in her mother's arms flooded into her mind and was satisfied.

"Yes. I am. And though you were not aware, I have watched over you your entire life. I have witnessed the many trials you have endured; I have watched you fight for justice and for others, and for your faith. It has not been an easy walk, but you prevailed at every turn."

"Oh, it was you who sent the blue bird, was it not?"

"Yes. I sent you the blue bird to mark that moment so you would remember you had experienced it before and more easily believe what An'Kru was telling you."

"I never knew you, yet I missed you all my life."

"I know. I felt your heartache as deeply as I felt my own at not being with you."

Adia realized An'Kru was no longer with them.

"I wish I could stay here."

"That day will come, my dearest."

"Where is Father? You are not with him?"

"I am at times. At other times I tend to my own path. This is only one in many steps on our journey to reunion with the Great Spirit.

"But for now, there is much yet for you to do, my beloved daughter. Hard times are coming for all of Etera and for you, too. An'Kru brought you here to me because it is time for my words and presence to comfort you through the difficulties to come."

Adia's eyes stung with tears, which surprised her; after all, this was the Corridor. "I wished so many times to be able to listen to your advice, to talk to you, to tell you how much I was missing you."

"I know, daughter. And though you did not realize it, I have never been far from your side. You have been strong for yourself and others; I was not there for you, and so in your moments of deepest despair, to whom did you turn? You turned to the Great Mother and prayed, asking for help and guidance and the wisdom to know what to do and the strength to do it. Your prayers were answered— perhaps not always in the ways you thought or expected, but every step has brought you closer and closer to her.

"Not everyone turns their hearts to her; somewhere along the way, many turn to the pleasures of Etera's realm to solve their problems. These pleasures are intoxicating, so tempting that we can lose ourselves if we do not rather turn to their source, for love, joy, and pleasure are the source from which all is created. They are given to us to be enjoyed, but when we lose sight of where they come from, we begin to focus on the pleasures themselves and take our eyes off the source. Then we move further away in our pursuit of what can only come from him."

Adia nodded her understanding.

"Once our eyes are turned to focusing on obtaining the pleasures themselves, it becomes harder to turn them back to seeking the Great Spirit. This, partly, is what has happened to the Waschini and all who are similarly lost. The further away they become, the greater the correction that is needed to bring them back into seeking the true source of all joy, love, and pleasure."

"Something terrible is going to happen. You are trying to prepare me," Adia said.

"Terrible is a word often assigned to something we do not fully understand the purpose of. You believe your son has come to bring unity to Etera, but he has come not to bring unity but to bring division. A division that will strip the masks off those who are evil but pretend to be righteous. The division between good and evil will be made apparent, and false pretenses will be dropped. The true hearts of all who inhabit Etera will be revealed."

"And the hardship that is to come will cause those masks to fall?" Adia asked.

"Yes. Because pretense takes much effort. Of course, there are those who are outrightly evil, and they are easier to see. But then there are those who are just as evil but hide it behind manipulations and cleverness. Because they live lives of relative ease, they have the energy and time to put their machinations into play. The hearts of the good are easily confused; because of the gentleness of their souls, they do not see what is right in front of them, and they are tempted to deny that evil is real."

The hardship to come will peel away the facades of those who do not seek the Great Spirit or wish to live in harmony with others."

"There is more, though, that you are here to prepare me for, is there not?"

"Yes, my wise one. And you may wonder why I am explaining all of this to you, Adia. It is time for you to grow from being a Healer to becoming a teacher. You must start sharing this understanding of life with the other Healers, so it can be spread throughout the communities of the People and the Sassen. Up until now, you have only been allowed to share with very few what you have learned here. But that is changing."

"Tell me, then. I am ready."

"This chance for the lost to turn to the Great Spirit will come at a great cost, for only in this way can the path be opened for them to find their way home. You have heard your son talk of how suffering breaks open the shell of arrogance that keeps people on a path of error. But the evil are not suffering enough to cause them to abandon their ways. Left unchecked, they will strip Etera of her resources and poison all that is left. They are enjoying their positions of power at the expense of others."

"But how can people who are committing evil enjoy doing so?"

"The same life force that is love, pleasure, and joy also enlivens them. So even in their twisted and destructive ways, the root of that life force exists. They do evil because they have lost their way, and the only pleasure they know is what their actions bring. The pleasure of dominating, hoarding, feeling superior, and competing is all they know of it, even, sadly, in some cases, the pleasure they experience in inflicting harm or behaving cruelly to others. And the more they are blind to the natural pleasures the Great Spirit has provided—love, companionship, contribution, the wonder of creation, the beauty of the night sky, the smell of rain, the song of the birds of the air, the stillness through which the Great Spirit speaks—the more lost they become.

"This is the last chance for the lost. Pray it opens their hearts, but make no mistake, evil will not be allowed to prey on good forever. In preparation for what happens next, pray for understanding, strengthen your faith, and hold on to it with all you are. Remember what you know so well when you are here, that love never dies, that all those you have lost are waiting for you here. Remember, too, that everything that happens, no matter how hard, ultimately is so you can find your way here and be reunited with all those you love, have loved, and will ever love."

"Krell. What is coming is to help save those lost ones from krell."

"They are already existing in a level of krell, but they do not know it. Their souls still search for something, which is why they continue to fight and scrabble for more and more. However, none of their acquisitions or addictions, or achievements can quench the thirst that is the emptiness of their souls because only reunion with the Great Spirit can fill that hole. The path they are on will take them only further in the wrong direction, and krell is a bottomless pit of isolation and despair."

"So, An'Kru has come to make a way for them to find their way back on the path home," Adia said.

The last thing she remembered before realizing she was back on Etera was the love for her shining in her mother's eyes.

Then her attention was drawn to An'Kru, who was standing waiting for her.

"An'Kru, I understand now. Thank you."

"I must now bid you farewell and leave you, Mother," he said, "and I must find Father and say goodbye to him, too."

"Where are you going? Why must you leave?" Adia asked.

"I have set in motion that which must be accomplished here. But there are other tasks I must complete between now and when I fulfill my destiny. I will not be far away; if you need me, I will know, and I will come back to you."

Not long after Ned left, Grace went into labor at her parents' house, and she delivered a beautiful baby girl, just as Newell had predicted. Dr. Miller declared her and the baby in fine health and left to let them both rest.

Newell and Grace agreed to name her Ruby after Grace's grandmother. The baby had brown hair, and Grace was secretly pleased Ruby had not inherited the Webb blond locks. She had always thought they looked washed out compared to the rich beauty of brown hair.

In the kitchen, Nora was preparing something special for Grace. "Finally, a girl," she said to her husband.

"Yes, though boys are important to help with the homestead, I understand a woman has a special relationship with a daughter. And a granddaughter."

"Oh, Matthew, if Ned has children, we will never see them unless we go—"

"Now, Nora, please, don't start. I know you would do anything for your children, and I love you for that, but this is more than a move across town. If what Ned says is true, we'll recognize the signs. And then we'll decide accordingly."

"You don't believe him."

"I do, and I don't. I agree with Newell; it is clear Ned believes it. But that doesn't make it true."

"You and Newell have already discussed this, just the two of you?"

"Yes, we are the providers and the protectors of our families. You know it falls to the men to make major decisions such as this."

"You and I have always discussed big changes. I don't like that it sounds as if Grace and I are being left out of what happens to us and our children."

"I don't want this to come between us, please. Let's just count our blessings and trust we will know what to do when the time comes."

"I'm going to take this up to Grace." Nora picked up the meal she had prepared.

Little Ruby was nursing, content in her mother's arms. Nora set the covered bowl on the bedside table.

"Look how sweet she is, Mama."

"I brought you something to eat. It will keep until she is done." Then Nora sat down on the edge of her daughter's bed.

"I miss Ned already," Grace said, carefully

adjusting the blankets Ruby was nestled in. "Oh, if he had only stayed a few more days. But I know; he wanted to get back to his wife."

"He is a good husband."

"Mama, what are we going to do? What if Ned is right? Newell thinks he is delusional; he has nearly said as much."

"Your father is not convinced, either. And, believe me, the idea of leaving everything and starting a new lifestyle at this point in our lives does not please me at all. I just want to live out my life here, surrounded by you and your family. That kind of change sounds exhausting; I can only imagine how hard an adjustment it would be. Although, Miss Vivian and Ben did it, and they were quite a bit older than your father and I are now."

"So you do believe Ned, don't you, Mama? Not just that he believes what he is saying but that what he is saying is true. That it is going to happen."

"I do; God help me, I do. And if it happens as he says, then life as we know it will be replaced by a struggle with who knows what end in sight."

CHAPTER 9

K alli took on with vigor her role as big sister to her brother, Srakkah. She helped her mother change him, and she sat and rocked him and told him stories. They were happy stories about little forest creatures and their lives. She turned them into people and gave them names and personalities. Of course, he didn't understand any of it, but her tone made him smile, and that pleased her.

Haaka knew her oldest daughter was still struggling over who to identify with. It was an undercurrent, but she got glimpses of it whenever Kalli saw her reflection on the water or in a polished rock wall as they walked by. Haaka decided to seek help sooner rather than later.

Adia listened carefully to Haaka's concerns. "I do so understand the challenge, Haaka. I am glad you came to me. Certainly, Oh'Dar had a similar situation; there was no one here with whom he could identify. The closest to looking like him were the Brothers. Kalli has Del'Cein, and the two of them are very similar, both more Akassa than Sassen."

"It is true," Haaka agreed. "But it broke my heart when she said she only belonged to Haan and Del'-Cein only belonged to me, but her brother belonged to both of us."

"I cannot imagine the heartache of how she was feeling. Does Haan know how Kalli feels?"

"Yes, I told him. It hurt him as much as it hurt me —for her sake, not ours. It was the last thing we wanted for either of them to grow up feeling as Akar'Tor did. Though Hakani and Haan were mates, I was part of his pod. I saw much of Akar'Tor's struggle. It wounded him deeply that he was so different. He felt he did not really belong anywhere. I thought their having each other, Kalli and Del'Cein, would be enough. But it is not."

"What about Del'Cein's seed father?" Adia asked.

"Lannak'Sor? Kalli knows he exists, but Del'Cein has no understanding of it. I have kept him out of our lives, but are you saying perhaps now that should change?"

"He seems to have a kind nature," mused Adia. "And he has asked about the two of you on and off but is respecting your privacy, as you agreed. He is no relation to Kalli, but there is the chance that, in time

Del'Cein may feel as Kalli does. Perhaps you should discuss with him how Kalli feels?"

"I have not spoken with him since the seeding. You told me he was pleased to hear that Del'Cein had been born healthy, but I saw no reason to include him, as the understanding was clear his involvement would be limited unless I asked otherwise. He *was* kind. He wanted to help me because he had seen Oh'Dar's struggles and because he had siblings and knew the value of those relationships."

"It might help them both if he were open to bringing both Del'Cein and Kalli into the community at Kthama."

"But he is a watcher stationed at the outskirts of your territory. How would he be around to do that?"

"He paired a year ago; he is no longer a watcher."

Haaka grew silent. She remembered the conversation in which Lannak'Sor had said whoever he paired with would know about the situation. He had promised to be there for the offling if she needed him to be.

"How would this sit with Haan?"

"He would do anything for them. He is not the jealous type. He would see how it would help both Kalli and Del'Cein, to be around others they resemble. They are both young; there is time to help turn this around. If he and his mate were willing to help both of them, it would also strengthen their bond as sisters. Perhaps they will be the bridge to bring our two communities even closer together.

"Thank you, Adia. I knew you would help me. Please give me a few days to speak with Haan, and then perhaps you would set up a meeting between Haan and me and Lannak'Sor and his mate."

Eyota was caring for all three offling while Haan and Haaka met with Lannak'Sor and his mate, Tisu. It was the first time Haan had seen the Akassa male who contributed his seed to create Del'Cein. The first time he had even heard the name. Lannak'Sor seemed to be strong, by the Akassa's standards, less puny than most. And there was clearly a close relationship between him and his mate.

Acaraho made the introductions. "You know why this meeting was arranged. Adia and I are only here to answer any questions you may have since we ourselves also raised an offspring who felt like an outsider within our community."

"My first son, Akar'Tor was an Akassa," said Haan. "He never found his place, either with us or with your People. But he had problems with his mind, which I believe were passed on to him by his mother, Hakani. If he had been raised with his own kind—well, I do not know if that would have mitigated his troubles. I will never know. But I do know he suffered from feelings of isolation, even though his mother was an Akassa like him. Now my daughter, Kalli, is struggling with the same feelings of not belonging. I cannot bear to see her suffer, nor her younger sister Del'Cein. If you are willing to help us help them, Haaka and I will be so very grateful."

Lannak'Sor looked at his mate. She was tall like him, with a figure far more lithe than many of the Akassa females.

Tisu introduced herself, continuing, "When Lannak'Sor and I were getting to know each other, he made it clear about the situation with his daughter—your daughter—Del'Cein. I assure you my heart is open to her and to your other daughter as well. If it would help them in any way, we will both be happy to bring them into our community to whatever extent you want."

Adia interjected, "If you decide to proceed with this, I suggest that, at first, you meet at Kht'shWea so your daughters are on familiar territory. Once Kalli and Del'Cein get to know you, then slowly start bringing them closer to the People's culture. I am sure all our offspring will also be glad to help welcome them."

Haaka said, "Though Del'Cein shows no signs of realizing she and her sister are different from the rest of us at Kht'shWea, she will no doubt in time. Hopefully, this will work. Hopefully, this will help Kalli and head Del'Cein off from developing the same feelings."

"I do not think it will solve all their problems," Adia added. "Realistically, Kalli and Del'Cein will always be aware they are different from the rest of your people—and ours to an extent. But they will have a place where they will not feel quite so different. Where they do not stand out so sharply from the others. And, no doubt, it will draw them closer to each other as well."

Over the upcoming days, Lannak'Sor and his mate began their casual visits to Kht'shWea. Both the young females were interested in the two strangers who appeared frail and yet were so friendly and kind.

The days passed. Routine returned to everyone's lives. Ned and Awantia set out for the Brothers' villages, taking Eralato and Taipa with them. At each location, the Healers used their abilities to ensure the harvest would be bountiful. By the time it was mid-summer, they were on their way back to Chief Kotori's village.

Everyone tried to keep busy, distracting themselves from the passing days and anticipation of An'Kru's first warning. However, conversation always quickly turned to what it might be, even among the most taciturn. There had been unusual events before, and the people wondered how this event would stand out from others. What would make it so unmistakable that this was indeed from An'Kru?

The People kept their discussion from the offspring as much as possible. They did not want to alarm their little ones, as these were adult concerns and not burdens for them to bear. The adults busied themselves making items that might be of use to the neighboring tribes of the Brothers—primarily skins and furs. They also gathered food and medicinals that could be preserved. No one knew what to expect, but they knew food, water, shelter, and health were basic survival needs.

As part of their preparation, Acaraho and the other Leaders each looked at their communities' layouts. They prepared the spaces where there were opportunities to cluster visitors together if necessary. Would these events be so severe that the Brothers' villages would need to be evacuated? No one knew. But there was no leaving anything to chance that they could prepare for ahead of time.

Iella was close to delivering. Nootau left her side only when she was in the company of Adia, Urilla Wuti, or Nadiwani. When the time came, he stayed in the hallway with his father and Oh'Dar, both of whom commiserated with him over the stress of waiting. Eventually, Adia came out and told them Iella was fine and that she and Nootau had a son.

Acaraho slapped Nootau on the back, and Oh'Dar gave him a brotherly hug. "Congratulations, I know you will make a great father."

"I hope so. I certainly had the best."

"Go in there and be with your Saraste' and son," said Acaraho."

"Come with me," Nootau urged him.

"I will be there in a moment. You first need to have some private time."

As Nootau entered, Adia and Nadiwani left to stand outside with Acaraho and Oh'Dar.

"Our family grows, Saraste'," and Acaraho pulled Adia to him.

Nadiwani was looking gloomy, and Adia took her hand. "Are you alright?"

"I am reminded of my own empty arms, that is all. Forgive me for thinking of myself at such a joyful time for your family."

Adia wrapped an arm around her friend, pulling her close.

Nootau hurried over to Iella, who was holding their son in her arms. He leaned down and kissed her on the forehead and brushed her cheek with the back of his fingers. "You have never looked more beautiful. How is our son?"

Iella took Nootau's hand and kissed it, then moved the offspring so Nootau could see him. She pulled back the blanket that had been covering his head.

Nootau just stared.

At Kht'shWea, great strides had been made with Kalli and Del'Cein on the part of Lannak'Sor and Tisu. Haaka started accompanying her daughters to the High Rocks to visit the Akassa couple. Del'Cein took it in with the wonder of a young offling, while Kalli was more discerning, noticing that though the People were much smaller than the Sassen, Kthama was as large as Kht'shWea.

"The Akassa are smaller. Why is their home as large as ours?" she asked her mother one day.

"Because a very long time ago," Haaka explained, "our ancestors lived here too. So everything is to the same scale."

"Scale?"

"Size. The tunnels are tall and wide, just like those back home. The Great Entrance is huge and spacious. We all came from the same ancestors, Kalli. We are all related."

Kalli smiled. "We look different, but we are all related?"

"Yes. We all have the same bloodlines in us, just in different proportions. You know, like when I make you willow bark tree when you do not feel well? Sometimes it is stronger than other times, and that is because sometimes, I put in more water than other times. It is always made of the same ingredients, but the change in the amounts I put in each makes it come out different."

Kalli tilted her head. "So, all of us have the same ingredients? Just in different amounts? And that is why everyone at Kht'shWea is bigger and stronger than the people here?"

Haaka smiled and nodded.

"Huh," Kalli said.

Later, when Haaka shared the story with Adia, the Healer was impressed. "What a great way to explain it. Perhaps next time you make something, you can let her help you, so she can see how changing the amounts of the ingredients makes it come out different."

"That is a great idea; I will. I really think it helped her, as she seems more thoughtful since then. Actually, I think it is all going as well as could be expected. She enjoys her time with her blood father and Tisu. And your twins play with her."

"The next time Oh'Dar and Acise are here with their family, perhaps we should let her meet them."

"Then she would have seen all of us. Sassen, Akassa, Waschini, and Brothers all getting along and enjoying each other's company. I agree. I think that is a good idea."

The mid-summer sun was beating down in a cloudless sky. Animals sought relief from the heat under trees or next to springs and creeks. Newell, sweltering in his office in town, decided to call it a day and head home before dark. He locked the door behind him, tested, as always, that it was really closed, and then trotted down the steps and into the street. It was too hot for a hat, so he clutched it in one hand. He squinted up at the blazing sun, shielding his eyes. Perspiration rolled down his forehead, and he wiped it with his sleeve. Not even a breeze to cool his face.

He started walking and then stopped and looked around. What was that sudden, ongoing noise? It wasn't thunder, but it was coming from relatively far away. He finally figured out the direction and squinted into the distance. He saw what looked like a dark cloud heading toward town, but it was more than a storm cloud. It was so low it almost touched the ground. He quickened his step, hoping to get home before it reached Wilde Edge.

The sound grew louder and louder and soon

became a roar. It didn't waver as an incoming storm might, with rumblings of thunder rising and fading.

As he turned into the street of their little yellow house, a gust of wind caught him from behind. His hat flew out of his hand, and his shirt turned up, almost covering his head from behind. He fought to keep his balance, but the wind was so strong he had to lean back into it to keep from being bowled over. He looked for anything to grab onto, a tree branch, a neighbor's fence. Suddenly, twigs and debris started pelting him. He ducked his head down and tried to shield his face with one arm while grabbing onto whatever he could reach to keep moving forward.

The sound had become deafening, and the skies had grown dark. Up in the distance, he could see their home, the lights now on inside, even though it was midday. Finally, he grabbed the porch railing and hoisted himself up the steps.

The door opened just as he was about to reach for the handle, and Grace was standing there, their sons huddled behind her. "Come in, hurry. I am so glad you are home; I was worried about you, and the children are scared."

Newell quickly picked the twigs from his hair and dusted as much dirt off himself as he could before stepping inside.

"What is happening, Pa?" their youngest son asked.

"It's just a windstorm, Tom. Nothing to worry

about. Nothing can keep up that much force for very long; it will stop soon enough."

Only it didn't.

Day had been turned to night, and oil lamps burned night and day. Animals were brought in to safety. The winds continued to blow nonstop, and no one was easily able to leave their houses. Normal routines stopped, and stores were shut down. On the coast, sailing ships had all been moored, and strong winds had brought the waters far inland.

As much as Grace was worried about her parents, it was too dangerous to go outside. Even Newell did not want to chance it. He assured her that her parents must be fine, having good sense and not being wont to foolishness, so they huddled together in the living room, even bringing the mattresses there to save the oil lamps.

"Newell," Grace whispered to him after the children were asleep.

"Stop; I know what you're going to say. This isn't it, Grace. It's just a summer windstorm, that's all."

"When is the last time you remember one that lasted this long?"

Newell couldn't lie to her but didn't want to admit this was an unusually long storm. Everywhere outside the windows, there were twigs and branches, even fallen trees. He thought of everyone else also trapped inside their homes. There were farm animals to feed, cows and goats to milk. He trusted that the farmers had seen the clouds coming and found a way, no matter how difficult, to get their live-stock to safety and continue to tend to them, just as he had.

Their animals were safe, but it was dangerous and treacherous, and they were skittish and difficult to handle. Each time, Newell came back in, covered with muck and exhausted. Every simple chore had become a debilitating task. By the time the buckets of milk were carried in, they were filled with dirt and mostly empty from the pails being sloshed around.

On the fifth day, even Newell was worried. This was excessive. How could anything go on that long? They weren't on the coast, and there was no reason for this so far inland. And he knew that with each passing day, Grace's concern about her parents was growing.

On the late afternoon of the sixth day, he said, "One way or the other, I'm going to make it over to your parents' house. I know you're worried sick, and I am also starting to be. We both need to know they're alright. I'll be as careful as I can but don't worry. It is going to take me a long time to make it over there, check on them, and get back."

Newell wrapped one of Grace's lace scarves around his face. It would protect his eyes but still be sheer enough to see through. It was unbearably hot, but he still covered his arms and legs to protect them from the flying debris.

"What is the ax for?" Grace asked.

"I can't assume they won't have the same number of fallen branches and trees as we do. I might need it to get through to their door."

Newell told the children to take care of their mother and, quickly as possible, stepped outside.

If it had been windy before, it was unimaginable now. Nearly all the bushes were flattened, trees bent over like dancers silhouetted in a performance of some kind. If he hadn't known it was morning, he would have thought it was the middle of the night. He tightened the scarf around his face again and carefully walked down the porch steps into the road. The sound was so loud he wanted to cover his ears, but he needed his hands to steady himself.

He took a few unsteady steps toward the Webbs, leaning into the wind, which was now blasting him from the front. Then suddenly, he fell forward and landed flat on his face. The ax in his hand skidded to the side as his palms dug painfully into the dirt and gravel road.

It had stopped. All of it. Absolute silence. Not even a whisper of a breeze remained. The clouds lifted, and daylight returned. In spite of himself, Newell said out loud, "How is this possible? This isn't possible. Nothing can just stop like that."

He pushed himself up and dusted the dirt from his hands, picking out small pieces of gravel that had become embedded into his palms. He brushed down his sleeves, shirt, face, and pants. Then he undid Grace's scarf and stood there looking around.

Gradually, birds started chirping. He saw several taking flight off in the distance, but he was transfixed, not yet able to move, waiting for the wind to start up again. But it didn't.

Almost as if nothing had happened, conditions returned to normal.

He heard their door open, and Grace called out, "Newell?"

"It's stopped," he turned and shouted back, then feeling foolish as clearly she had to know this. "Do you want me to come back in?"

"If you are up to it, can you still go and check on Mama and Papa?"

"Yes. I want to know as much as you do that they are alright. I'll be back as soon as I can."

He picked his way through the obstacles blocking his path until the familiar Webb farmhouse came into sight. Matthew was out in the yard looking at the damage.

Newell called out, "Matthew!"

"Newell! Are Grace and the children alright? We've been so worried."

"Yes, all fine, though it's been a tense time for everyone. Nora?"

"Same. It seems to be over now, though."

"Do you need help checking the barn?" Newell asked.

"Yes, but first, let's go inside and let Nora know you are all fine."

Matthew called for his wife as he stepped through the door. Buster came running toward him, then Nora.

"Oh, Newell, tell me everyone is alright? Grace? The baby?"

"Everyone is fine. The boys, Grace, Ruth, even Pippy and the pups. The goats stayed put, but the chickens were a bit roughed up with all the high winds. Nothing they didn't handle, though."

"Ours seem to be fine, too. Darn things just kind of hunkered down inside the stable with the other animals. As far as I can tell, they're all there."

"Do you need anything right away?" Newell asked.

"I reckon we're alright. Just glad it's over. Try as I might, I have to admit it did unnerve me."

"Nothing like this has ever happened before that I know of. I don't remember my parents or grandparents ever talking about anything like this," Nora said. "Do you think—?"

Newell did not want to start a fight, so he kept to himself the remark that came to mind. But Matthew said it anyway.

"Don't start, Nora; I know what you're going to say. It was just a windstorm. Maybe it was unusual, but that doesn't mean it was some kind of warning. I know you've got your mind made up that what Ned told us is going to happen."

"I know you and Newell think this is Ned's imagination, but don't tell me about having my mind made up when you both already have yours made up. I think we all should try to keep an open mind about this; what if he was right?"

Matthew looked at Newell, then said, "You're right. I'll tell you what; Ned said there were going to be three events. So, if this is really one of those, then we can expect another by fall. Until then, I still don't think there's anything unusual about it. Out of the ordinary, yes, but not mystical."

Matthew and Newell remained convinced it was just a windstorm until later on when the two went to the general store in town and started hearing stories from other townspeople.

"It wasn't only local," the banker said. "My nephew just rode in from Appleton and said it had reached all the way over there."

Newell shifted uneasily on his seat at the counter. It was one thing to dismiss Ned's claims as a young man's misunderstanding, but hearing it as fact from the businessman unnerved him. If it was this wide-spread, then perhaps there was something to it. He felt his stomach twist at the thought.

"Keep us posted, please," he said. "Anything else you hear, I want to know about it. You know where to find me."

The Brothers, the People, and the Sassen communities had all experienced the same wind-storm. Only, they had no doubts it was one of the signs An'Kru had warned them of. In addition to the severe weather, the People and the Sassen had all experienced physical effects. First, a sense of agita-tion, followed by lightheadedness. Then they felt a wavering in the magnetic lines that snaked throughout Etera like a giant web. A surge, as if something was tugging at the magnetic field of Etera.

The Healers at the High Rocks were gathered together. Nadiwani, Urilla Wuti, Adia, and Iella.

"The vortex. The magnetic lines and fields are tied into the vortex," Urilla Wuti said. "Perhaps the great winds were a result of something shifting in the magnetic lines. Some energy was moving about deep within Etera, causing the windstorm."

"No doubt there are many wonders of which we know nothing," Adia remarked. "Perhaps, in some way, the forest creatures could feel this same shifting, and it was that which alerted them to take cover. The birds of the air all roosted. None of the watchers have found any dead or injured animals, which seems impossible."

"Perhaps what seems impossible is just something we do not yet understand," Urilla Wuti answered.

"They did know it was coming," Iella said. "Just before it started, I felt some type of knowledge to take cover moving through all of Etera's creatures."

"An'Kru said no creatures would be harmed," Nadiwani remarked. "Perhaps this is why. He knew they would know that something major was going to happen."

"Or the shift in the magnetic lines alerted them, and they took cover out of instinct."

"Either way," Urilla Wuti said, "since this was the first, then we can expect another toward the change of season."

While the People and the Sassen had experienced physical symptoms, the Brothers and the Waschini had not. Neither Awantia nor Ned knew of any changes other than high winds and nearly perpetual nighttime.

They had returned to Chief Kotori's camp and had sheltered with the rest of Awantia's people. An'Kru had prepared them so the Brothers were not afraid. Instead of seeing it as a bad event, they hailed it as reassurance that the terrible events of the future An'Kru had told them of would not come to pass.

Awantia squatted down next to her life-walker. "You are worried about your family."

"They know enough to stay inside," Ned answered. "They will do what they have to do to make sure everyone is safe, but yes, I am. Not as much for their physical safety, but whether they will recognize this for what it is, the first of the three warnings."

"None of my people remember anything like this happening before. Winds, yes. Dark clouds covering most of the sky, yes. But not day becoming night and endless winds howling for days. And the sound; how can they dismiss this as something ordinary?"

Ned shrugged. "As An'Kru said, many of my people have lost their belief in the Great Spirit. Others have become so disassociated from a sense of wonder that they dismiss anything extraordinary as having a logical reason. And from what he said, that distancing is only going to get worse."

"I wonder what this great discovery is that he warned us about? Something that will cause them to move even further away from Etera's silence and beauty? What could be more enthralling than our world?"

"I don't know. I can't even imagine. It is obviously something no one has discovered yet, whatever it is. Or if someone has, its use has not spread very far. I almost wish I knew; it sounds magical."

"That is interesting," said Awantia. "Something magical. Yet he said it will become so commonplace as to become ordinary. Another loss of the sense of wonder you just spoke of."

"That is true. Perhaps that is how we start losing our connection. Starting to take for granted the amazing wealth of blessings already provided. Look at the firebugs. How do they light up? And rainbows, the night sky, the shooting stars, lightning!"

Awantia added to his list, "The intricate beauty of the flowers. How plants grow from tiny seeds. How is any of that not a miracle? Oh, and the smell of the soil after the rain. Birdsong!" She laughed with glee. It had turned into a playful game of listing all their favorite things.

"Rest after a long day of hard work," Ned continued, "Plunging into cool waters in the heat of summer. Or the beauty and warmth of the fire in the cool evenings. My mother's biscuits! The Great Spirit's blessings are all around us, yet how easy it becomes to rush past them every day."

He took her hand in his. "Waking up with you in

my arms, because the most precious of all is love and belonging. One of the most important things I have learned from coming to live with your people is that everything we truly need to be happy is already provided.

He leaned back on their sleeping mat and pulled her down with him until they were lying face to face, their limbs intertwined. He noticed she looked suddenly sad. "What is wrong?" He placed a finger under her chin and raised her face to his.

"Not everything we need to be happy. I have not given you a son. Or a daughter," she whispered.

"It will happen when it happens. Please do not be concerned about it; it should not affect our happiness."

"Do you not want the joy of seeing our children running through the summer meadows, trying to catch the firebugs, or gathering the beautiful flowers for our shelter? To hear their laughter as they play with the other children?"

"If it happens, I want all of that. I just do not want you feeling bad that it hasn't happened yet, and if it never does, my life is complete by sharing it with you."

CHAPTER 10

Oh'Dar and his family had sheltered at the Brothers' village, but the storm had left him uneasy. Was the first to be the worst or the least of the warnings, or were they all to be of this magnitude? There was no way of knowing, but it troubled him. But An'Kru had promised no one would be harmed. Still, the children could be frightened.

"I know my father," he said to Acise one morning when the children were with their grandmother, Honovi. "He is making plans for us to move to Kthama if it gets worse."

She frowned at him. "I cannot leave my family. My mother. Ithua, who is on her deathbed."

"No, I mean everyone here. Everyone."

"Oh. I am just nervous. Even though my faith told me no harm would come to us, it was still a frightening experience. The wind never before blew or howled as hard. And having it dark for days—I do not know what is coming next, but I do not look forward to it. I'Layah and Tsonakwa seemed to bear up well, but Ashova was frightened."

"I know," Oh'Dar said. "And I think they would feel safer at Kthama."

"But, with Ben and Miss Vivian—"

"Yes, it will be sad, but An'Kru spoke with all three children, and I think they are convinced life goes on. Letting go is part of life, even though no one wants to see their children suffer in any way."

"There is just one problem," Acise said. "We do not know exactly when the next warning is coming. Let alone what it will be."

They decided to speak with Acise's parents, Chief Is'Taqa and Honovi.

"We seek your advice, Papa," Acise said. "And yours too, Momma. We are concerned about the next event. How severe it might be. Knowing it will come does not keep us from being affected by it."

"Of course. I understand," her father said. "Even normal events that we see happen all the time, like thunder and lightning, can still be scary. Even if we know we are safe, our bodies sometimes think otherwise."

Oh'Dar spoke up. "My father will be making

room at Kthama for every one of us. Perhaps, before it is time for the next event, we should move there. All of us."

"The horses and ponies," Honovi said. "Noshoba could care for them there, with help from others, of course."

"He will have made provision for those, too. And it would only be for a little while," Oh'Dar said. "Once it passed, we could return home."

As Oh'Dar had said, his father was making plans to house the members of the village if Chief Is'Taqa wanted to move his people there.

"They may not wish to, but they are welcome," Acaraho said. "They may feel safer being out in the open than inside Kthama."

"Khon'Tor once said Kthama had stood for thousands of years, and she would stand for thousands more."

"Yes, it was when Kthama Minor was being opened. The walls of Kthama were shaking as the Sassen moved in union, joined by the One Mind. Many of our people were frightened, and he calmed them down. They had such faith in him," Acaraho said.

"They have faith in you, too, Father," said Oh'Dar.

Acaraho smiled at his son. "Take time to visit

with your brother while you are here and share his joy in the birth of his son."

Oh'Dar found Nootau outside with High Protector Awan. They seemed deep in conversation, but they noticed him, and Awan called him over.

"I do not mean to interrupt. It looked like you were having a serious talk."

"We were—are—and there is no reason you cannot join in. I would value your opinion, too," Awan explained.

"We were talking about what is coming," Nootau said, "and what it means for our offspring."

Oh'Dar nodded slowly, "I think I understand your concerns. What have we brought our children into? What challenges will they face that we cannot imagine?"

Awan rubbed his chin before speaking. "Nootau, I am sure I am not supposed to ask, but I am going to. You said you lived twenty years with the Mothoc before returning with An'Kru. In all that time, many things happened."

"Of course, yes," Nootau answered. "But what did happen has no influence on what may or will happen next."

"I know, I know, but I still have to ask. In all that time, did Nadiwani and I ever pair?"

The question that so many had wondered about was out in the open. Clearly, Awan and Nadiwani were enamored with each other and had been for years. They spent nearly all their free time together, and others saw them laughing together, embracing in the shadows, yet they had not asked to be paired. The High Council had long ago revoked the Second Law forbidding Healers and Healer Helpers from pairing and having offspring. It was not that.

"Why do you ask?" Nootau answered with a question of his own. "And what difference does it make? If you did or did not is irrelevant."

"I do not think it is irrelevant. I need to know what path I took in the other timeline."

"And if you knew, how would that affect the decision you are apparently trying to make now, in this one?"

"Oh," Awan gritted his teeth. "I feel like I am talking to your father! Where did you learn to avoid answering a simple question so cleverly!"

Nootau chuckled. "I am not avoiding answering it; I am trying to help you find for yourself the answer you are seeking. What you may or may not have done at another time does not matter. What is it you want to do, Awan? What is it you want to do? Do you know?"

Oh'Dar raised his eyebrows and grinned at Nootau. "Welcome to the conversation, brother." They all laughed.

Awan bent down to pick up a couple of rocks and pitched one into the foliage. "I do know. But I do not know if I should."

"What is keeping you from doing what you want to do?"

Awan pitched the other stone further than the first. Leaves rustled as it passed through the bushes ahead.

"Myself," Awan answered. "Me and my fears."

"I see. So what you want to know is, did you and Nadiwani pair and have offspring, and were you happy?"

"Yes!" Awan practically shouted. "That is exactly what I want to know. So please tell me."

Nootau ran his hand through the crown of his hair, a habit he had unconsciously picked up from Khon'Tor. Oh'Dar and Awan both stared at him.

"What?" Nootau asked.

"Are you going to answer Awan's question?" Oh'Dar said.

"Awan, what do you think the answer is?"

Awan frowned. "That we did not. We never paired, and we never had offspring." He turned away.

Nootau asked, "Why do you think you did not?" He saw his brother squinting at him hard and held up his hand for Oh'Dar to be silent.

"I supposed what you and I were talking about when Oh'Dar came up. I was afraid to, just as I am now, so I never got my courage up to pair with the female I love. As a result, we never experienced the joy of being truly one, and the joy I see Nootau going through, having a son. What I have seen countless others go through. All because I was afraid. What a missed opportunity. What a shame."

Oh'Dar and Nootau remained quiet, letting the High Protector have his feelings to himself.

Finally, Awan said, "Thank you, Nootau. That is what I needed to know. And I am not going to make the same mistake this time. I am not going to let our lives pass us by because I am afraid of something that may or may not happen. Maybe the world is not a safe place. But cheating yourself out of life's greatest happiness because of fear does not make it any safer. It just makes it more lonely. I am going to pair with Nadiwani."

Even though Awan was still standing there, Oh'Dar could not hold it in any longer. "Nootau! Were you not at Lulnomia all that time? Did you come back to Kthama and learn this? Did someone tell you? How did you know they never paired?"

"I did not know; you are right, brother," Nootau said. "But Awan wanted an answer, and he got one. And his reaction to it helped him figure out what he wanted to do. Was that not the point of the conversation?"

"You tricked him!" Oh'Dar accused his brother.

"Oh no, Oh'Dar," Awan laughed. "I am not angry. He did not trick me; he only helped me find the answer within myself. Oh, Nootau, you are your father's son for sure!" Awan laughed again. "Now, if you will excuse me, there is someone I need to talk to right away."

Awan hurried back to Kthama and ran through the halls looking for Nadiwani. She was not hard to find, usually in the Healer's Quarters tending to someone or preparing concoctions. She turned when she heard him fly in through the door, and he practically skidded to a stop in front of her.

"Oh my, what is going on?" she laughed. "I have never seen such a sight!"

Awan closed the distance and swept her up. She barely had time to set down the plants she had in her hand before he spun her around.

Her arms tightened around his neck, and she laughed.

Finally, he put her down and said, "Nadiwani, we have wasted enough time. I love you, and you love me. It is time we asked to be paired."

"Really? Is that what you want?"

"I have wanted it for a long time, my love; I just let fears keep me from what could be. But no longer."

"Why have you never talked to me about this? What have you been afraid of?"

Awan could not stop smiling. "Life. Being happy, perhaps. Having even more to lose than I do as we are now. But that is no way to live, and I am not going

191

to hide from life any longer. We can be paired at the next Brotherhood meeting; they will not deny our request."

"I am sure they will not. They have probably all been wondering what has taken so long."

"What is it Adia always says? Fear and faith cannot exist at the same time. I need to let go of my fear and lean into my faith. I know we belong together, and, as one, we will face whatever comes."

Still outside, Oh'Dar turned to Nootau. "I came to hear how your son is doing! I still haven't gotten to see him. Whose coloring does he have?"

"My father's," Nootau said.

"You mean our father's."

"No, I mean my father's. Khon'Tor's. He has Khon'Tor's black hair and that residual white Guardian streak down the crown."

"Are you upset about it?"

"I do not know how I feel. Partly concerned that I do not wish to hurt our father's feelings. Relieved that Khon'Tor has confessed to what he did to Mother. At least it has been out in the open for some time now, and he came forward himself."

"Khon'Tor has redeemed himself over and over, brother. Anyone who has a different opinion is not someone whose opinion should be counted."

"It will just be a constant reminder," Nootau said, "that he is not Acaraho's descendent."

"It is bothering you far more than it should, I think."

"Please tell me why you're saying that. I do not want this to cast a shadow over my joy at having a son."

"First of all, Acaraho was the greatest father anyone could have. We both know that. He raised you knowing you were not of his blood. He raised me, obviously not of his blood. No father ever loved his family more than he did. What we looked like, whose blood was in our veins, never mattered to him. He is a saint."

"But I wanted to be the first to give him a grandson. I do not want Laru'Tor's resemblance to Khon'Tor to take that away from Father."

"You mean an Akassa grandson," Oh'Dar corrected him, thinking of his own sons, Tsonakwa and Ashova.

Nootau smiled. "You are right. What difference does it make? And if it does, in time, Aponi will pair, and then Father will have a grandson of his own blood."

"It is all 'Tor blood, Nootau. It is not as if they are not related at all."

"My feelings are mixed, though. Yes, I have forgiven what Khon'Tor did; I mean, if Mother can, how can I not? But it is hard to forget."

"A terrible mistake in a lifetime of service. Is that to be his legacy?"

"It is terribly unfair, I know. When Urilla Wuti asked for mercy for Khon'Tor, when he confessed to what he had done, I think it resonated with everyone because it is true; it is what each of us would want if our greatest sins were to be revealed to others."

"Have you talked to Mother about how you feel?" Oh'Dar asked.

"No. Neither of our parents; I'm still sorting out how I feel."

"And Iella?"

"It does not bother her at all. She thinks Laru'Tor looks distinctive."

"Talk to our parents. It will help; I am sure of it."

Both Acaraho and Adia were sure they knew why Nootau had asked to talk to them, but they patiently waited for him to get around to it. After some mundane conversation, he finally said, "I need to talk to you about Laru'Tor. His hair—"

"The 'Tor streak," Acaraho said. "Are you worried it will cause him trouble? Possibly being identified as of Khon'Tor's blood?"

"Not at the Far High Hills, because it seems the people did do as Urilla Wuti asked and kept the knowledge of my blood father inside the walls of the

High Rocks. But here. We now live here at the High Rocks."

"People may well accept it as part of the 'Tor line, which is also my heritage. But that aside, I think you do not give our people enough credit. Your son is just a tiny offspring. He is innocent. No one is going to hold Khon'Tor's sin against an offspring."

"How can you be so sure?"

"Because I went through it, Nootau," Acaraho said. "Your mother and I both lived through years of the People thinking that she and I had violated her sacred vow as a Healer. That I had seeded her. Yet they forgave us. It may have taken a while, but they worked it out. And I believe they did with Khon'Tor too. What else is bothering you?"

"How you feel about it. About Laru'Tor not being your blood relation."

"You should know your father better than that," Adia scolded.

"It is alright," Acaraho said. "I understand; you are concerned for my feelings because you love me. But it makes no difference to me any more than it did to you. Despite what everyone else thought, I knew I had not seeded you. Yet you were and are my son as much as if I had seeded you. And Oh'Dar too."

"Perhaps, right now, when you look at him, all you see is that streak," Adia said. "But in time, you will learn who he is, and you will see him as himself. As your son. And nothing else will matter."

"None of us is perfect, Nootau," Acaraho said. "Not me, not your mother, not the Overseer, and not Khon'Tor. But no one's worth should rest on judgment of the worst mistake he or she ever made. Khon'Tor was a great Leader, perhaps the greatest Leader of the High Rocks ever. Perhaps of all the People ever."

"Father—"

"No, do not object. I know I am a good Leader. Maybe, in my own style, as you have said, even a great Leader. But there is only one Khon'Tor, and he deserves every accolade that has ever been given him. He led our People through some of the worst times in our history. He went with Moart'Tor and Paldar'Krah to try and reach the rebels and to rescue the Sassen female, Eitel, walking into what we all believed to be nearly certain death. And he knew it, too. But his love for our People took precedence over everything else. If anything, you should be proud to have his blood in your veins. That is how I see it."

Nootau stepped forward and hugged his father. Adia placed a hand on her son's shoulder as Acaraho continued speaking.

"We are all of the House of 'Tor. A House that has produced some of the greatest of our People's Leaders. From Moc'Tor and Straf'Tor to the first Akassa Leader, Takthan'Tor. And Moart'Tor will always be remembered as reuniting the rebel Mothoc with those at Lulnomia. The Guardians of Etera come through our line. Hold your head up high, son. And teach your son, and any other offspring you may have, also to do so."

Haaka was walking back home with Del'Cein and Kalli after their visit with Lannak'Sor and Tisu. "Did you have a good time today?" she asked her daughters.

Del'Cein took her finger out of her mouth long enough to answer yes.

Kalli said, "We enjoy going there, but Mama, I cannot understand everyone. A lot of them talk in gibberish."

"That is called Whitespeak, honey. It is the language of another people."

"But I want to know what they are saying."

"I am sure if you want to learn it, someone there can teach you. I will ask your father, alright?" Seeming to be satisfied, Kalli continued walking, holding her mother's hand.

"I am not against it," Haan said to his mate. "They both look far more Akassa than Sassen, and I think we both realize they will eventually spend more time at Kthama than here with us. It is where they will be more comfortable. If they have any chance of pairing, it will happen there. As for it being Whitespeak, it does not make any difference. If it helps them merge into the culture and feel more comfortable at Kthama, then I agree they should both start learning it. I will speak with Acaraho tomorrow."

"Why just Del'Cein and Kalli, then?" Haaka asked. "Perhaps we should all learn it. What could it hurt?"

So, Whitespeak classes were started for Haan's people. Though, with their huge fingers, they would most likely not be able to master writing it, and their mouth structure and large canines made for different pronunciations of some words, it was an undertaking that would bring the two communities even closer together.

CHAPTER 11

The hot summer days gave way to the cooler fall weather. Across the land, all the communities were busy with harvesting and gathering. Thanks to Taipa and Eralato, the bounty was the best anyone remembered. Brothers, Sassen, Akassa—all storehouses were overflowing. The sense of security lifted everyone's spirits.

Everyone was on watch for the next event promised by An'Kru. The first had been the violent dust storm. What the next might be was the most popular discussion everywhere. Then, on one particularly clear fall evening, they had their answer.

Awan had been out making the last rounds before going to bed. The watchers were at their posts, their calls to him confirming all was well. Suddenly one of them let out a screamcall. Awan immediately tensed up and started toward the call. It didn't take him long, though, to realize it was not a warning of danger but an alert. Overhead, the sky was shimmering with color. Purples, blues, and greens. Nothing like he had ever seen in his lifetime, something never mentioned before, even in tales or legends. Awan stood transfixed, unable to take his eyes off the display until he realized he should answer the screamcall. He let out a long-drawn-out response; the watcher had been heard and understood.

Not knowing how long the wonder would remain, Awan pulled himself together and ran into the Great Entrance. Once inside, he called out to any within earshot. "Do not be alarmed, but wake the others; come and see what is happening!"

All the People were streaming out of their cave systems and staring up at the night sky. The same was happening outside Kht'shWea and at the Brothers' villages.

Adia and Acaraho stood with their family, astonished at the beauty blazing overhead. Offspring everywhere laughed and pointed; no one had ever seen anything so beautiful. The colors danced, wavered, climbed higher, then dipped down. No one doubted this was the second warning. But many were embarrassed that they had assumed each warning would bring trouble. This was one of joy and one that would be talked about for generations.

Not everyone saw the display. Many had already gone to bed. Newell only heard about it the next day while picking up supplies at the General Store, the main source of news and gossip in Wilde Edge. He walked into the middle of a conversation between several customers and the shopkeeper.

He stepped into the circle and interrupted. "What are you all so excited about? What did I miss?"

"Oh, you didn't see it?" someone asked.

"See what?"

"The light display last night. The most beautiful thing I've ever seen—any of us have ever seen. Sweeping colors in the sky, lighting up the countryside. How could you have missed it?"

"We went to bed early last night. It sounds pretty amazing."

"It was," another chimed in. "But you'd have to see it to fully appreciate it."

Newell pushed from his mind the thought nagging at him.

"We're going out tonight to see if it comes back; you should, too. You never know!"

Newell was torn over telling his family about the display they had missed, yet if there was a chance it would return, he felt he owed it to them.

When he returned home, he and Grace made plans to go out after dark and see for themselves.

Dark fell quickly, so it wasn't long before it was time. Grace bundled up Ruby and made sure the others all had warm enough coats on, and they set out.

They didn't have to search for it. Soon, a moving banner of turquoise, blues, greens, and some gold stretched across the night sky.

Transfixed by the dazzling performance, no one said anything for some time. It was everything the men said it had been. A once-in-a-lifetime spectacular.

After a while, Nat said, "My neck is tired. Can we lie on the ground?"

"I'll tell you what," Grace said, noticing the children were clutching their jackets tightly around themselves, "let's go inside, and I'll make some hot cider. Then, tomorrow, we can bring some blankets out and lie on the ground."

"What if it doesn't come back?" Nat asked.

Grace didn't say what she was thinking, that this was the second warning and, if so, might last as long as the first one had. "I have a hunch it'll be back for a few nights. Besides, you are all close to shivering, so I need to get you inside."

"Mind your mother," Newell said, and they

followed her inside.

Later, with the children in bed, Grace and Newell were sitting at the kitchen table.

"You know what I am thinking," Grace said.

Newell swirled the leftover cider around in his mug but didn't look up. "I do."

Grace pursed her lips. Apparently, there was not going to be any discussion. No matter; she would bide her time. If she was right, and the lights continued for six days, as the high winds had, then she'd bring it up again.

Four nights later, the show was still going on, but the next night, there was nothing. Grace had been right; six times, just as the windstorm had raged for six days. In her mind, everything Ned had said was coming true. So this would be the second warning, but this one hadn't been dangerous as the first had. Did that mean anything? If so, what? Maybe the term *warning* was only meant in terms of counting down the time to prepare for whatever was to come. Something that in the future would be dangerous.

She vowed somehow to keep her mouth shut and pray that her husband came to his senses. In the meantime, she would talk to her mother, and the two could prepare in the background. There were many things they could do. Gathering non-perishable supplies over a period of time, taking inventory of their warm and cold weather clothes, and mending those that needed fixing.

And, together, they would think about what to take with them that would not be available where they were going. Goats? Chickens? Did the Locals have livestock? When Grayson was on trial, Grace had been to the local village with her brother looking for Ben and Miss Vivian, but it was so stressful she didn't really remember much. And even if she had, that didn't mean all the Locals lived the same way. She kicked herself for not asking Ned more about what living with them was like.

No matter. The two women would just have to do their own research, as quietly as possible, of course. She tried to think of who she could ask, and only one person's name came to mind.

The next day, Grace was standing in Sheriff Moore's office.

"Good morning, Mrs. Storis; what can I do for you?" he asked.

"Please, you've known me all my life, Sheriff Moore. Please call me Grace."

"I didn't want to be dismissive, seeing you are a married woman now."

"It's fine, really. It will make me uncomfortable if you address me as Mrs. Storis," she smiled.

He extended his hand toward the chair next to his desk. "Sit down, please."

Grace set her market basket on the floor and sat down. "I came looking for some information; you were the only one I could think to ask."

"What do you need help with?"

"I want to learn how the Locals live. I know you have visited their villages many times. Could you tell me, please, about their lifestyle?"

The Sheriff tilted his head and looked at her sideways.

"Oh, I know, I know. My brother and I went to one looking for Grayson's grandparents. But that was only one village, and I was too upset really to remember much. I figured you have been to more than just one, and probably several times."

"I am not an expert, Grace. But I have been among the Locals many times, it's true. The best I can tell you is that it looks to be pretty basic. Close to the land, I suppose, is a way to describe it. They have individual shelters covered in hides and sometimes bark. And then there are larger buildings, perhaps where they meet as a group? Lots of fires. Everyone seems to be doing something. Usually, the women are cooking and stirring something, fetching water, weaving baskets or blankets, tanning hides, or making tools. The men go out hunting, and the older children learn to help their parents. The younger ones run about and play games just like ours do. Other than that, I don't know what to tell you."

"Do they have livestock? I mean, did you ever see any goats or chickens?"

He closed his eyes and frowned. "No, I can't see that I remember any of that. Ponies, horses, wolf cubs sometimes. That doesn't mean some villages don't have them, though."

Grace folded her hands in her lap. "I suppose you think it strange I am asking these questions."

"None of my business, really. I wish I could help you more, though."

"I don't think it's that much different than how we live. They grow their own food, harvest, and store up for the cold months. I'm sure we have skills they don't have, and they have skills we don't have. We probably could learn a lot from each other, given the chance."

"It is good to hear you say that. I think most people look down on them, think they are somehow less important than we are."

What she didn't say, and couldn't, was that her brother was living among them. And that soon, the rest of her family might too.

At Chief Kotori's village, Ned was also contemplating what the third sign might be. Unlike Newell or his father, Ned had no doubt that these events were exactly what An'Kru had told them to watch for.

Something out of the ordinary. The timing and the duration convinced him—every three months and for the exact same number of days.

Taipa and Eralato had done their jobs, and no one had ever seen such a surge of growth or such healthy and robust plants, so the village had an abundance of preserved food, herbs, and plants stored up. The women had woven extra blankets, the men had brought in as much firewood as possible, and shelters had been reinforced. There was clearly more provision than they would ordinarily need.

Ned turned to Awantia, who was sitting at his side. "The third warning is not long off. I need to visit my family and see if they have changed their minds."

"Winter is just around the corner. Is it wise to set out now, not knowing what the last event might be?"

Ned got up and paced around. "I do not know what to do. Spring will complete the year, and An'Kru will return to the High Rocks and finish what he said he would do. Do I wait and go after the third event? Will there be enough time? And I do not want to be caught on the way there. There is no way of knowing if it will be benign as this one was or as threatening as the first."

"If you are worried about me, I will be fine."

"I am. I am worried about everyone. I know how Grayson felt. No matter which place you are, you feel like you should be in the other. And you are right; what if I get caught on the way?"

"We were warned so we could build up all these provisions. I doubt whatever is coming is going to damage or undo all our efforts."

Ned raised an eyebrow. "You are right. That would be counter-productive. So whatever is coming, it should not be damaging. Frightening, perhaps, like the first. But in retrospect, no harm was really done. Nothing was destroyed." Then his thoughts went to An'Kru's words that destruction was part of the creative process and that there would be destruction, but not yet.

"The timing puts the next one at mid-winter," Ned said. "So what winter-related events take place that are a hindrance but not deadly?"

Awantia replied, "Heavy snowfall, sleet, hail, blizzards. Avalanches, freezing rain? I cannot think of any other."

"Neither can I. And unlike the others, there's no guarantee the effects will just go away after six days. If there is heavy snowfall, it will most likely linger until we get a warm streak. But that could go one of two ways. If I leave now, I could get trapped there. And I do not want to be kept away from you. If I wait and go afterward, I may not be able to get there at all."

Ned sat back down and dropped his head into his hands.

"Seek Chief Kotori's counsel, perhaps?" she suggested.

Chief Kotori listened to Ned's concerns and then said, "In your imagination, you see only troublesome outcomes, no matter which path you decide, so either choice is one to be avoided. Your soul is not in peace, which is making it hard for you to determine your path. Set your fears aside, and let us reason together."

Ned closed his eyes and focused on his breathing. "If I go before the next event, there is a chance they will not be convinced. And I would have to go back again after it occurred and hope it convinced them to come with me." He opened his eyes and looked at the Chief.

"You cannot convince them to come with you. They must convince themselves. If, and once they do, they will readily accept your help instead of refusing it."

"You are right. My words are not enough. Somehow I thought they would be."

"Had you not heard the Promised One speak, met him, seen him, would you have believed another who told you such things?"

"No," Ned admitted. "I would not."

"Return to your home fire. Prepare to leave after the next event. In the meantime, ask for help building them a shelter to live in."

"In all my worry, I had not thought of that. It will still be cold weather; how could I have not thought of that."

"A mind full of worry is like an overgrown field. There is not much open soil for new seeds to take root."

They built two shelters for the two families. One for Ned's parents and another for Grace and her family. Seeing the shelters completed, Ned felt deep satisfaction. There was nothing more he could do but offer his help once again. As soon as the next event was over, he would head to Wilde Edge.

Winter had set in, and it was a hard one with more snow than people remembered in a long time. All who knew to expect it discussed whether this was the third warning. But the consensus was no, as it was not that unusual, and it lasted more than the expected six days.

Ned's peace had been replaced by anxious anticipation. If the next event came soon, travel would be an impossibility. Cold weather was one thing. Miles and miles of deep snow was another. And traveling alone made it more dangerous.

Everyone in the village knew of Ned's plans. And they knew that, no matter how supportive Awantia was, she must be worried for her life-walker's life.

One night at their fire, Sakinay—Sourface— approached. Both Ned and Awantia looked up at him and Ned gestured for him to join them.

"Ned Webb," Sakinay said. "We are aware you are about to make a dangerous journey to save your Waschini family. It is not right that you should go alone. I will go with you."

Ned and Awantia looked at each other.

Ned spoke. "Sakinay. I am honored by your offer, but where I am going, the people may not look kindly on you."

"I am not afraid of the Waschini. It is not wise for you to travel alone."

Awantia rested her hand on Ned's arm.

"Thank you," Ned said. "I will be glad of your company."

Later, lying next to each other in their shelter, Ned wondered aloud, "What prompted that? There was a time when he vehemently resented me. He even attacked me."

"I remember, but time has passed. You have proven yourself. You came with Oh'Dar and rescued us when the Waschini soldiers took us away. The Chief declared you one of us. Sakinay hates the Waschini, but he no longer sees you as one of them."

"It will complicate things, but it will also be a help to have him along."

"Perhaps it will be good for your people to meet him."

Then the thought crossed both their minds that of all the Brothers to take to meet his family, Sour-face was probably not their first choice.

Awantia added, "Or not—" and they both laughed.

It was a starlit night, and without the nightly blanket of cloud cover, it was even colder than usual. Everyone had retired early, as not even the warmth from the fires was enough. Distracted by the upcoming trip, Ned had neglected to bring enough wood in to keep the shelter fire banked for all night. He wrapped a brightly colored woven blanket around him and quickly stepped outside. He looked overhead at the amazing display of stars. It was the new moon, and the sky was an inky backdrop to the sparkling array.

Just then, a streak of bright light raced across the evening sky. Then another. Then another. It was the yearly meteor shower, he told himself. Beautiful but nothing unusual. He walked over to the stockpile and gathered up as many logs as he could carry. When he looked back up, more light caught his eye. This time he stood for a while watching it. This was more than the usual display. Yes, some years were more active than others, but this was beyond that. He started to believe this might be the last warning.

His feet were getting very cold, and his teeth were chattering, but he couldn't tear himself away; he had never seen so many falling stars. They were coming in groups now. He thought about waking Awantia but decided against it. If she was warm, he wanted her to stay warm. And if this indeed was the third warning, it would follow the same pattern and return for several nights. That, and the tremendous number of streaks overhead, would tell him if it was out of the ordinary.

He stepped through the opening as quickly as he could, not wanting what little heat there was inside to escape. When he finished fixing the fire, he pulled his blanket up around him and got as close as he could to his mate without waking her with his chilled frame.

When he awoke, his first thought was how warm it was. Then, in a panic, he threw his blanket off and sat up, afraid the shelter might be on fire. But it wasn't. The fire was still giving off heat, but not enough to explain how warm it was. He went outside as quietly as he could. It was warm outside, too. Silvery-crusted, the snow was showing signs of melting. Then he noticed others were also up and about, talking about the sudden change in temperature.

He remembered the shooting stars last night. There couldn't be a relationship, could there? He didn't see how. It was just a peculiar coincidence. But if the warm weather continued, it would make traveling much easier. There were still enough grasses under the snow to feed the horses, and the melting snow would provide more than enough water.

He decided that if the shooting stars continued over the next two days, far longer than any other time, and if the warm weather continued, he would ask Sakinay to set out with him for Wilde Edge.

Three days later, Ned and Sakinay were on their way.

In every community of the Akassa, Sassen, and Brothers, someone had mysteriously woken on the first night to notice the shooting stars. So when they continued night after night, coupled with the unseasonably warm weather, it was deemed to be the third sign. However, the same events that had enthralled their communities had a different impact elsewhere.

What had been another beautiful nighttime display for the Brotherhood had been a nightmare for the Waschini. The meteors that streaked harmlessly across the night sky had elsewhere plummeted to earth.

As bad as the windstorm had been, this was far worse. The first night, all were enthralled with the beauty of the shooting stars, but that was until they started hitting the ground.

For the next five nights, everyone huddled inside. Children were kept in the most protected part of the homes or hustled away to root cellars. Families stretched their supplies. Where possible, animals were brought inside. Only the stretch of warm weather made it bearable, as they were not suffering from the cold, and caring for animals was easier. Churches were holding prayer vigils, but for the most part, everyone was housebound. Though they were only seen at night, the meteor impacts continued during the day. When it was over—after the sixth day, as with the other events —people came out to find their roadways and bridges annihilated. But, miraculously, it seemed no person or animal had been hurt and no buildings destroyed.

In all the White communities, talk started about the regularity of the events. How they were each spaced three months apart and lasted six days. Religious leaders spoke of it being a warning to people to make themselves right with God. Teachers struggled to come up with an explanation that didn't involve a supernatural element.

Even Newell was starting to have doubts. And when he joined the men in the feed store, he felt his denial crumbling. Outsiders passing through reported that this same event had happened everywhere they'd been and for the same six days. They also spoke of how, by chance, the weather had shifted as it started, which kept many people and animals from freezing to death. Then there was the most peculiar of all, the accuracy with which the meteors had hit. There was damage—a lot of damage

—but it created an inconvenience, not life-threatening situations.

All these elements, individually and collectively, convinced many that this was something more than a fluke of nature. While some speculated these events had a spiritual component, others ridiculed them.

The division had started.

The meteorites had caused serious damage to the roads, holding up supplies and transport. The warm weather had held up, so the prison Louis and Riggs were in had prisoners out repairing the roadways. It was grueling, backbreaking work, and Louis could hear Riggs swearing under his breath. He was used to his soft job, not manual labor.

All the time Riggs was complaining, Louis was looking around. There were not enough guards to manage the large number of prisoners. Though he had said he would wait for Riggs to be paroled and take him to where his nephew, Grayson Morgan, was last seen, he was getting older with each passing year, and lately, he had occasionally been coughing up blood. He never said it out loud, but he feared the worst. However, something other than whatever sickness he had, was gnawing at him. The possibility of not living long enough to take his revenge on his nephew. What if he didn't have another year to wait for Riggs to be on parole?

Despite the winter snows, high grasses still stood tall, rimming the road on both sides. The prison was in the middle of nowhere, and everything grew wild. Past the grasses were tall stands of fir trees, beyond which the elevation changed, rising to form hills and mountains.

It was the third day the crew was working, and Louis had planned it carefully, using a lot of his best contraband to buy the cooperation he needed. He hadn't told Riggs what he was planning. What would happen to Riggs without his protection? Louis didn't know and didn't care; all he knew and cared about was that time might not be on his side.

He picked his moment and signaled his lead man that now was the time. Just then, a fight among the prisoners broke up, with three men threatening and ganging up on another, escalating as more joined in. While everyone was staring at the distraction, Louis disappeared over the side of the road into the tall weeds. He could hear the uproar continuing and knew this was the time he needed to get as far away as quietly as possible. It was a terrible risk, as it was possible one of the guards would see through the distraction.

Louis figured once they noticed he was missing, they would start looking for him in the direction furthest away from the prison and toward the nearest town. So he headed back to the prison instead. Luckily, the terrible road conditions would make it difficult for them to pursue him by horse, and the equal risk of a horse breaking a leg in a meteorite hole in the fields would also hold them back.

The fight expanded, forcing all the guards to get involved in breaking it up. As promised, none of those in on the ruse looked to see if he had gotten away. Louis knew that would be a dead giveaway and had made them vow to keep their eyes on the fight. Poor Riggs stood watching with his mouth open, having no idea his protector was getting further and further away.

The price Louis had paid his cohorts was far less than the punishment they would receive, but there was more in it for them. To be rid of Louis and his overbearing control of everything in the prison, including the guards, would be relief enough. And they now had access to Riggs. Those still alive whom Riggs had helped put away still remembered, and they were not the forgiving type.

A shot rang out overhead. "Break it up!" the head guard shouted, firing off another round. The prisoners stalled long enough for the other guards to rush in and restrain the offenders. "You're in for it now. Damn idiots! What's gotten into you?" To the others, he barked, "get back to work; we're not done here."

The on-watchers picked up their shovels and got

back to work. Unseen by the guards, a few exchanged knowing glances. Despite the punishment coming, those involved knew that, in the long run, it would be worth it to be free of Louis' domination.

Riggs, whose only goal had been to stay out of the limelight, was the first back to work. He had never wanted any trouble, and with a year to go until his parole, he certainly wasn't going to cause any now. He kept his head down, not daring to look around. Only later would he realize his protector was gone.

Louis moved as stealthily as he could through the weeds, belly crawling where they were too low to let him walk stooped over or travel on all fours. Each step took him closer to freedom and his revenge on his nephew, Grayson Stone Morgan III.

He didn't know how long the warm spell would last, and he was far from any town. Louis knew the odds were against him. He might well freeze to death or be killed by a bear or poisonous snake. But even that was better than a slow death in the prison as his health waned away. Even in the infirmary, without being able to carry out the threats holding everyone at bay, he wouldn't be safe. He had made many enemies inside, and they knew there were worse things than death, one of them being torture. So even if he died out there, it would most likely still not be the agonizing death that awaited him back behind those stone walls.

Louis had never been a man of faith, but if he had been, he would have thought providence led him to what he came across. As he breached the first hilltop, he could see smoke in the valley below. It was too small to be a forest fire. He scrambled down the hillside as carefully as he could and worked his way in that direction. It was nearly quitting time, and he knew the guards would soon figure out that he was gone. No doubt they knew whatever it was down there existed, but whether they would think he found his way there or not, he didn't know. Neither did he know if any of the roads going to the prison were connected to this valley. No matter, it would increase his chances of survival, so there was no decision to be made.

He finally found the source of the smoke. It was the chimney of a little cabin. A homestead of some type. Louis knew whoever lived there was most likely armed, and his work clothes gave him away as an escaped prisoner. He would have only seconds to take control of the situation inside the cabin, so he ignored his pounding heart, barged up to the door, and kicked it in.

Inside were four startled people, one a man who quickly glanced over to the wall at his right. That was all Louis needed, and he lunged for the rifle hanging over the mantle. Louis was determined, and despite the struggle and the wild screaming in the background, he won the firearm.

He cocked the gun. "Now everyone calm down, and no one gets hurt, understand?"

The mother had gathered her two children behind her over by the cookstove. They were crying and clutching the back of her dress.

"Shhh," she tried to sooth them. "Please, don't hurt us, mister; please."

"I have no quarrel with you. I just need some help, and then I'll be on my way." With the gun, he motioned to the man. "You, get over there with your family where I can see you all."

The man inched his way over, not taking his eyes off of Louis, and stood protectively with his family behind him.

"I need some different clothes and a satchel to carry whatever food you have. Give me those, and I'll be gone. And no one gets hurt."

"I'll get them for you," the man said.

"No," Louis barked. "Not you; I need to know where you are. She goes," he nodded to the woman.

She left the huddle and went into another room, coming out with a leather tote and some clothes draped over her arm. She held them up for Louis to see. "Will these do?"

Louis took his eyes off the man long enough to glance at what she held out. "And a coat. I need a warm coat; this weather won't hold up long." He knew he was taking precious things from them as no one had a spare coat, but he didn't care.

The woman fetched what was probably the only coat her husband had and stuffed it into the bag with the other items. "We don't have much food, mister."

"You can get more." And then a spark of humanity flared in him. "alright, keep enough for your young'un's dinner and give me the rest. I'm not going to hurt you; just don't come after me, and this will all be over in a few moments."

With the satchel now filled with what he had asked for, Louis snatched it out of the woman's hand as she extended it to him.

"Good. Now, do as I said, and don't come after me. And if anyone shows up looking, tell them I went downstream."

Louis backed away toward the door, the barrel still aimed their way. He saw the man staring at the gun and knew he was hoping Louis would leave it. The man had a family to feed, but Louis had a mission to fulfill. He had seen the traps hanging outside; they wouldn't starve. He backed out of the door and took the weapon with him.

He had ordered them to tell anyone looking for him that he'd gone downstream, so if the family should be questioned, his trackers would most likely do the opposite and head upstream. So, downstream he went.

As he ran away, he could hear wailing from inside the cabin.

CHAPTER 12

Ned and Sakinay were headed toward Wilde Edge. As they approached the small Waschini communities along the way, they noticed lots of damage to the trails and roads. Their rate of travel slowed as they couldn't risk one of their horses breaking a leg in the deep holes that scattered the landscape.

It was nearing twilight as they rode into Wilde Edge, and, as anticipated, they drew stares from the few townsfolk around. Sakinay stared proudly ahead and rode tall. The townsfolk would recognize Ned, so he had little fear for Sakinay, at least in this town. Ned was shocked at the damage done, yet amazed that it seemed none of the buildings had been hit. Truly, this had been an extraordinary event. He only hoped his father and Newell had accepted that.

"We'll go to my parents first," Ned explained. Sakinay just nodded and kept his stoic face.

Arriving at the Webb farm, he and Ned dismounted. Ned went to the door first and, though he was family, knocked. Barking ensued inside, and Ned could hear footsteps coming to the door. "Ned!" his mother exclaimed, reaching out to embrace him while eyeing Sakinay.

"Oh, you came back. I am so glad. And who is your friend?"

"This is Sakinay. He lives in the same village as Awantia and I."

"Welcome," his mother said, before asking Ned, "Does Sakinay speak English?"

"I do," Sakinay answered, causing Nora to startle somewhat.

"I apologize; you are very welcome."

"Is Father home?"

"Yes, yes, oh, please do come in," Nora stepped aside.

"You're staring, Mother," Ned whispered as he passed her as indeed she was. She had never met a Local or been this close to one.

Ned's father had heard his wife's voice and came out from the back room. After introductions were made and everyone greeted, Buster suddenly ran out from the kitchen and started sniffing Sakinay's boots.

"Small curly wolf. It has Ned Webb's hair," Sakinay said, bending over a bit to get a better view of the little creature circling him.

They all laughed together.

"They find my hair an oddity," Ned explained.

"You must be tired; do you wish to rest or clean up? Or both?" Nora asked. "I have supper on the stove, but you have some time." She asked Ned to show Sakinay around, and the two left with Buster at their heels.

"I am relieved to see Ned, I admit," Matthew said.

"So, do you now believe these three events have not been normal occurrences, and there is something to what he told us?"

"I would be a fool not to. Yes, at first, I brushed them off, but the identical duration, and that during this last one, no one was hurt, and none of our buildings were destroyed. That can't be a coincidence. And I know what you are going to say next."

"Yes; it's more of a question, though. When will we be leaving?" Nora asked.

"We have to talk to Grace and Newell, of course, but otherwise, I would say, weather permitting, as soon as we are ready. However, we all have a lot to think about and to prepare."

There were bowls of steaming food already set out, and Ned wondered just what of it Sakinay would eat. To his surprise, his companion tasted it all, and as he put a buttered biscuit into his mouth, his face went slack, and he stared ahead, eyes unfocussed.

"Do you like it?" Nora asked, concerned.

Sakinay chewed some more after swallowing and said, "It is good. What is it?"

"The fluffy part is similar to the cornbread you make," Ned explained, "which I think is also good. But I suspect you mean the butter. The yellow stuff on it. I could teach the Brothers to make it if they had cows or goats."

Sakinay answered, "Perhaps our Chief might consider getting such cows and goats."

"We will be taking our cows and goats with us," Matthew said, "so we will share them with you."

"What?" Ned almost dropped his fork midway to his mouth. He had thought it too early in the meal for serious talk, so he hadn't brought it up, though everyone knew the possibility of their going back with him was the reason he had returned home.

Matthew wiped his mouth with his napkin and laid it back on his lap. "I know I gave you a hard time about this, son. And I hope you understand why it was so hard to believe you were correct in your understanding, but I do believe you now. Though part of me still can't accept it is happening, and as hard as it will be to adjust to an entirely different life-style, your mother and I are willing to return with you."

"What about Grace? Have you had time to talk to them?" Ned asked.

"We planned on visiting them tomorrow after

Newell gets home from work. You will come with us, Sakinay?" Matthew added.

"I came so your son would not travel this distance alone. But I will come, yes. I want to see the ways of the Waschini as they are before they are destroyed."

Ned heard his mother gasp and saw her wide-eyed look.

There was not much dinner conversation after that.

Later, in the privacy of their bedroom, Nora sighed, "What Ned's friend said."

"Sakinay," Matthew answered. "I know. I saw the look on your face, and it affected me the same way. But, as shocking as it was, it is also somehow reassuring to hear."

Nora finished his thought for him. "Because someone other than our son also believes it."

"I am sorry to admit it, but yes. I do now believe him. I would be a fool not to, and yet at the same time, it seems impossible. Even though we lived through each of these events, my mind can't quite accept this situation as real."

He sat on the end of their bed and took off his socks, anxious to get under the covers, which were now probably nicely warmed by his wife's curvy body.

He slipped under the thick comforter and turned toward her, propped up on one elbow. "But you believed him all along."

"He's our son. He has never made up stories, and he has always been an honest boy, not one given to drama. No matter how incredulous my mind was, my heart knew differently."

"We will leave as soon as we can," Matthew said. "Load everything we can on the wagon. But we will have to leave room for Grace and her family, and that will be a lot of the space."

"The Lanes have a wagon and team they want to trade, but maybe they will sell it instead."

"Hmmm. I suppose we could afford that. We still have that money Grayson set aside for us. I don't suppose it will be of any use to us once we leave here."

"We should take our best goats and our best laying hens and a rooster. If the weather doesn't hold up, it will be a cold trip, but if they're huddled together and covered, they should survive it."

"Everyone will think we're mad," Matthew said. "But I suppose, after a while, it won't matter anymore." He let out a long sigh.

"What is it?" she asked.

"Now that I believe him, I wish I could warn the others, but they wouldn't believe me any more than I believed my own son—and then they will think I'm mad, that we all are. Best we prepare as quietly as we can and pray it is not as bad for them as it sounds it might be."

"Matthew," Nora lowered her voice. "I have a confession to make."

When he said nothing, she continued, "Grace and I have been preparing all along. Please don't be mad; I didn't mean to defy you. We both just believed differently than you and Newell and felt we had to do *something*."

"What do you mean, preparing?"

"Gathering up extra supplies, items we won't have there but will be helpful. I'm sure they have their own ways of doing things, but at first, we will need many of our own things. I also made a list for you to look over. Things like seed corn, ointments, your farrier supplies, and tools for repair. It is just a start."

"I am not angry; I am glad you listened to your heart, and I will look it over. We also need to speak with Ned. No doubt they have ways of accomplishing the same things we do, so we may not need to bring as many items as we think."

"That would be good," she smiled. "More room for goats and chickens and their feed! But Matthew, what will happen to the farm?"

"I doubt anyone will bother about it. They won't know where we went to or why, and it will just run down over time. We could give it to someone else, but it sounds like everyone is going to be struggling on their own as it is."

Nora pulled her covers up and rolled over, scooting back up to her husband, who laid his head down and put an arm around her.

"We're leaving behind all our memories."

"But we'll be making new ones," he answered.

When Newell arrived home, he saw the Webbs' horses tethered out front. There were two others he didn't recognize, but he did recognize their blankets and harnesses from his time with the Brothers. Ned was back. Had he brought his wife with him?

Newell stomped his boots on the porch to clean them off before opening the door and walking in. The sweet cozy home Grace had created for them and their children provided a soothing welcome at the end of his day. The warm yellow walls were cheery and bright, whatever the weather was doing outside.

Grace came out of the living room to greet him. "We have company! Ned is back home."

"I could tell by the horses. One for Ned, but whose is the other? Awantia?"

"No, a fellow named Sakinay."

"Sakinay! He came all the way here with Ned?"

Newell exclaimed as he shook off his coat and hung it on the entryway peg.

"He seems enamored with Pippy and the puppies —although they are hardly puppies anymore. He clearly enjoys playing with them. It seems peculiar coming from such a fierce-looking man."

"I guess everyone has a soft side," Newell commented. "Where are the boys?"

Grace explained that when her parents, Sakinay, and Ned showed up, she had taken the boys over to a neighbor they often visited and asked if the three could stay with her for a while.

"Mama is in the kitchen; she brought a pot of leftover stew, and she's warming it up."

They walked hand-in-hand over to where the men were sitting, and Matthew rose to greet Newell.

"As you can see, our son has come home and brought a visitor."

Newell greeted Ned and his companion and said to Sakinay, "You have come a long way; welcome to our home."

"I will let you all talk," said Grace. "I'm going to help my mother make some biscuits."

Sakinay turned to Grace.

"What did I say?" she asked.

"Sakinay has only recently discovered home-made biscuits and fresh butter." Ned smiled.

"Oh," Grace answered. "I'll make sure we have

more than enough." She bustled through to the kitchen.

"I am glad to see you, Ned," Newell said. "And you too, Sakinay. Though, six months ago, I didn't expect to be saying that. Well, you know what I mean."

Ned nodded. "I take it to mean that you have now become convinced that what I told you was true," And you are coming back with me and my parents."

"Ah. Your parents are returning with you. Well, I am not surprised; it is the reasonable decision to make. No, that isn't the right word; there is nothing reasonable about this whole situation. It is completely unbelievable, though here I am, realizing everything happened as you said it would. Now I have no choice but to believe the rest will happen as you say."

"You are a logical and orderly man, Newell," Ned said, extending an olive branch.

"Thank you, but I have seen things the others here have not seen, and of all of us, I should have believed you, Ned. For that, I apologize."

"Apology accepted. Now, after dinner, we all need to talk about how to make sure you take only what you truly will need and also how we can pull this off without drawing too much attention."

The others tried to include Sakinay in conversation but soon found out he was a restless man of few words. He did seem to be looking over everything he could see. He tested the wood floors with his weight and closely examined the fit of the stones in the hearth and how they were sealed together. He stared out of many of the windows, tapping on the glass and carefully fingering Grace's ivory lace curtains.

Grace had made sure to set the biscuits and butter close to Sakinay's plate. Once they were seated, though he didn't realize it, the others each took only one, leaving the majority for him.

After supper, the rest of the evening was spent making plans. Ned explained as well as he could the Brothers' way of living, pointing out what they would not need to bring as the Brothers had ways of achieving the same results.

When the subject came around to keepsakes, he had a different take. He remembered how much it had meant to Grayson's grandparents to have their favorite items with them. Miss Vivian's teacup, her mantel clock, Ben's pocket watch. He, therefore, encouraged them to bring what they cherished most.

Somewhere in the middle of the discussion, Nora's eyes became misty. "It is just hitting me what we are doing," she said, "and that we are never coming back."

"I know it's hard, Mother," Ned gently said. "And it is best if you consider never coming back. If there were any chance of it at all, it would be years down the road, and there is no telling what we might find."

Grace got up and put her arm around her

mother. "I know, Mama. I've had the same thoughts, but we have each other, and we'll get through it together. As for the children, they are still young enough and will adapt. No doubt they will find it a grand adventure."

"No one will object to Buster or Pippy? Or the puppies?" Nora asked.

"No," said Ned. Where we are going, everyone has far more reverence and consideration for animals than we do, and the Brothers do tame wolf cubs. As you can see from Sakinay's reaction, there is no doubt they will be wildly popular."

"We have a short while before the boys come home," Newell said. "They don't need to hear our concerns or bear our burdens, so let's see how much of this we can figure out before they get back."

In the time remaining, they debated together whether to tell their friends and neighbors they were leaving. No one wanted to leave with goodbyes unsaid, but in the end, they agreed the best approach was to say nothing. Even with a cover story, there would be many questions requiring untruths and complex explanations. Newell's business was booming, the Webb farm was doing well, and they could think of no emergency that would cause them to pack up and leave together.

By the time the three boys returned, everyone else had left, and Newell and Grace were sitting in front of the warm hearth, with Ruby falling asleep in Grace's arms.

"There are lots of horse tracks outside," Nat exclaimed. "Who was here? Who did we miss?"

"Your grandparents and Uncle Ned. And a visitor. You'll all see them soon, so wash up and get ready for bed," Grace said.

Each of the boys came over and kissed little Ruby before they filed off together.

With their plans made, the men started putting them into action. Not wanting to draw attention, Ned and Sakinay stayed with the Webbs and took care of things there. Matthew took some of Grayson's money and bought the extra wagon and team of four horses from Farmer Lane, who was happy for the cash and didn't question why Matthew needed it.

Since they didn't own a billy goat, using the Baxters' goats for stud, Matthew went to trade one of his year-old heifers for a billy.

They would sell the cows just before they left. They knew too much buying and trading would raise suspicions. The Webbs had never been big traders or gone much outside their homestead for things. Luckily, Grace and Nora had planned ahead, so there was no need to buy much else except new leather boots for Nat. Those he had were still in good shape and would be handed down to Luke and then to Tommy.

The biggest problem in loading the two wagons was the feed they needed for the animals on the way. Ned knew the route well by now and knew where the potable water sources were, but they still had to bring barrels for the dry stretches. Matthew wanted to wait for warmer weather, but with Ned and Sakinay having come all that way, he didn't want to ask them to come back later. So they would have to make it work, though it would take up precious space in the two wagons.

"Now I understand what Miss Vivian went through," Nora said. "It is so hard deciding what to take and what to leave behind, knowing you'll most likely never see it again."

"I know," Grace agreed. "With Luke and Tommy, it is not too difficult, a favorite toy, a blanket. But Nat is old enough to have stored up memories tied to something physical. Also, there will be a lot of us crammed into two covered wagons."

"Nat and Luke can sleep with us and Buster. We'll have room. There is no way you can fit all six of you plus Pippy and the puppies in one wagon."

"I know they would like that. They will probably think it is some grand adventure."

"Well, it is, isn't it?" said Nora.

Grace lowered her eyes, and color filled her cheeks. "You're right, Mama. I need to look at the upside of this and stop focusing on the challenges. The children will learn so much from the Locals; it can only help them in life. From what I saw, their community is very close-knit. Nat, Luke, and Tom will eat it up. As for their future wives, hopefully, they will be as lucky as Ned has been. The same for Ruby."

"I am not sure your husband feels the same," Nora said.

"Yes. I know he has agreed this is what we have to do, but I still sense some hesitation. I never thought of him as prejudiced, but perhaps that is it."

"I noticed you didn't tell him you and I had already started preparing?"

"I know. I didn't want him to think I was forcing my opinion onto him. Newell doesn't like to be pushed. If he thinks he is being pushed, he digs in harder."

Nora didn't say anything but was concerned Grace didn't feel she could be open with her husband. However, they had not been married so very long, and perhaps Grace was underestimating Newell. It could take a long time to truly get to know someone, but also, not being honest with each other only created problems down the road. But then, in all fairness, Nora hadn't immediately disclosed her preparations to Matthew, either.

Grace went back to helping her children decide

what they could and could not live without. She started with the two older boys.

"Nat, have you collected the things you want to take with us? And have you, Luke?"

"They're right here, Mama," Nat said.

"Show me, please, starting with the most important."

Nat picked up the first item. It was the first tool his father had given him, a small hammer. "Papa gave this to me."

"You should bring that. It has a good memory associated with it, and it will be handy to have, no doubt. What else?"

Next, he picked up a coonskin cap, also something his dad had given him. It was small and wouldn't take up much room, and it was another strong memory. "Do you think the Brothers would feel bad about my wearing it? Because it came from a raccoon?"

"We can ask Sakinay or Ned, but my first thought is no; they wouldn't because they wear animal hides. But that is considerate of you to think of how it might affect others. I'm proud of you, son."

Nat put the cap down and picked up his last item, a slingshot.

"Another very practical choice. Are you sure you aren't missing something sentimental that is just for your comfort?"

Grace was surprised to see her oldest son blush.

"Well, there is this—" He pulled out a stuffed toy Grace had made for him when he was a baby. It was in the shape of a baby goat, and she had made it from scraps of Matthew's worn-out shirts.

"I am sure there is room for that, Nat," Grace didn't want to embarrass him anymore, so she didn't elaborate on the sentimental value of it. "How about you, Luke?"

Luke went over to the closet and carried out a pile of things.

Grace looked at the collection of Luke's treasures. There was a fallen bird's nest he had found on his own last summer. She didn't know he had saved it. A pretty field stone he had found helping her in the garden last spring. An old Harmonica that had belonged to her father and a drum her father had made for him. Grace wanted her sons to learn to think, so instead of deciding for him, she talked to him about each item.

"Let's start with this one." She picked up the bird's nest. "I remember when you found it."

"I really like it. But, I guess I could find another one where we're going."

"Alright, so how about this harmonica and the drum. They're both musical instruments. And your father and I know how much you like music." Grace could see Luke was thinking hard.

"I don't know," he said, looking from one to the other.

Grace couldn't help herself. "They won't take up much room if you want to bring them both, honey."

"I really like the harmonica. But will the other children have them? It might make them feel bad. I'm sure they have drums, though!" he brightened at the last sentence.

"I am sure you're right."

"I'll take the drum and drumsticks. That way, I'll still have something from here. Something to help me make friends there!"

Grace was proud of both her sons. They had shown good judgment, and instead of thinking only of themselves, they had also considered others. "Do you think you could both help your little brother make his choices?"

"Sure we can!" Nat volunteered.

"I will let you help him then, but let me know if you need help."

"We will, Mama. But come and check at the end. I don't want to make him leave something behind that he'll be unhappy about later."

"I'll be glad to; just let me know when." Grace left the boys to their task.

She sought out her husband. "Newell, you should be so proud of your sons. They just showed me the keepsakes they want to take with them, and they've made very wise choices."

"I'm glad to hear that. I wish someone could help me decide! This is hard."

"When Ned and I visited Ben and Miss Vivian, I could see how much sentimental things meant to them. So while you're being practical, don't forget the things that warm your heart and feed your soul."

Newell kissed his wife on the forehead. "You are so wise; the boys come by it from you. How is your end going?"

"I've made some pretty hard decisions," Grace said. "For me, it's my grandmother's hand mirror, brush, and comb set. They were the finest things she ever owned and were a wedding gift from my grandfather. An old compass of his, which I'll probably pass on to Nat someday. My journal. That's about it."

"We only need enough food to get us there and then some," added Newell. "Ned learned so much from Sakinay about hunting; I am sure that is the first thing I will learn—and how to make a good set of bow and arrows."

"I think we should have Ned look at what we've collected. We may be bringing things we won't need or forgetting things we should take," Grace mused.

"Another great idea. I think we'll be ready in a couple of days. I am sure as much as Ned knows how important it is to get everything right, he is anxious to get back to his wife."

Newell was right. Ned was anxious to get back home. He was also aware that Sakinay was feeling quite out of place. Ned remembered how he felt the first few weeks at Chief Kotori's village when he didn't know any of the Brothers' ways. At least Sakinay could speak English, and the two were more than happy to look over the inventory.

The horses would pull the wagons, four on each team. Matthew knew oxen would be better, but they had done far too much business in town lately, and they had no real need of oxen. As many of the healthiest goats as could be fitted into a cart would be pulled behind one of the wagons.

They knew horses were a mainstay to have where they were going, and he felt they should bring their own. Ned and Sakinay already had mounts, and Ned had offered to lead two more of the Webb horses. It was going to be slow going as it was, with the wagons. Not counting those of Ned and Sakinay, that meant they would have ten horses altogether. Enough to rotate into pulling the wagons and enough that when they arrived at Chief Kotori's village, they would not be arriving empty-handed.

Matthew would drive the first wagon, and Newell would drive the other with Grace sitting up front. If she wasn't sleeping, Ruby would join them or play in the back with her brothers.

It was almost time to leave, and Ned wanted to speak with his sister in private, so he pulled her aside. "I know it is late to ask this, but I'm worried about you. Are you sure this is what you want?"

"I believe you, Ned; I always did. We can't stay here; I want my children to have long lives with as much stability as they can, whatever that looks like."

Ned scuffed the heel of his boot in the dirt. "It is just that I remember, when I was deciding whether to go live with the Brothers, how I mentioned I wanted you all to come with me. I remember you said that you loved your life with Newell and you didn't want to go off exploring old caves and such."

"I know, but things have changed, and if it's what you're saying, I have never thought for even the briefest moment that you made this up to get us to go with you. Besides, we might end up living in caves!" and she let out a little laugh.

Ned's stomach clenched. But what if it came to that, even for a little bit while An'Kru released the vortex? Could his sister adapt? Would she be angry with him forever? But they were about to leave, so they would have to cross that bridge if they came to it, and besides, there was nothing he could say to prepare anyone for the People, the Sassen, or An'Kru.

His family would have only a short while to adjust before An'Kru released the vortex. Would it be enough?

It was nearly time to go. Everything was loaded, and Grace and Newel had closed up their little yellow house and said goodbye. Grace tried not to cry but couldn't help it. Their first years as newlyweds had been there. Her children had been born either there or at her mother's. No longer would the soft light of the oil lanterns breaking through the ivory curtains in the windows greet her husband as he came home from work. Her little garden out back would go untilled, in time overcome with weeds until nature reclaimed it. And they weren't allowed to say goodbye to anyone or leave any note of explanation; they would simply have left. It wouldn't take the neighbors long to realize they had taken all the animals.

With the animals loaded, Grace and Newell left before first light, hoping not to be seen. In the back of the wagon, the chickens and rooster clucked and bobbed their heads around. Their supplies were packed as tight and as level as possible, with the bedding making the top layer. Oil lanterns swayed suspended from the hooped stays that supported the canvas top.

Newell drove their wagon over to the Webbs' house, where Grace quietly went up to the door and tapped lightly. Nora came around from the back where the barn was.

"Oh. You've already locked up?" Grace winced.

"You wanted to say goodbye one last time? I'm sorry," her mother said. "I'll have your father let you in through the back."

"No, it's fine; I have to let go. Seeing it again isn't going to make it any easier. Are you all ready?"

"Yes. Matthew is pulling the wagon up now. How did you do with getting Pippy and the pups settled down?"

"Right now, Luke is holding Pippy, and Tommy is in the back, entertaining the others. We have a crate that they will eventually have to go in, but they'll cry, and we're trying to leave as quietly as possible."

"Ruby?" Nora looked around.

"In the back, sleeping. For now."

"I can look after her whenever it would be helpful."

Matthew brought around his wagon with the goats in the cart behind. Ned and Sakinay followed on horseback, Ned with the two horses he would be leading.

"This is it, I guess," Nora said, looking around.

"If we're ready, let's get going," Matthew said gently.

Grace bit her lip as tears started rolling down her face. She was grateful her back was to her boys.

Newell put his arm around her and pulled her close. "I know it's hard. We all know."

She indulged herself for another moment before wiping her eyes. "I'll be fine once we've left; then I'll only be looking forward. If you're ready, I'm ready."

The caravan started its long journey to their new life.

CHAPTER 13

"Where does An'Kru go?" Adia asked her mate.

"I do not know," Acaraho answered. "He said he would be back, but nothing about where he was going. I doubt he goes back to Lulnomia, as he is still a young offspring there. Perhaps we will never know."

"The last sign was just a few weeks ago, so he'll have to be back soon. Spring is just ahead, and that is when he said he would return."

"We are as ready as we can be, with all the room in our various communities to shelter the Brothers if they so wish, the shelters Haan's people built, and those bountiful harvests—thanks to Eralato and Taipa.

Adia nodded. "I do wonder what happened with Ned and his plans to bring his family back? Was he successful? Are they already at Chief Kotori's village?

Are they on their way? It is frustrating not knowing what is going on in the outside world."

"We are very cut off. It has not mattered much before, but with all the big changes coming—"

"And we have no one but Oh'Dar to send into the Waschini world to find out what is going on."

"Ned could as well."

"Perhaps it should be discussed at the next Brotherhood meeting. Maybe Oh'Dar and Ned could take turns going, but I hate to ask that of either of them. It is a long trip and will no doubt be fraught with risk, based on what An'Kru explained will happen."

By the time the light broke over the horizon, Ned and his family were far enough away that Wilde Edge was cleanly out of sight.

Ned was dealing with his own feelings about never coming back. His family home had been at Wilde Edge, and it had always comforted him to know he could go home if he wished. Now that was gone, though, on the upside, he had everyone with him and Awantia waiting, and together, they would make new memories.

It was cold, but not unbearably so. The warm weather had tailed off but had not been replaced by the biting cold that preceded the meteorite storm. Burlap bags thrown over the chicken cages kept the heat in, and they seemed to be doing fine, though they were creating quite a smelly mess. In retrospect, Ned wished they had thought to make one wagon just for sleeping, though it would have been tight, and the other for the animals. Too late now; the damage had been done. Luckily the breeze passed the smell behind them, but at night it was something else.

They passed over long stretches of tedious terrain, mostly flat land with a few clumps of trees. They crossed the streams, which were low, as Ned had expected. Had they waited until spring, they could have ended up in a dangerous situation with rivers and streams swollen by the winter melt-off. The trip was so far uneventful, which was a blessing, but that brought with it boredom. The children had sung every song they knew of and told every joke over and over again. When they could, they slept. They usually made camp early, so the men had time to hunt and have whatever they caught cooked early enough for the children to get a good night's sleep. Ned and Sakinay were used to sleeping under the stars and kept the fires banked through the night.

One day, as they were on the way again, Grace said to her husband, "Surely by now they've noticed we're gone. I wonder what they're thinking. I hope they don't think we came to any harm!"

"There would be no reason for them to think that. There was no sign of a struggle, and our houses were shut up tight and tidy. Even the barns were left in good order. But you are right; I did think of that and that we wouldn't want them snooping around. That's why I told a few of the businessmen in town the day before we left that I was moving my family and my business elsewhere."

"What?" Grace clicked her tongue. "We agreed we would not say anything—none of us."

"I know, but the more I thought about it, the more I felt it would just create too much mystery, so I came up with that plausible story. I didn't say when we were leaving, only that we were, and I planned it with no time for people to ask many questions. By the time they realize we are gone, it will have been several days, no doubt."

Grace squeezed her jaw tight to keep from saying what she wanted to. How could he? They had all agreed. The least he could have done was ask her father about it. Or maybe he had.

"What did my father say when you told him you were going to do that?" she asked.

"I didn't tell him. Look here, Grace, I know I made a decision that was out of line with what we all discussed, but I don't think it was a mistake. You don't know; we might be back someday. I am still in charge of the Morgan Trust, and what if he needs me to go back and make other arrangements for his wealth? I felt it was what I needed to do."

Grace rode in silence for some time, going over

and over in her mind how he would do such a thing without at least consulting her father. They were one unit now, and what one did affected the others. If he had already veered from the direction they'd all agreed on, what might happen down the road? And did this mean Newell didn't truly accept this as a permanent move? For the first time, Grace started to see a part of her husband she wasn't comfortable with.

Newell was also silent. He was the man of the house, and it fell to him to make the difficult decisions. He knew she was right that he should have discussed it with Matthew first, but it had just happened. He hadn't planned it. Well, he hadn't planned it for very long. He was confident that, in the long run, they would be glad he'd made up the cover story. He silenced his conscience with the thought but did note that he probably shouldn't make any more unilateral decisions.

The days and nights passed. Ned knew they would come to Chief Is'Taqa's village before Chief Kotori's, and after conferring with Sakinay, he brought the subject up at the evening fire.

"We are several days out from the first village, which is the village Grace and I visited to help free Grayson. We could push on through, but I think it would do everyone good to have a break from the wagons. Does anyone object?"

Grace looked hopefully at her parents. She doubted Newell would object as he had been to this village more than once and knew the people there.

"I think that is a wise idea," Matthew said. "Best to break up the trip and maybe get warm again for a while. Will the animals be a problem?"

"No," Ned assured his father. "They have never seen goats, so they will be an oddity, but the village children will really enjoy seeing them and the chickens."

"Won't the chickens get lost?" his mother asked.

"Oh, they might wander a way a bit, but we can ask the children to help us round them up and put them back in their cages before nightfall."

"I would support dunking those cages in a nearby stream if we could. They really need to be cleaned before we set out again," his father added.

Ned looked at Sakinay and said a few words they didn't understand, to which Sakinay replied, "Good choice. Wise Waschini."

It wouldn't be long before their wagons would be seen by the Brothers' scouts. Ned was confident they would recognize him even from a distance due to his curly blonde hair, which set him apart as much as

Grayson's sky-blue eyes. He breathed a long sigh of relief when he saw the scouting party up on the ridge ahead, hands raised in welcome.

"Is that them? Is that them?" Luke blurted out. "I can see them! Look!"

Nat hoisted Tommy onto his lap and pointed to the distance.

Nora reached over with her free hand and grabbed her husband's. He squeezed it and gave her a reassuring smile.

"Hi-yah," Matthew cried out and snapped the reins, urging the team on and up the small incline to the top of the ridge. He pulled them to a stop a little way from the waiting party.

"Greetings, Ned Webb," said Pajackok.

"Greetings, Pajackok. This is Sakinay from Chief Kotori's village." He waved to the rest. "This is my family. They are coming to live at Chief Kotori's village."

Pajackok and his party turned and rode toward the village, their signal to follow.

Even those who had grown sleepy were now wide awake. The children were excited, their eyes darting everywhere, not wanting to miss a thing. Nora held Ruby tight and moved as close to her husband as she could.

"Mama, Mama, look!" Luke pointed first at one thing, then another as more parts of the village came into view.

Newell turned back to see what Luke was trying to draw attention to. "Don't point; it's rude," he admonished his son. "You have to be on your best behavior now, so please try to calm down. We'll be here a few days, no doubt, so there's no need to discover everything at once."

The closer they got, the more of Chief Is'Taqa's people started gathering around. Ned was riding in front, and he stopped the wagons on the outskirts of the village. While everyone climbed out, he dismounted and went to greet those waiting.

Oh'Dar was standing with Chief Is'Taqa and Honovi.

"Welcome," the Chief said.

Ned greeted him, Honovi, and Oh'Dar and asked the Chief if he and his family members could stay a few days before traveling on to Chief Kotori's village. The Chief agreed, and introductions were made.

The men then moved the wagons to where Oh'Dar directed. With the wagons and trailer situated, they set about taking care of the horses.

Noshoba, now nearly a grown man, went over to join them. "I will help look after your horses while you are here."

While the men had been moving the wagons, Honovi and her younger daughter, Snana, were greeting the women.

"I apologize; we did not prepare shelters for your

family," said Honovi. "Had we known you were coming, we would have."

Nora answered, "Thank you, but we simply appreciate your help. This is all so different for us."

"I remember you from when my brother and I came to help free Oh'Dar," Grace said.

"You have a family now." Honovi smiled at little Ruby on Grace's hip.

"Yes, I have four children now. This is our daughter, Ruby, and our boys over there are Nathan, Luke, and Tommy."

The boys were following their father's directions to unload some of the items from the wagon so they could set the chicken coops out, but upon hearing their names, they came running over.

As they exchanged greetings, Nat's attention was drawn to a figure who was apparently coming to join the group.

"Who is that?" he blurted out. Honovi turned to see her granddaughter, I'Layah, walking toward them.

"This is I'Layah, daughter of Oh'Dar and my daughter Acise."

Nora gently nudged her son and whispered, "You're staring, Nat."

No one could have blamed Nat for staring. The young girl's unusual red hair glistened in the winter sunlight as she approached.

"I am I'Layah," she introduced herself and turned

to her grandmother, "I am going to help my mother fetch more water."

Nat noticed a small crowd of children and some women, most likely their mothers, gathered around their livestock. Standing a safe distance away, some of the little ones were pointing and chattering in excitement. Nat went to explain about the chickens and goats and why they had brought them.

Luke, in his lighthearted, easy-going way, opened one of the coops and took out a chicken. He carried it over to the children and told them how to pet it. First one, then another, patted the chicken's head and pulled their hands back, giggling.

Newell came back from helping with the horses and joined his wife. "Grayson sent me back to make sure you were all fine."

"We are," Grace said. "Look at your oldest son; he is a natural with children and animals and has already made friends. And Luke is taking after him. He let Pippy and the puppies out for the children to meet. It's a great start!"

"We really have to stop calling them the puppies, you know. But Grace, who in the world was that red-headed girl?"

"Grayson's daughter. A surprise, to be sure,"

Grace answered. "My goodness, she's the image of Miss Vivian."

"She certainly doesn't look anything like one of them. It's a shame," Newell said.

"What's a shame?"

"That she's being raised—" Newell stopped himself. "Never mind. Just a stray thought."

"None of us expected to see a red-haired, blue-eyed girl here," Grace answered.

Newel thought of the other surprises in store for them, far more unexpected even than a red-headed child among the Brothers. He wondered how long before his family would learn of the People and the Sassen. Would it be possible to keep that from them forever? He wished it were so, but he was certain it was not. He only hoped they would have more than enough time to adjust and feel comfortable in their new lives before they had to make that discovery.

"The Chief's wife, Honovi, said the village will feed us while we are here. How kind they are. Just as I remember."

Newell put his arm around his wife and pulled her close. "How is Ruby doing? I see she's awake."

"I should feed and change her," Grace replied.

"I'm going to see if the boys need help with the livestock. Grayson told me where we could put the goats to graze. I'm glad the billy isn't grown. I don't look forward to that."

It had been a long day by the time they bedded

down in the wagons for the night. They had set their supplies out, so their mattresses and bedding sank down between the side boards, making it much cozier and warmer. Newell and Grace could hear the boys talking in her parents' wagon, but before long, there was only silence.

Ruby was safe and snug in her layers of clothing, and Grace cuddled up against her husband. "We made it," she whispered. "Sleep now, while we can, before the dogs wake up."

Newell hugged her tighter. "Tomorrow starts our new life among the Brothers."

Grace woke up to hear Tommy calling for her. She sat up and saw the oil lamp was on in her parents' wagon. Then she realized why. A chorus of yips and howls was coming from one of the ridges. Grace tossed her covers off and rose.

"Where are you going?"

"I'll be right back; Tommy's calling for me." Grace checked on Ruby and eased herself out of the wagon, though waking the dogs as she did.

Nora met Grace with the oil lamp held high. "He's fine. He's just a little scared."

Grace leaned into the back of her parents' wagon and lifted Tom out. His arms and legs wrapped tightly around her.

"I'm sorry; I'll take him back with me." Grace padded back to the other wagon. Newell was sitting up now, trying to hear what was going on.

When Grace arrived, he took Tom from her. "It's alright, son. It's just coyotes. You've heard them a hundred times."

The little boy buried his head against his father's shoulder.

"Here, you can sleep between us," Grace said and made room for their son. "You know your Papa won't let anything hurt us, and there is also an entire village here. If we were in any danger, there would be people out chasing them away."

By now, Ruby had woken up, so Grace tended to her while Newell settled Tom down next to him.

"The chickens and the goats!" Tom whispered.

"The coyotes aren't going to come this close," Newell assured him. "Not with so many people around. It'll be alright, I promise."

Newell immediately regretted promising his son that. What if something did get the goats and chickens? What a horrible start to their new life, not to mention how it would be for the goats and chickens. He wished Ned and Sakinay were sleeping outside the wagons as they had on the way here, but they had been invited into the Chief's shelter for the night.

It took a while for the dogs to settle back down, but no matter, Newell knew he wouldn't sleep the whole night worrying about the livestock. He assured himself that Oh'Dar would not have let them camp where they had if the livestock was in danger, but it didn't work. He got up and took his firearm outside to sit watch and vowed that in the morning, he would ask to move the wagons further inside the village.

It was only when the first light broke across the horizon that he let himself sleep.

As she and her mother were standing outside their wagons, talking, Grace saw Honovi approaching. Honovi invited them all to the Chief's morning fire.

Grace gathered the boys, and, with a trail of dogs behind them, the families soon joined Chief Is'Taqa and his family. They settled around the fire with Buster, Pippy, and the other dogs gamboling about.

"How long will you be staying with us?" the Chief asked.

"We're not sure," Ned answered. "We only wanted a short rest from traveling."

"What my life-walker is trying to say," Honovi interjected, "is that you are, of course, welcome to stay as long as you like, and some of our women have made arrangements so a shelter can be freed up for your use. It may be a little crowded, but it will be warmer, and you will no doubt find comfort sleeping inside."

Grace looked at her mother and replied, "We would greatly appreciate that; thank you so much."

"We had no way of knowing you were coming," said Honovi, "but last night, you should not have had to sleep in the wagon with your little ones."

"The coyotes did frighten Tom," Grace volunteered. "But, it's not like we haven't heard coyotes before."

"You do not need to explain," Honovi said. "We will show you to the shelter after you have all filled your bellies."

Nat raised his hand to speak. Grace saw Honovi smile at him. "Yes?"

"What about our chickens and goats? They will be unprotected."

Noshoba spoke up, "The chickens are more at risk from other predators than the coyotes."

"Racoons, for one," Honovi said. "We can move them for you."

"They will be safe, and the watchers will—" Noshoba stopped himself.

Ned froze. Honovi froze.

Newell stepped in, "Yes, we should have known you would have scouts around, even at night. Thank you, that helps."

Luke quietly added, "And we have Buster, Pippy, and the puppies to protect us." At hearing their names, Buster and Pippy came frolicking over.

Honovi smiled. "We have raised orphaned wolf

cubs here before. Oh'Dar was given one when he and my daughter were bonded. Her name is Waki; she is full-grown now and comes and goes."

Grace watched Luke's eyes widen at the mention of a wolf cub.

Oh'Dar and his family joined the group. He sat next to Ned, with Acise and the children in a line to his right.

"This is my life-walker, my wife, Acise. You have met our daughter, I'Layah. These are our sons, Tson-akwa and Ashova."

Grace said, "Your sons look to be about the same ages as our two oldest." She then introduced Nat, Luke, and Tom.

"I'Layah and Tsonakwa are only a year apart," said Acise. "They are eight and seven years old, and Ashova is five."

"Nat is nearly seven. Luke is four, and little Tom is three. And then, of course, Ruby. She has just turned one."

"Children are the blessing of the Great Spirit," Honovi said.

"My mother says that every day," put in Nat.

After they had all eaten and were being taken to their new shelter, Oh'Dar pulled Ned aside for a moment. "Let's make time to speak later this morning."

Soon, Ned and Oh'Dar were talking.

"I am very happy that you convinced them to come," Oh'Dar said.

"The Great Spirit did the convincing; I only showed up at the right time. Newell and my father were the hardest to convince. I think my mother and sister believed me from the start. But, if it hadn't been for telling them about An'Kru's warnings, they would not be here. Not even my father could dismiss the unnatural nature of those three events."

"There is so much more to come, Ned. But you have been through it yourself. You know the adjustments that are coming."

"I'm not worried about my nephews; they will make friends easily enough, and they love the outdoors, even little Tom—though my father and Newell may have a hard time being over-protective of Ruby. Grace and my mother have each other. It will all work out."

"And there's Awantia. She will be a stabilizing force for your mother and sister."

"I miss her terribly. It feels as if I have been gone for so long. I now understand what you went through during all those years of traveling between Shadow Ridge and Kthama."

"Yes, Kthama." Oh'Dar let out a long breath. "More hurdles to come. Just take them one at a time."

"I can't imagine what will happen when they meet An'Kru," Ned said.

"Are you smiling?" Oh'Dar laughed. "You are!"

"Oh, I am just picturing the sweet unspoken moment of *I told you I wasn't making it up*," Ned laughed back.

Over the next few days, the families rested and relaxed. Knowing they were safe within the Brothers' village was more of a relief than any of the adults had anticipated, but sadly, soon it was time to move on, and the goodbyes were heartfelt.

Everything was packed up, dogs, chickens, and the goats in their cart. None of the livestock had been lost to predators, and Matthew promised that once their numbers had increased, he would give the Brothers some goats and chickens.

CHAPTER 14

Louis was surprised he was still alive. If he hadn't stumbled on the trapper's cabin and stolen the man's coat and rifle, he wouldn't have been. He figured by now the prison guards had found the cabin and questioned the man, and believing Louis was headed downstream, were now miles in the other direction.

He realized he had picked the worst season to escape. But the winter weather would also make it harder on the guards as well. Leaving the trapper and his family with only enough food for the children for a few days and taking the man's precious coat and gun had started to prick his conscience, but he told himself this was not the time to get a conscience.

The cold air burned his lungs and made his coughing worse. He was also perpetually hungry. He made a fire only during the day and melted snow over it. He knew enough not to eat the snow directly as it would lower his body temperature, and he could likely die, and if it weren't for his burning desire for revenge driving him forward, it would have been an easy way to go. But he was not ready to die. Not before Grayson Stone Morgan the Third.

Louis followed the little river downstream, believing that, in time, it would lead him to a town or at least a small settlement, but he didn't know how long he still had to travel to find any information about where he was. He made snow caves at night to preserve his body warmth, but he knew time was not on his side.

Next to food, water, and shelter, his next goal was to get out of the clothes he had stolen from the trapper, which were wet, dirty, and torn. But that would have to wait. He motivated himself with fantasies of the light leaving his nephew's eyes as the life was squeezed out of him. Oh, it didn't really matter how Grayson was killed. He had multiple scenarios, and those images were what kept him going.

He had lost track of the days, but finally, he reached the crest of the ridge before him and spotted buildings at the bottom. There was a small grouping of establishments, more like a settlement than a town. He could see several houses spread out quite a bit from each other. As anxious as he was, he knew darkness was his best ally in finding what he needed, so he waited.

When it was dark, he crept down the ravine, being careful not to lose his footing and go into a slide that could prove deadly. He would have to be very careful and make a quick exit once he'd found what he needed.

Despite it being winter, the women had still hung clothes out to dry. They were frozen into their shapes, which helped Louis find the sizes he needed. He didn't have gloves and was excited to find a pair on the clothesline. Everything was frozen stiff and left his fingers painfully cold as he took them down. Louis tucked the bundle under his left arm, knowing it would only get him wet as it thawed, and hurried to the next house to see if there was anything else he could use.

The full moon gave him enough light to see where he was going but also made it easier for him to be seen. He heard a low growl as he approached the next house, and realizing there was a dog whose barking would no doubt wake the residents, he moved on.

Whether out of courage or desperation, at the next house, he tried the kitchen door. It opened, and he eased inside. On the counter were a bowl of biscuits and a dozen or so eggs. He scooped up the biscuits and put them in his satchel but had to pass on the eggs. He wanted to open the cupboards, hoping to perhaps find a jar of honey, but instinct told him he was pushing his luck. He spotted a crock of butter and scooped out a big gob, and smushed it in his mouth. He knew his finger marks would show but didn't have time to care. He crept back through the door and left as quickly as he could with his stolen bounty.

Louis forced himself to travel most of the night, getting as far away as he could, picking his way on hard ground as much as possible to avoid leaving footprints.

Finding another small town, he decided to creep around what seemed to be the main street and see if he could find out where he was. He was in luck, as the postal service office had the town name on it. He couldn't believe his eyes. Could he be that lucky? He wasn't far from Shadow Ridge. He knew Grayson wasn't there, but he knew the ranch better than anyone and might be able to steal a horse. Not only would it be worth a lot of money, it would get him that much faster to where he was going. But where was that exactly? Without Riggs, he had no idea where his nephew was, but he had to do something. Then it occurred to him he didn't have to wait to steal a horse from Shadow Ridge; he could steal one from this town. So, back he went toward the homesteads, looking for a barn large enough to be housing what he needed.

He stood outside the biggest one he could find and listened carefully through the barn door. He could not hear anything, but he was certain they would have horses. He was also hoping there was a heated tack room, as he fully intended to take a horse, and an ice-cold saddle was not healthy. It could even cause a horse to act up. He gently eased the bar that lay across the doors and opened one just wide enough to slide inside. Whinnies of various tones greeted him. He looked down the line of stalls to see heads bobbing up and down, no doubt expecting a treat as a result of the surprise visit. He almost congratulated himself out loud when he did find a heated tack room, the small wood stove still putting off heat from the last burning embers.

He picked a saddle, the one most broken in, grabbed a blanket, bridle, bit, and saddle bag, and then walked between the row of animals. He wasn't as good as old Ben, but Louis did know horses. He picked the one that seemed most amiable and gently eased into the stall. It was a long time since he had saddled a horse, but it came to him as easily as if he had last done it the day before. Soon, he was walking the horse out into the cold air and on his way.

Now he only needed to get safely away to set up camp, thaw out the clothes he had stolen, and ride into Millgrove. He could be there in a day.

Louis started to believe luck was turning his way when the next day brought high winds. He had not dared to stop, riding slowly and carefully through the night, doing his best to see the road damage made by the meteorites before the horse stepped into a crater and broke a leg. But now, the snow would drift over his tracks. Horse stealing was a terrible crime.

He saw a thick stand of fir trees a way off and rode in that direction, traveling partway into the forest until he came upon a large rock overhang. It was as good a place as any, so he dismounted and started a fire. He kicked himself for not looking around the barn more; there had probably been many items he could have used. Then he remembered the saddle bag and opened it. He found a knife, a canteen, and some jerky. He would fill the canteen with water from the snow he melted.

With the jerky eaten, he looked after the horse, leaving the blanket on for warmth. He knew there were still shoots of grass under the snow, but he also hoped it had recently eaten back at the stables.

His mind wandered back to Dreamer, the unbroken stallion at Shadow Ridge. Louis had tricked Grayson into mounting the stallion, then whipped Dreamer to make him bolt, only to be dumbfounded when the boy took control of the animal. Ben Jenkins had witnessed the whole thing from afar and somehow set him up to make a confession in front of the entire farm crew, then turning him in to Miss Vivian. Louis would like to pay back old Ben if he could, but Grayson was his real target. He wondered how many of the Morgan horses were still at Shadow Ridge and if he had changed enough that Mrs.Thomas wouldn't recognize him. He didn't remotely resemble the man he had been, though his red hair could be a giveaway. Showing up at Shadow Ridge was a serious risk to take, but without Riggs, he knew of no other way to learn where Grayson Stone Morgan III might be.

CHAPTER 15

Ned let his family know they were getting close to Chief Kotori's village. He knew they were all exhausted, sick of traveling, tired of being jostled about in the wagons, and tired of never feeling really clean. Tempers were also at breaking point. He wanted to let them know it was almost over.

He thanked the Great Spirit every day for Awantia and found his heart racing at the thought of seeing his beloved again. He knew he would first have to stay focused on getting his family settled and comfortable, but in time, they would enjoy each other again as life-walkers.

Pakwa was a familiar site, and Ned called out to him. The brave raised his arm in acknowledgment and disappeared to let Chief Kotori know Ned had returned and had others with him. Sakinay rode ahead in pursuit.

By the time Ned and the wagons arrived, Chief Kotori, his Medicine Woman, Tiponi, and Awantia had assembled with most of the village behind them.

Sakinay had already dismounted and was also waiting with them. Ned had the wagons stop just outside the village before he dismounted and went to greet the Chief. "I have returned, Chief Kotori, with my family."

"Your family is welcome here. We have hoped for your success, and believing in the Great Spirit's guidance, we prepared shelters for them."

Ned kept his attention focused on the Chief out of respect. He knew Awantia would understand. "I wish to thank Sakinay for making this quest with me."

Sakinay stood stoically with barely a tip of his head to acknowledge the thank you.

"Do your people need help getting unloaded?" Tiponi asked.

"I think they do. We have also brought animals with us; you will see," Ned said before scooping Awantia into his arms. After greeting his life-walker, he looked around for one other face. "Where is Kele?" he asked.

"Kele is here!" a voice shouted, and out from behind his mother, who had been holding him back, Kele sprinted toward Ned, who gave him a warm embrace. "Awantia has a surprise!"

His mother shushed him from a few feet away.

"She does? I can't wait to see it!"

Then Ned returned to his family and ushered them to meet the Chief and welcoming villagers. He first introduced Chief Kotori, then Tiponi, and, finally, his life-walker.

"This is my wife, Awantia."

She responded, "Welcome. You are all so welcome here."

Nora looked up at her husband and whispered, "She's so kind—and a handsome woman."

Matthew took off his hat. "Our deepest gratitude for letting us live among you and learn from you."

When the rest of the introductions were over, several of the Brothers went to help Ned, Matthew, and Newell unload. Awantia and Tiponi led Grace and Nora over to the newly-constructed shelters. Along the way, other women joined them, wanting to get a peek at the little girl on Grace's hip.

Tiponi held back the covering of the first shelter's entrance. It was large, and Ned assumed it was for Grace, Newell, and their family. Grace stepped inside and looked around. Ned watched her walk over to the walls and touch them lightly. "There's a vent up top, so you can have a fire in the center there," he pointed to where a place had already been prepared.

Then they went to the next shelter, which was only slightly smaller. "The larger the structure, the harder it is to keep warm," Tiponi explained. "But if this is not large enough, we can build another."

Nora spoke up. "This will be fine for my husband and me. Even if the boys visit, we will have enough room. Thank you so much for doing this for us."

"We all have much to learn," Grace mused.

"Yes, you have much to learn of our ways," Awantia said, "but our people will teach you, and we will provide for you until you are ready. Rest now."

Just as at Chief Is'Taqa's village, the livestock and the dogs were a fascination. Nat explained to everyone around what the purpose of the chickens and goats was and that the dogs were just for companionship.

Finally, when everything was unloaded, stored properly, and the livestock secured, Ned excused himself to have a few moments alone with his life-walker.

He led Awantia away to their shelter and drew her down to sit next to him on their sleeping mat, pulling one of the blankets up for warmth.

"I thought about you every day. Every moment," he said.

"So did I. Did you have any trouble?"

"Not from anyone. It is peculiar, though, that what was to us a beautiful night show of shooting stars wrought havoc in the Waschini world. The roads they use to travel and move goods were all but made impassable. Perhaps that is why they did not pay Sakinay much attention. People were in shock, not knowing what to think."

"How could that be? I do not understand," she frowned.

"Small rocks left those streaks of light in the sky. They did not land here, but they did elsewhere. The closer we got to Wilde Edge, Sakinay and I started noticing the damage. I cannot explain it other than it is what the Promised One said would happen. The three signs took place right on time. They were what finally convinced my family to join us."

Awantia slid closer and ran her hand through his curly mass of hair. "I am happy for you that you have your family with you now. Hmmm; I wonder if our child will have your bright curly hair or my dark straight hair?"

"What?" Ned's head snapped up. "Are you— Are you—"

"Yes, my love. We are finally going to have our own family."

Ned leaned over and pulled her onto his lap, and kissed her. Then she wrapped her arms around his shoulders and leaned into his embrace.

"How long have you known?"

"I only recently realized I was pregnant."

"How did I not notice?" he asked, pulling the blanket back enough to look at her belly.

"I am hardly showing, and with the cooler weather, I am dressing with more layers."

"What wonderful news to come home to." Ned kissed her again. "Who else knows?"

"Tiponi. And my parents and Myrica, of course. Well, everyone here knows," she confessed, and they both laughed.

"My mother, in particular, will be thrilled to hear this."

"It seems women are much the same everywhere, then."

As he rode into Millgrove, Louis spotted the local inn. He wanted a hot bath more than anything, but he had no means to pay for it. He needed a job but was not hirable in his current state. He knew he was filthy and stank, and he was sure even his more recently-acquired clothes smelled, too. The only things he had of any value were the stolen horse and the rifle. He decided he could get another one, and it would probably be best if he did, so he went to the innkeeper and asked to trade the horse for a few days' lodging.

The innkeeper came out to look at Louis' horse. He ran his hands over its legs and picked up the hooves to examine them. "Looks healthy. It's a deal.

You can stay for five days, room and board, but that's it."

"Five and a hot bath?" Louis bartered.

"Fine. Take your saddlebags and saddle; I don't imagine you meant to include them."

"Thank you," Louis said, surprised at the man's sense of fairness. He wasn't used to being treated like a human being.

After the longest hot bath he remembered, even compared to Shadow Ridge, Louis used the remaining bath water to wash and rinse out his clothes. They didn't rinse well, seeing the water was soapy, but they would still be in far better condition for it.

Exhausted, he hung the clothes up as close to the wood box as he could and flopped into bed. He couldn't remember the last time he had smelled clean sheets and bedclothes.

When he woke up, Louis couldn't work out what time of day it was. It was either just getting dark out, or the sun was just rising. He walked over to the window and determined it was sunset. He hoped he had not slept a whole day. He checked the clothes, and they were dry but not as dry as if they had been hanging there for a whole day.

He dressed and went downstairs.

The innkeeper was also the barkeeper and greeted him. "Good afternoon, mister—? Never did catch your name."

"Taylor. Bud Taylor," Louis lied. He had picked a very common surname, figuring it wouldn't stand out.

Louis sat at a small table in a corner. An older woman dressed to indicate she was available for company brought him a bowl of meat stew and some biscuits on a platter. She took one look at him and didn't ask if he was interested in her services, no doubt because he didn't look as if he could afford them.

Louis wasn't going to ask what the meat in the stew was. It was cooked, and there was a lot of it. He did his best not to wolf it down, also fighting the inclination to keep looking around for fear of someone taking it away from him. It felt like decades since he had been able to eat a meal in peace.

As soon as the bowl was empty, the woman brought him another one, which surprised him. She realized she couldn't make any money off him, yet she was showing him a kindness.

He finished the second bowl more slowly, this time enjoying it. He crammed the leftover biscuits he couldn't finish into his pockets for later.

As the woman walked by again, he interrupted her. "Excuse me, miss."

She turned and cocked her head, "Miss? Alright;

what do you want?"

"I need work. Is there anyone hiring around here?"

"Down at the lumber company, they're always looking for workers. End of town, turn left, and it's about three miles down."

Three miles and no horse. Not today, Louis thought. It was too late anyway, but after a good night's rest, he would head there in the morning. He didn't know what they paid, but right now, he needed something coming in. He only had four more days of hospitality left from the trade for the horse. He must stay long enough to find out what he could, if anything, in the hopes of not having to go to Shadow Ridge.

And he must buy another horse.

It was a long walk, but worth it in the end. The lumberyard manager hired him on the spot. It was hard work, and at first, Louis wondered if he was working off more than he would gain back at mealtimes, but as a bonus, they fed the workers at midday and fed them well. He also learned that if he worked hard, they had some bunkhouses in the back where he could stay for free. It saved time with the men not having to come and go, especially with the short number of daylight hours.

So, by the time Louis' bed and board ran out at the inn, the stockyard manager had decided to keep him on. Louis figured that within a couple of weeks, he would have enough money to buy another horse. But then what?

Most of the men working there were like him, just passing through. They didn't seem to have wives or families and stayed where they found work and moved on when it dried up, so they weren't any source of information. But the manager had grown up in Millwood, and he definitely knew of the Morgans. He hadn't met any of them, but he knew the story well.

"Sure, everyone here knows about them. Had that fancy place called Shadow Ridge. Bred high-end horses. The grandson was raised by Locals and wasn't socialized, I heard. After Mrs. Morgan took him back and civilized him, it turned out he murdered them for the money. The old woman left the place to her housekeeper. We all often wondered if she was in on it; imagine that, a housekeeper getting that whole estate."

This was not the story Riggs had told him, and Louis realized he was listening to gossip and couldn't take what the man was telling him for the truth. This also meant the only way to find out was to go to Shadow Ridge and hope no one there recognized him.

The hearty meals were building weight he had lost on the way there, and the work would put enough money in his pocket to buy a horse sooner than he'd hoped. It was still cold weather, but that would be breaking soon. It meant the timing would be right for him to work there a while longer, visit Mrs.Thomas, and then, in gentler weather, travel wherever he was to go next. But all that changed the day he went to buy a horse from the local stables.

"What can I help you with?" the stable master asked.

"I need a good horse, healthy. Don't try to trick me; I know my horses."

"No need to get testy; I'm a fair man. I'll show you what I've got."

Louis looked over the selection and decided on a bay mare. He checked her all over, and not all her adult teeth had come in yet, which told him the man was being truthful about her age and asking a fair price.

"When can you have her ready?"

"She's ready now. Where you headed, mind I ask?"

"I have some family out at a ranch out here named Shadow Ridge; you may have heard of it. I'm related to Mrs.Thomas, who inherited it from the Morgans."

"Haven't you heard?"

"Heard what?" Louis, who was getting his money out, paused to listen.

"Mrs. Thomas died some time ago. Her sons had moved there to help her run it, and after she passed, they sold it all. You didn't know?"

Louis didn't have to pretend to look shocked. "No, I didn't. I live out— West. They used to have a lawyer in town. I should look him up and see what else I can find out."

"Newell Storis? Oh, he moved away some time ago. The grandson was put on trial for suspicion of murdering both Mrs. Morgan, his grandmother, and the stable master, Ben Jenkins, and he was found innocent. Not long after, Storis moved to a little town called— Oh, what was it?"

Louis counted to ten to keep his temper down. He hated waiting.

"Wilde Edge. That's the town where the grandson was tried. I'm not sure if that was the reason he moved there."

"You just saved me a lot of trouble," Louis said.

"Don't see how seeing as I had to tell you your relative died. What relation was she?"

"Great aunt once removed," Louis lied. He wasn't sure if that even was a term or what it meant, but the stable master seemed to buy it.

Louis handed him the money. "I'll be back in the morning to get her."

It was starting to add up. Wilde Edge was where he had taken his grandmother to meet Grayson. It was at a family's home. The Webbs, he thought. He was sure he could find it again or at least find out if Newell Storis was somehow involved with them. The only other piece of information Riggs had divulged in all the years past was that Grayson had married a Local. One who was part White. That led Louis to believe he was living in a village of Locals, as law-abiding White people likely wouldn't accept her. But there were so many, and Louis didn't have time or the health to travel to them all. Right now, his next best hope was to pick up some gossip in Wilde Edge.

He had escaped recognition at Millgrove, and he was pretty confident that if he ran into Storis, he would not be recognized either. Louis hadn't had that much contact with his mother's lawyer, to begin with, and with his current rough looks, he bore no resemblance to his former refined self.

Everything he owned was now either on his back or packed in the saddlebag and about to be on its way toward Wilde Edge.

Nootau and Iella had never been happier. Their hopes of having a family were a reality. Nootau dreamed of all the things he would teach their son, Laru'Tor, just as Acaraho had taught him. Acaraho's point of view had turned around Nootau's shame about the white streak in his son's hair. There were times when the old feelings still rose, but he pushed them away. He focused on the proud history of the 'Tor line that Acaraho had pointed out.

High Protector Awan and Nadiwani were equally

happy. She was looking forward to moving out of the Healer's Quarters and into a new living space with Awan. It would be a fresh start for both of them and allow her to separate her private life from her work life, something she had not experienced before.

Everyone was aware that spring was around the corner, the time of An'Kru's return. Every possible idea about where An'Kru had gone had been discussed. Perhaps he was traveling to all the Brothers' villages to speak to them directly. Perhaps he had gone to Lulnomia to teach his younger self there. The conjecture entertained the People many a dark night, but though they might never know where he had been all this time, the anticipation of his return was now foremost on their minds.

Adia and Acaraho spent as much time as they could with their family, knowing their future was uncertain. What would happen to their way of life, their culture? The prospect of the People no longer inhabiting Etera was sobering to everyone, and the question Urilla Wuti had posed at the last High Council meeting remained unanswered. Which path would they choose? Try to breed with the Sassen? The Waschini? Or let their people pass into history.

How sad that as time was running out for the Waschini, it was also running out for the Sassen and the People.

CHAPTER 16

Louis arrived at Wilde Edge. It was a small town—smaller than Millgrove. It had a single main street with a handful of shops running up and down both sides. A General Store, a small bank front. He looked for any signs of Storis' office but found none. A small jail cell told him there was a local sheriff still in residence, and he looked carefully but didn't see any posters with his resemblance on them. It had been long enough; they could well have been posted by now, but this was quite a way from the prison, and news traveled slowly.

For a brief moment, Louis thought of Riggs. What had become of him after Louis' escape? Without his protection, Louis figured the man had only lasted about a day. And the warden. With Louis and his threat of exposure gone, there was nothing hanging over the warden's head.

Louis had enough money left to buy some

lodging for a few days and put his horse up at the stables. Whether that would be enough time to find Storis, he didn't know. But he did as he'd done in Millgrove and took up residence at the inn. It had become run down since the time he and his mother stayed there, clearly not having enough business to keep it in repair. He associated only bad memories with it, but Ruby's Inn was the only place in town to lodge. The food turned out to be serviceable, and no one seemed inclined to bother him, being a stranger and all.

As it was often a good place for finding out what was going on, Louis asked the barkeeper if anyone was hiring. "Check at the General Store. They don't pay much, but it's honest work."

Louis went directly there and was smart enough not to use his real name. He was hired right away to help with unloading goods that came in and stocking the shelves. The barkeep had been right, it didn't pay much, but it was enough to keep him and his horse housed and fed.

The General Store was one of the best places to overhear town gossip. Louis made sure he worked hard and didn't talk much; he knew he wouldn't learn anything by being the one doing the talking, and it was in his best interests to stay in the background and give the storekeeper no reason to send him elsewhere. He planned his work so that at its busiest times, he would be inside the store stacking shelves and hoping to overhear a conversation or, even better, catch Storis in the store. He kept his head close-shaven for fear the auburn hair he'd inherited from his mother might be a giveaway. Unless he was standing in direct sunlight, it would pass for brown.

It didn't take long before he heard a name that caused his ears to prick up.

"Storis' family just up and left," a woman's voice said behind him.

"They didn't tell anyone anything?" he heard a man ask. "Not anyone?"

"You haven't been back here for a while, Mr. Nelson," the storekeeper addressed the man. "But no, not the Webbs. At least, no one I certainly know of. Though Storis did say he was moving his business. But their leaving was the talk all over town; they shut up the houses and left."

"Houses? Who else left?"

"Not just Storis and his family, but also the Webbs, Matthew, and Nora. Even took the goats and chickens—at least, they are all gone, too, and the horses Matthew still had after he sold those fancy ones.

Louis started moving a little slower to stretch out what he was working on.

"They each came in within a few days of each other and paid off their tabs, which makes me think they planned it together."

Louis knew this might be his only chance to find out what he needed to know, so he turned away from the sacks of grain he was stacking. "Excuse me. Please forgive me, the fellow you are talking about, Storis?"

The three turned to Louis. The storekeeper answered. "Do you know him? Darndest thing. His business had really been booming lately, too."

"I used to know someone of that name, but it couldn't be him. He lived in another town. Was a lawyer man."

"That's him, no doubt. He was involved in the trial of the Morgan lad."

"How did he get all the way out here?" Louis asked, trying to sound casual.

"The trial was held here, and then he got involved with the Webb girl, Grace. She and her brother somehow testified and got Morgan off, and then he married her. And now the whole family up and left with no warning."

"If you don't mind my sayin', it sounds crazy," said Louis. "And it's getting more and more peculiar. My wife had a sister named Nora, who married a Webb guy out this way. My wife lost touch with her sister, and it seems too odd if that were to be her."

"Is that why you came here?" the woman asked. "Looking for Nora Webb?"

"Partly. I was just working my way in this direction. My wife died, and I couldn't bear to stay where we were any longer. Wasn't much of a place to begin with. Seems everything was a struggle for us. I didn't know what else to do but thought I could at least try to find this Nora Webb and tell her that her sister died."

"Nora Webb," the woman said. "Did you ever meet her?"

"No, I only heard my wife talk about her. She moved away before we were married."

"I don't know how it can't be the same person," the woman said to the storekeeper.

"The Webbs were—are—fine people," he agreed. "Nobody knows where they went, but I can't believe they won't be back someday. In the meantime, their place is just going to go to ruin. Seeing that you're kin and all, I think they would want you to stay at their place. Look after it, you know? They planted a fine garden; it would be a shame to have it all go to waste."

Louis made himself hesitate. "Oh, I don't know. Seems like I don't really have a right—"

"No, you should," the woman said. "I've known Nora and Matthew a while. They would want you to; I know it. They were always helping others."

"I'll take you there when you're done today," the storekeeper said, "and I'll let others know you'll be staying there. It's better for you, and it's better for the homestead not to be left abandoned like that. No one will give you any trouble."

"Well," Louis said. "If you really think it's what they would want. It sure would help me. In a way, they're the only family I have left."

Louis had smartly transitioned himself from a stranger to someone nearly kin. The storekeeper not only took him to the Webbs' house but he also gave him a raise for being a hard worker and being related to the Webbs.

After the storekeeper left, Louis looked around. It had been a long time since he was there, but nothing much had changed. The wood floors creaked as he walked into the sitting room where he, his mother, and his wife, Charlotte, had waited to meet the vagrant boy whom everyone else hoped was his nephew Grayson Stone Morgan III. Everyone except him and his wife. He remembered looking at Charlotte when the boy produced the blue blanket with the Morgan monogram on it and the locket. The damn locket sealed the deal. Everything went downhill from there.

It was all the Webbs' fault, but they were gone, and at least he had a place to stay. As bad as the memories were at Ruby's Inn, they were worse here. It would serve them right if he burned it all down after he had accomplished what he needed to. If they ever did come back, they would learn what it felt like to lose at someone else's hand everything they had worked for all their lives. Just as Louis had when the damn kid showed up alive, and the Webbs helped figure out who he was.

There wasn't much to eat in the wooden cupboards except some canned peaches and tomatoes, but it was better than nothing, and he could always go back to the inn to eat. It looked as if they had taken some of the oil lamps but not all of them. At least he would have light and soon a fire to keep him warm.

After years of prison living, the little Webb homestead may as well have been Shadow Ridge. Louis had forgotten what it was like to be in a home and to be free, to walk from one place to another, not under guard. For a moment, the idea of remaining there crossed his mind. It was a possibility. No one knew who he really was, and he would have work at the General Store, a soft bed to sleep in, and a vegetable garden. He could get some horses and breed them; he knew how. He could let go of all the anger and hatred and live out what was left of his life in peace. Maybe other people would even help him, and he wouldn't have to die alone one day.

But then it passed, killed by the hatred for his nephew that still burned in his heart. No. Louis knew he was dying, and the thought of Grayson enjoying life as his own came to an end was more than he could bear. Before he died, he would do all he could to make sure Grayson Stone Morgan III and whoever he cared about died first.

A warm front came through, and all across the Brotherhood, people were wondering if this was an early spring—or a false spring. Several warm days had coaxed the new sprouts out of the ground, and tiny green nubs began appearing on the bushes. As much as they tried to keep their minds off it, it was impossible. An'Kru would return soon. And then what?

It was on Ned's mind too. What would An'Kru do, and how much upheaval would it cause? Enough to shake people to their roots, it sounded like. Enough to get them off balance and open their minds to accepting help from the Locals. It would be a chance to make the Waschini see the Brothers for who they were, untainted by propaganda, just as his family was experiencing.

Awantia's pregnancy couldn't have been better timed. It was a chance for Ned's mother, his sister, and his life-walker to bond over a topic they both had in common and through which they could easily get to know each other. Ned knew no one kinder than his mother and his sister. The three of them, with Ruby in tow, were quickly becoming close friends.

Matthew was having a harder time finding his place. With his back injury, he was not able to hunt or chop and carry wood. He was too young to be old and too old to be young. It had been different at Wilde Edge, where families lived apart, and the men didn't work in community as they did at Chief Kotori's village. Seeing other men his age and how active they were, made him even more aware of his disability.

Newel had it better; he was young enough to learn to hunt and provide for his family. Between him and Newell, Ned's parents were also provided for. Nat, Luke, and Tommy seemed hardly to need any adjustment at all and ate up everything they were being taught. Ned chalked it up to their age and their inherent love of the outdoors and animals. So, on the whole, it was going well, except for Matthew.

That the entire village spoke English made the transition immediately easier than it had been for Ned—and also that they all had each other. But in the back of his mind, Ned felt they needed to learn the Brothers' language, too; it would further their integration into the community and would help them let go of the lives they had left behind. They would never be Locals, but in time they would no longer be entirely Waschini, either.

As Ned was hauling firewood back to the village one day, Sakinay, with a stack in his own arms, caught up with him.

"Ned Webb, your father is lost."

"My father is lost?" Alarm spiked Ned's tone. "When?"

"Now. Your father is lost. He is no longer Waschini, so who now?"

Ned was relieved. "Oh. Yes."

"You must help father find his way, as father helped son find his way. Men have more value than lifting, carrying, hunting."

Ned knew Sakinay was right, but how to help his father find a place? It was such a physical lifestyle, and he didn't know what the answer was. Perhaps Awantia could help him.

That night, in the privacy of their shelter, Ned talked to Awantia about his father, who had become disabled some time ago at Wilde Edge. He couldn't farm or even garden much at all, and while Ned knew it was hard for his father not to be able to do all those things, back in Wilde Edge, Matthew seemed to have accepted it and occupied himself elsewhere.

"What did your father do in Wilde Edge?" Awantia asked.

"He went into town and talked to the other men. Mostly at this one place called a General Store. It's a place where you can get supplies—things you don't make yourself. Perhaps like when the Brothers have pau-waus. They trade stories, tools, goods."

"And who are these men he spent time with? Were they strangers?"

"No. They were men he grew up with, who he'd known for a long time."

"Ah. So they held the memory of your father for him as he was before he was hurt."

"I suppose. Wait; I think you are on to something. Yes, they knew him as he was. For most of their lives together, they knew him as strong, robust, and a hard worker. It is only in more recent years that he hasn't been able to do all those things."

"None of the men here carry for him the memory of who he was. He is who he is now only because he has no other memory of himself here being other than— *Disabled* is the word?"

"Yes, disabled."

Then Awantia asked, "What do the men do together at this General Store? Are they working there?"

"No, they talk. They share stories and ideas. He often came home and told us about his conversations there."

"You must help him find this other side of himself, the side that provides value, so he can become that man."

Ned thought long and hard about what both Sakinay and Awantia had said. His father needed to make a space for himself in the village, or he would never belong. Ned had encountered that struggle himself when he first arrived, but it was even harder for his father, who was a mature man, someone to look up to. Someone to inspire others. That night, Ned stepped out into the dark and said a prayer for guidance that he might help his father discover who he was there, among Chief Kotori's people.

Adia and Acaraho had talked late into the night about An'Kru's expected return, and at the end of the conversation, Adia told her mate about the meeting in the Corridor with her mother.

"You immediately knew it was her?" he asked.

"No, I did not; she told me who she was. Meeting her and realizing her love had never faltered or left me helped heal something inside me. All my life, I have wondered about her, what she was like, if she was watching over me, if she would have been proud of me."

Acaraho put his arm around her and pulled her close. "You did not have to hear it from your mother for me to know that she would be—that she is— proud of you."

Adia shared everything her mother had said about why An'Kru was born and that the division to come was necessary for the true evil in the world to be revealed. That, also, this evil would not be allowed to prey on the innocent forever.

"What does that mean?"

"When he returns, hopefully, we will learn more; it will not be long now."

And it wasn't.

I'Layah and her brothers were out scouting for a perfect spot to plant raspberries in the summer. Their mother loved them, so there could never be too many raspberry patches.

It was a beautiful spring morning; the sun was just beginning to throw gentle rays of light through the budding trees and bushes as birdsong sprinkled the air. Tsonakwa was walking ahead, using a stick to knock the dew off first, so their clothing wouldn't get as wet as they passed through. Just up ahead, a patch of light was breaking through the canopy above. A perfect site.

I'Layah brought up the rear, behind Ashova. She thought it must be her imagination when she saw the light flash, but as they stepped out into the sunlit grove, there stood An'Kru.

The three of them stopped and stared.

"An'Kru." It was I'Layah who spoke. "You have come back."

"I have."

"Does anyone else know?"

"You three are the first."

I'Layah looked at Tsonakwa as if he might

explain why the Promised One had appeared to them first.

An'Kru knelt down so he was not towering over the children, and he opened his arms, welcoming them to come closer.

"Listen to me carefully. What is about to happen must happen. No other solution has manifested. Do you know what that word means?"

"Shown up?" Tsonakwa offered.

"Yes. I wanted to speak to you directly to remind you of our visit to the Corridor and remind you to hold tight to it. No matter how bad things look, no matter how frightened you might be, remember fear and faith cannot exist at the same time, and I want you to choose faith. Anchor your hearts in what you know to be true about life and about the lie that is death."

"Who is going to die?" I'Layah's eyes widened. "Not Momma or Papa?" Her lip started to quiver.

"No, my dear one. Not your momma or your papa. No one is going to die, ever. They will only step into another room and wait there for you to join them. Your parents will be with you for a very long time yet. I am leaving this realm, and I want you to be prepared."

"But you will be in the next room waiting for us?"

"Yes, always." An'Kru stood up.

"But will we ever see you again like this?"

"I do not wish to speak of what my abilities make

possible. Now, continue on your mission, and never forget I am always with you, even if you do not see or hear me."

With that, An'Kru turned and walked away into the bushes, which didn't seem to part but which he just faded into.

Tsonakwa said, "Are we to tell Momma and Papa about this?"

"He did not say we could not, but I think we should wait. I think we will know very clearly if we are to tell them."

"I want to go home," Ashova said. "We can look for a planting spot another time."

"Yes," agreed Tsonakwa. "I also want to go home. I want to think about what just happened so I do not forget it."

Acaraho was with Adia, taking an early morning walk to enjoy the return of spring. As much in love as ever, they walked hand-in-hand and stopped to kiss each other from time to time.

"I am enjoying this moment of peace together," he said. "It seems we seldom have quiet any longer, and I suspect that in the future, it will become even harder to find."

"And yet, if what is about to happen is as impactful as it sounds," Adia said, "it will be even more imperative that we do find this time to be together. You are my strength. My refuge. My comfort."

"As you are to me."

They both turned as a bright light flashed and then faded away.

"An'Kru!" Acaraho exclaimed.

The father looked upon the son who towered over him, who had been born to make a way for all people to return to the loving arms of the Great Spirit.

Acaraho's voice dropped. "So the time is upon us."

"Father, Mother, yes, but before I do what I came to do, I must once more address the entire Brotherhood and as many others as wish to come. No doubt the walls of Kthama will not contain them all."

"I will send messengers, and there are plenty of open areas in which you can address them. When do you wish this to take place, my son?"

"At the full moon. That will give everyone time to travel to the High Hills, and as they do, it will light their way during darkfall. I have some others to visit, and then I wish to spend time with you and the rest of our family."

As soon as they returned to Kthama, Acaraho sent word to Iella to ask if she would, as before, send messages to the outlying communities about the upcoming meeting.

Pakwa was in his favorite spearfishing place on the river. The winter run-off had caused the waters almost to breach the riverbed. The currents were fast-running, and he had to be quick to catch anything, but he was having unusual luck that morning, and his basket was nearly full. As he removed the last fish from his spear and added it to the rest, he said his thanks for the giving of their lives for his and his people's sustenance. Then he bent over and picked up the heavy basket. He stopped, frozen in place.

It was as if his arms and legs had taken root in the warm spring ground and were holding him fast. He was transfixed, overcome with the sight before him; he opened his mouth, but nothing came out. Taller even than the People, with long silver-white hair and striking grey eyes, stood a being the likes of which he had never seen. The basket of fish slipped from his grasp and landed on the ground with a thump.

The giant spoke. "I am An'Kru, the Promised One. Do not be afraid." His voice was gentle and soothing, and Pakwa felt his muscles unlocking as fear left his body.

"My Chief speaks of you. You have spoken before to the Brotherhood about the destruction that must come and our role in helping the Waschini find the Great Spirit."

"It is true; I have returned to complete what I was born to do, but first, I wish to address your village. Would you please ask Chief Kotori for permission for me to do so?"

Pakwa started to leave but heard a voice reminding him, "Your fish. You forgot your fish."

Flustered, he clumsily stepped back and retrieved his basket, then quickly went on his way to find Chief Kotori.

He knew if he entered the village running and out of breath, it would only create alarm and confusion. He made himself slow down, counting between paces to measure his steps. His heart was pounding, and his hands were shaking, but he hoped his slow pace would not draw attention.

"Tiponi," he said, coming upon her at her loom, where a circle of children sat watching her and asking questions. "I wish to speak to Chief Kotori. Do you know where I might find him?"

"He is in the Chief's lodge with his Elders. You must wait until they are done."

"It is urgent," Pakwa answered.

"What is it? Your hands are shaking." Tiponi stood up and took one of his hands in hers.

"A visitor," Pakwa stammered, "unlike any we have ever had. He waits by the river. He said his name is An'Kru."

Even Tiponi could not hide her reaction. "Wait here."

She slowly pulled back the entrance cover of the Chief's lodge and entered. Pakwa heard her speak.

"Please forgive my interruption." Her voice sounded shaky. "The Promised One is here."

Normally a man of subtle reactions, the Chief blurted out, "We must go now."

Out of respect for Pakwa, to whom the Promised One had appeared, the Chief let him lead the way. And there An'Kru was. Those Elders who had not been to the Brotherhood meetings had only heard him described, and the closer the group approached, the slower they all walked, partly in reverence and partly in awe. They could feel the power emanating from him.

"I am An'Kru. Chief Kotori, Healer Tiponi, I am pleased to see you again."

"We are honored by your presence," the Chief answered.

"As I am by yours. I came to tell you that the season of change is at hand. Now will come your greatest challenge, to help the Waschini find their way back to the arms of the Great Spirit."

An'Kru turned his gaze toward the Elders who had not seen him before. "The Chief has explained the hard times that are coming. They are necessary not only for the Waschini but also for your people. What I have come to do is not just for their good but for yours as well, for without my intervention, in time, your people will be all but annihilated by those who nurse evil in their hearts."

"We have prepared our stores as you asked, and we are ready to help them," the Chief answered. "Is there more you require of us?"

"I would like to meet your people. I believe it will help them in the times to come."

The Chief invited An'Kru to follow them back to the village while Tiponi ran ahead to gather everyone.

Ned heard the news with trepidation. Was his family ready for this? Was anyone? Would this help them when and if meeting the People and or the Sassen became unavoidable? He would know soon enough.

He had only a few moments to prepare them, so he quickly called them together. "When I first came home, I told you what was to happen. You have come to believe me, or you would not be here now. I never told you how I knew it was going to happen, and only Newell asked me. There were many of us who were told about this at an assembly called the Brotherhood. It is made up of communities of people, and it was told to us by one known as the Promised One."

He waited for their reaction, but they were

distracted by the parade of people passing by, heading toward the center of the village.

"Where are they all going?" Nora asked.

"There is nothing I can say to prepare you for this. But you are going to understand why I have been so certain of what I told you. Come on."

By the time Chief Kotori and the Elders made it to the village, trailing behind Pakwa, everyone was assembled.

The Chief addressed them. "My people, Tiponi has told you of the difficult times to come and of the emissary who brought us that news. Today is a great day, as today you will meet him for yourselves. The Promised One, the Akassa Guardian, An'Kru."

The Chief turned back to invite An'Kru forward, but there was no one behind him. Ned felt panic rising. Oh no. A lot of his credibility hinged on the next moments.

Just then, a distortion began to manifest between the Chief and those gathered. Within moments, a bright light, followed by the figure of An'Kru, appeared.

Ned's heart started pounding. He was certain everyone there was also deeply affected by the presence of the Promised One.

He turned to look at his family's expressions. Ruby was sleeping safely in her mother's arms. His two older nephews were standing still, slack-jawed.

Only Tommy looked relaxed; he was pointing at An'Kru and smiling from ear to ear.

As An'Kru started to speak, Kele came running out of the gathering and leaped toward him, smiling with glee. An'Kru bent down just in time to catch him. Kele's mother and father had rushed forward to retrieve their son, but the Chief signaled for them to stay where they were. It was clear to everyone that Kele was in no danger and had been inexorably drawn to the stranger—a feeling they were all experiencing but had not acted upon.

"I am An'Kru," he said, smiling at Kele, who was now fingering the long silver-white hair. "You were told of my purpose and of the three signs I would send."

Ned saw Grace edge closer to her mother until their shoulders were touching.

"The three signs were not to frighten you but to assure you that I have come to do as I said and to remind you to prepare, for the day would come when that preparation would be called into service. They were signs to remind you that the time was coming when you would be called on collectively to serve the Great Spirit with the sole purpose of returning the wayward Waschini to their path home.

"People of Etera," An'Kru continued, "look after each other and listen to your spiritual Leaders. Do not lose heart; unprecedented change is coming, and you will need all your faith to stay on the path required of you. For your sakes, for the Waschini, and for all of Etera."

An'Kru gave Kele a hug and then set him on the ground and pointed him in the direction of his parents.

"The Brotherhood will be meeting at the full moon," he continued. "At that time, I will address all the peoples, the Brothers, the Akassa, and the Sassen. Bring all who wish to make the journey, for what I tell you must be remembered by as many as possible so you may shore up each other's faith through the times to come. I must leave you now, just for the time being."

There was a pause, and then a wave of energy swept through the crowd. People placed their hands over their hearts, some over their foreheads. Others reached for a loved one's support. An'Kru turned and walked away. All eyes followed him until he faded from view as if walking into a dense fog. Yet there was no fog.

Some people immediately started talking, while others simply stared at the place where the figure had disappeared. There were some tears of joy, some of relief, and all were filled with wonder. The crowd didn't disperse; they were processing what they had witnessed.

Ned felt someone's hand on his shoulder.

Grace said, "I didn't doubt you when you first told

us what was coming, but this is beyond anything I could have expected."

"I couldn't tell you about him. What would I have said? No one would have believed me."

Nora was with them now. "Your father and I owe you a big apology."

"No, Mother, you don't. If you had told me about someone like An'Kru, I wouldn't have believed you, either." Ned leaned over and kissed her on the cheek.

Matthew interjected. "I understand why you couldn't tell us; as it was, I had a hard enough time accepting what you told us. But, Ned, who was he referring to? The Akassa, the Sassen? Are these other tribes of Locals? And what is *he*?"

Ned swallowed hard. "I will explain it all to you, and sooner rather than later. I just need a few days to figure out how." To the side, he could see Newell eyeing him closely.

The Chief raised his staff to speak, and all fell silent, parents shushing their children.

"All of you have witnessed a great event, one that will be passed down through the generations to come. The Promised One will open a new age, not just for our people but for all of Etera's inhabitants. May we do what we have been called upon to do. May we serve the Great Spirit in this task without faltering, with the undying dedication of our hearts and souls."

It was clear nothing was going to get done by the

villagers except talking about what they had just witnessed. But the day's chores were not what was important now; they needed to sear the events of the morning deep in their hearts to carry them through the long journey ahead.

Ned had tossed and turned for several nights, and he knew his time was up. He now had to reveal to his family the existence of the People and the Sassen. Perhaps An'Kru's appearance would make it easier for him than he feared. The illusion that the Waschini were the only people on Etera had been shattered. The door to new possibilities had been opened; he only had to lead them through it into a new world.

Looking for support and a sounding board, Ned sought out Newell, who had already crossed into the world that contained such miraculous creations as the Akassa and the Sassen. In addition, Newell also had responsibility, as the emotional welfare of his wife and children was at stake.

Both intentionally rose very early, at a time when neither Matthew nor the women and children were up. "I had hoped this day would not come," Newell said, bending over to stir the morning fire.

Ned squatted down and carefully laid another log on the flames, careful not to force a cloud of hot embers from the fire pit. "Did you think it possible that our families could live their entire lives and never know of the Akassa or the Sassen?"

"Think it possible? I don't know if I thought it, but yes, I certainly hoped it might be possible. I just want them to have a normal life, Ned. Can you understand that?" Newell stabbed at the embers so hard that the stick broke.

"I did not know it would upset you so much. I am not one to advise you about that, as I never thought a normal life, as you call it, was that attractive."

"But there was a time, though. There was a time when you wanted to be an animal doctor like Mr. Clement, have your own practice, maybe marry Alice Baxter, and have young ones running about. But somewhere, that all changed. It was Grayson's influence that killed that dream, wasn't it?"

Ned frowned. "Killed is a strong word, don't you think? If a normal life is so intoxicating, why are so many people unhappy in it?"

"I didn't know they were," Newell snapped. "I certainly wasn't."

This was going in the wrong direction. Ned was looking for Newell's support, not his opposition. He needed Newell to help the others make the transition. He stood up.

"I didn't know you felt that way. Maybe I should have. You were so anxious to leave and get back home. I took it as normal homesickness, wanting to be with Grace, not as a rejection of what you had discovered. The People, the Sassen."

"I'm not you, Ned. I don't seek adventure. I don't want my horizons expanded. I wanted a quiet life with the woman I love, raising our children. To watch them grow, find true love, and marry. I wanted to bounce grandchildren on my knee, not live out here among—" He stopped himself.

Ned felt sick to his stomach. He was starting to think that he not only didn't have a supporter, he might well have an enemy.

"Do you blame me for this then?" he asked. "If I had just let go of my crazy idea of living as Grayson did, none of this would have happened, would it?"

"No," Newell said angrily. "It wouldn't have. And my children would be living in the same world I did. Going to school, growing up, just as I said."

Ned ground his teeth. He counted to ten. He intentionally took in and let out a long, slow breath.

"I can't do this without you, Newell. Like it or not, here we are. And this isn't about what you want any longer. It's about accepting what has to be. Nat, Luke, Tommy, and Ruby *can* live full, rich lives here. They will grow up and marry and have children of their own. Maybe not in the same world you grew up in, but it doesn't mean they can't thrive in this one. They can be happy and fulfilled, but not if you make it impossible for them."

"I would never do that!" Newell's voice was getting louder.

"Not on purpose. But they will be watching you, and if your resentment comes through, and it will, they'll pick up on it. Please pull yourself together and lower your voice. You're going to wake the rest of the family, and then how will we explain what we are fighting about!"

Newell stood up and shook his head. With his hands on his hips, he turned his back to Ned and tilted his head back, looking up to the sky.

Then he turned around. "I can't deny what I saw yesterday. *Who we* saw. Whatever he was, he was as real as you and me. I thought I had seen it all after the People and the Sassen, but he was something else altogether. I guess you're right, Ned. You're right about all of it. I am being selfish because it's not about what I want for my children or how I think it has to be. You're happy here, and no doubt they will all find it a grand adventure. After all, what child doesn't want monsters to be real."

Ned clicked his tongue. "Monsters?"

"I'm sorry. You're right, I am angry and resentful, and it is coming out as it did just then. None of them are monsters."

"No, they're not, "Ned answered sternly. "The monsters are those like Commander Riley who kidnapped this entire village, women and children and the elderly, and marched them through the cold, providing them with neither sufficient shelter nor sustenance. Driving them to exhaustion, not caring that they were falling ill and starving. Just doing what they were told. From everything I have seen, the real monsters on Etera are us."

Ned picked up a stray log that had rolled away and tossed it back onto the fire, causing a burst of embers to float into the sky. "I guess we'll talk later; I hear the women getting up." He walked over to his parents' shelter.

Grace came outside with a light-colored hide wrapped around her shoulders. "What's going on out here, Newell? It sounded as if you and my brother were arguing."

"No, not really. A discussion, maybe, that got out of hand. But I was in the wrong. I apologized before when we got into it, and I'll do so again. Please don't worry about it. Where's Ruby?"

"My mother came and took her in the middle of the night. She was fussing, and Mama remembered what it was like not to get enough sleep when they're still this young. I should go and collect her now."

"They should be up; Ned just went to see them."

Grace called good morning into her parents' shelter and was greeted in return. She pulled the flap open and stepped in. It was warm inside; her father had perfected the center fire, and she was glad to be out of the cool morning air.

"Ned and Newell have a good fire going outside," Grace said. "Are you ready for breakfast?"

"Ugh," Nat said, then quickly added, "Hello, Mama. I'm sorry, but we're not having fish again, are we?"

Grace laughed. "No, at least not for breakfast. Tiponi and some other women are teaching me to make cornmeal bread. We don't have any yeast, so it won't rise, but it's not fish, right?"

"I like fish!" Little Luke poked his head out from under his blankets and belly-crawled far enough to sit up. He had enjoyed sleeping like that since he was born, making a little cave out of his covers and leaving just a small breathing hole. He said it was cozy and made him feel safe.

Tommy popped his head out from the same blankets. "I do too!" He must have crawled in with his older brother sometime during the night.

"Can we sleep with Gramma and Grampa again tonight? It was fun!" Luke asked.

"That's up to them. Now get dressed." Grace turned to leave.

"Wait, Mama," said Nat. "The furry man we saw yesterday. Who is he?"

Grace didn't know what to say, but Ned stepped in.

"He is called the Promised One. He is not like us, is he?"

"No. He is really big and hairy, but nice, though. He was kind; I could tell immediately. And he seemed to like us all. A lot. And he doesn't even know us!"

Ned sat down cross-legged next to his nephews. "Does it bother you to know there are other kinds of people in the world?" he asked.

"Not me. I thought he was fascinating!" Nat answered again.

"Fascinating?" Grace asked and smiled at her mother. "Where did you learn that phrase?"

"It is something the other children here say. Fascinating. I think they really like that word."

Ned said, "What if I told you there were even more kinds of people than us, the Brothers, and the Promised One? Would you like that?"

"Ned, where is this going?" asked Grace, concerned. "You're really not making any sense."

Ned addressed his sister and parents, "Remember how I explained I was afraid to tell you about An'Kru, the Promised One because you would have thought I was crazy. Well, there are even more I haven't told you about that will sound even crazier than if I had told you about him."

"Son," Matthew spoke up. "I am not sure we can take anymore. We're about at the end of our flexibility. We haven't even mastered living here, and now we have met this— I don't even know what to call him. Being? Man? Who looks like something out of a children's fairytale. Please don't tell me there is more we have to adjust to?"

"I wish I could," Ned answered. "But I can't. And time is running out. You heard An'Kru speak of the Brotherhood. It is a community made up of leaders of their own kind—-of their communities— that comes together periodically to help each other."

"Of their own kind?" Nora repeated. "What does that mean?"

"The Brotherhood is not just composed of Brothers from different villages coming together. It is made up of other— Other types of people, too."

"No, no, I've heard enough," Matthew said. "Now, stop it, son. I can't take anymore, really."

Just then, the curtain pulled back, and in stepped Newell.

"No, Matthew. You have to hear him out. Like it or not. Ready or not, you have to hear what he has to say."

"And what do you know of it, Newell?" Matthew asked.

"More than you realize. More than I have revealed. And as much as I hate for you to have to learn this so soon, it can't be helped."

"Learn what?" Nora said. "Boys, maybe you should leave," and she looked meaningfully at Grace.

"No," Newell disagreed. "They are probably the best able of any of us to handle what we are about to tell you. They need to hear it. Heck, everyone here knows about it; you six are the only ones who don't."

Nat was counting on his fingers. "You forgot Ruby!"

"I didn't forget her, son; I just didn't count her, as she's still a baby. When she grows up, this will all be as normal to her as growing up in Wilde Edge was for you."

"So what is it we need to hear; what is it that everyone knows about?" Matthew asked. "And what do you mean by *we are the only ones here who don't know about it*?"

"It's actually not an *it*. It's a who. A who you don't know about," Newell said. "And, yes, everyone else here knows about them, and soon you will, too. You will meet them at the Brotherhood gathering."

"We have to go to that? Another long journey? More changes to face?" Nora sounded frustrated.

"Oh, I didn't want you to go through this yet," said Ned. "I wanted you to have time to adjust, to get used to being one of the Brothers, settle in, find your bearings. I'm sorry."

"Just tell us," Grace pleaded. "The suspense is only making it harder."

So Ned began. "When I learned of them, I was even more shocked than you're going to be, as I had no one preparing me. I learned about them by chance and by necessity. My first experience was when Newell and I were traveling with Grayson to rescue Chief Kotori's people from the outpost riders. We had made camp for the night. It was bitterly cold, and I woke up to get another blanket and noticed Grayson was missing.

"When time passed and he hadn't returned I started to worry, but then I heard his voice. At first, I thought he was praying, only it wasn't English, and it wasn't exactly the Brothers' language, either. Then I heard someone reply. Grayson was out there talking to someone in the dark, only the voice that responded was deeper and more guttural than any of ours could ever be. I was terrified. I listened a while longer, then quietly crept back to the fire. I never mentioned it. But it shook me to the core."

"You're scaring the boys," Grace admonished.

"No, he's not! Tell us, pleeease!" Luke was bouncing up and down.

"The next morning, we found the soldiers," Ned continued. "Chief Kotori's people were in terrible shape. The elderly were sick, and we feared many of them were dying. It was despicable, the condition they were in, with mothers and children going hungry, the men not allowed to sufficiently provide for them. I was ashamed to be a White person—one of those who had abducted them and treated them so poorly."

Ned paused.

"Keep going," Newell said.

"The soldier released them to us, and we started

back, but a terrible storm kicked in. Visibility was only a few steps, and it was impossible to erect shelters for everyone. There was also no food and no way of getting any. Without a miracle, many were going to die. But then help appeared."

Ned paused, and Newell took the cue and stepped in. "It was a whiteout, and then there was all this snapping and crashing in the woods, and Grayson came and took our rifles. At first, we didn't understand why. Grayson started telling us that time had run out, and he had to let us in on the secret of his past. He said he had no choice and told us not to panic. Then came this whooping sound, and then Kele, the same boy who ran and jumped into An'Kru's arms yesterday, ran right into the brush. The Brothers were chanting, Oh'Mah, Oh'Mah."

"Don't you mean Oh'Dar? Grayson's name?" Grace corrected her husband.

"No. It was Oh'Mah. It means Master of the Forest."

The boys' eyes were like saucers, and they were all leaning forward with rapt attention.

"Then what?" Nat asked excitedly.

"Then this person stepped out into view."

Ned breathed a sigh of relief that Newell had said *person* and not anything like monster or creature.

Luke couldn't keep still. "Like the man yesterday? Tall and hairy like him?"

"He was tall like him, yes," Newell continued.

"Only much, much hairier. He had hair from his head to his toe, and his eyes weren't grey; they were dark brown. His name was Nimraugh, and he was carrying little Kele on his shoulder, oh so protectively."

Ned took up the story. "And there was not just one of him; there were many like him. They had come to help Chief Kotori, and they built strong, tight shelters for all of us. And those people were so big that with a single one of them inside each shelter, their body heat warmed the entire area. They also hunted and collected food for us. If it hadn't been for them, so many of the people living here would have died."

"How big were they?" Nat asked.

"Big!" Ned exclaimed. "Tall like An'Kru yesterday, but with wider shoulders and big hearty chests. And they were so, so strong. Nothing can harm you when they are around; they won't let it. They are friends of us all, and you have nothing to fear from them."

Ned glanced from the enthralled gazes of his nephews to the more cautious expressions of his sister and parents.

"I think that's enough for now," Matthew said. "Come on, boys, let's gather some firewood for the rest of the day's fire." He stood and shooed the boys out. Then he threw a stern look back at Ned and exited the shelter.

Suddenly, Ned felt deflated and looked helplessly

at Newell. "He thinks I'm making this up, like some bedtime story or who knows what. But I'm not."

"I assure you both, Nora and Grace, Ned is not making this up. I was there; it was just as he said. It's all true, and you will see for yourselves soon enough. I'll talk to Matthew."

"About now," Newell said, "you're thinking he is crazy after all, aren't you?"

Matthew called out to Nat and Luke. "Go on, boys, watch your little brother."

Once the boys were out of earshot, he said, "You want to know the truth? Yes—except you're backing him up, and you can't both be crazy."

"I assure you, neither of us is crazy. It's all true, every bit of it. Just as true as that unbelievable figure we both saw materialize out of thin air yesterday and then walk off into nothingness."

Matthew pinched the bridge of his nose and squinted at Newell. "I feel like I should be waking up about now."

"I understand completely," Newell agreed. "And Ned wanted to give you more time before it got to this point. Me, I hoped it would never come to this; I would have been perfectly happy to let my children grow up as things are now. This, living among the Brothers, seemed adjustment enough."

"But the boys seem excited about it."

"Yes, their imaginations are still pure. They haven't been scared by the real world, by knowledge of the horrible things men do to each other, so their imaginings aren't filled with terrifying monsters or criminals with devious intentions and nightmarish outcomes. I'm grateful they are still innocent, and I wish we could all be that way. The world would be a better place without the horrors we bring into it."

"Horrors like you saw with the Chief's people. How they were treated," Matthew said.

Newell was nodding. "Yes. It changed me. I always knew there was evil in the world. Look at what Commander Riley did to the members of this village, as well as Snide Tucker and what he did. Grayson's uncle, Louis, who had Grayson's parents killed and who intended for him—an infant—also to be murdered, and then tried again to kill Grayson at Shadow Ridge.

"But those are exceptions, few and far between. They are twisted people, men who posed as being honorable and of good caliber. People I would never have thought capable of the cruelty they inflicted."

"But the soldiers didn't intentionally mean to harm the Brothers; they were just following orders," Matthew said.

"Just following orders. And how does that make what they did any less monstrous?"

CHAPTER 17

As before, Iella's messengers were on their way to all the communities of the Brothers and the People, calling them to the Brotherhood meeting at the next full moon. Not knowing how many to expect, High Protector Awan was working feverishly with Mapiya and other volunteers to free up as many living quarters as possible. The weather was warming, so no doubt the Brothers would lodge outside. Haan's people had built temporary shelters for them, in a pleasant location away from the wind and near a quiet stream.

At Lulnomia, Thord had been feeling shifts in the energy that coursed through him. What it meant, he was not sure, but something was afoot. He approached Wrollonan'Tor and Pan.

"I also feel it," Wrollonan'Tor said.

Pan agreed, "So do I."

"It is as if the magnetic center of Etera is moving. Well, not moving exactly," Thord clarified, "but twittering. Oh, what is the word? Some type of shift is happening on a low scale, but occasionally, it increases. As if something is waxing and waning or building up to something. You have lived for eons; have you heard of anything like this happening before?" he asked Wrollonan'Tor.

The ancient Guardian nodded slowly. "There is a tale of it, so very long ago, yes. And if that same effect is building again within Etera, then there is little we can do to protect ourselves because cataclysmic events are about to come to pass. But out of that long-ago destruction also came wonders. It was that same event that created the first Guardian, the first protector of all of Etera."

"If whatever happened before is preparing to happen again, what can we do to get ready—or somehow to help?"

"You and the other male Sassen Guardians must go to Kthama, to the High Rocks, for it is beneath Kthama that the strongest vortex exists. Within that vortex lies the power to destroy Etera or to save her."

"What of you, Pan?" Thord turned to her. "Will you be going with us?"

"No, I will not be going with you; I gave my word

to Adia," Pan answered. "But you no longer need me as you think you do."

"If we are to leave Lulnomia, does this mean our training is complete?"

"There will always be more to learn, but, yes, it is enough for what lies before you at present. Now, go and prepare the others. If you are being called to your destiny, remember the Great Spirit is with you all, always."

So it was that Thord called the other five male Sassen Guardians to him. Clah, Norir, Zok, Jokant, and Tarron.

"When will we return to Kthama? How will we know it is time to go? Will Wrollonan'Tor tell us?" Clah asked.

"Listen, please. Under the instruction of the Guardians Wrollonan'Tor and Pan, we have grown in our abilities and knowledge, and we have been blessed by all of it. However, now it is time we learn to hear our own guidance; we must trust we will know when it is time to go and when it will be time to return here to continue our training."

And Thord was right.

Time was running out, and Ned had to decide whether to introduce his family to the Sassen beforehand or wait until they arrived at Kthama for the

Brotherhood meeting. However, if he waited until then, there would be the added shock of the underground community of Akassa. They had seen An'Kru, and at least the existence of others not quite like the Waschini or the Brothers had been partially breached.

If he introduced the Sassen to his family ahead of time and they could not accept them, then all hope of getting them to go to the Brotherhood meeting was probably lost. And he needed them to hear for themselves An'Kru's message of what was to come.

Knowing his mind was clouded because it was his family involved, he sought the wisdom of others.

"Your fears are not unfounded," Chief Kotori said. "My people have known of Oh'Mah for generations. Though we have not had contact with them for many centuries, their existence was never questioned. But let me ask you this; who among your family are you most concerned about?"

Ned looked at Awantia sitting next to him. Her presence grounded him, comforted him, and calmed him. "My mother and sister are the most open-minded. My nephews see this as one big adventure. They were not frightened by what their father told them about the Sassen a few nights ago. Newell already knows of them. So the answer is my father. My father will be the one who will take more convincing that they mean no harm."

"As he should be," the Chief answered. "It is his

duty to protect his family. He cannot afford to displace his own judgment with another's when the safety of his loved ones is at stake. Whether they are friend or foe, he must decide this for himself. To expect him to do less is to expect him to be less than the Great Spirit created him to be."

The late morning sunlight filtered through the trees. The smell of the earth, warmed by the rising spring temperatures, rose up from under Ned's feet as they disturbed the soft soil. He found a deer path and took it. When he had said he was going into the forest for a while, Kele, always close by whenever possible, asked to go too. Ned didn't have to turn back to see if Kele was still with him; he could hear him chattering, greeting the flowers and birds along the way.

The deer path wound down a little ravine, and patches of sunlight lit the spring green of the new leaves just recently bursting forth. A brown rabbit bounced across not far in front of him, flushed out either by Ned's presence or Kele's happy conversation behind him.

After Ned, Newell, and Oh'Dar had rescued Chief Kotori's people from the military, the Sassen promised to station watchers around the Chief's village and territory. Even with Oh'Dar's help, Ned had never quite perfected the Sassen call, but it was close enough. Besides, he knew the watchers were aware of his approach, though, in contrast, he would never be aware of their presence unless they wanted him to be.

Now far enough away that he would not be overheard, Ned let out his best call. Now he just had to wait. A moment later, a knock came back, the kind made from a piece of wood hitting against a tree trunk. Soon, the bushes off to the side started moving, and a large Sassen stood not far from him. He had never gotten over the impact of their size. He no longer feared them, as he had at first, but though the fear had left, the sense of awe had not and probably never would.

"Thank you for answering my call," Ned said in the Brothers' language. He squinted to see who it was because the Sassen before him was backlit by the sun's rays.

"Greetings, Ned Webb." Ned recognized the voice. It was Nimraugh himself, the leader of the Sassen group that had come to help them save Chief Kotori's people. Ned did not know he had stayed in the area, and felt as if he were meeting an old friend.

"Nimraugh, I am pleased to see you again. I have a favor to ask. No doubt you know the Promised One has returned to warn us that the events he spoke of are about to come to pass?"

"Yes. We all know."

"My Waschini family is here, at the Chief's village. They returned with me, and they are learning to live as we do. They are adjusting, but now I must introduce them to something even more unimaginable and unexpected to them than life among the Brothers. I must take them with me to the Brotherhood meeting because they must hear An'Kru speak for themselves."

"Yes, and my people will frighten them."

"You understand it is not a judgment; it is based on ignorance."

"I understand. They have much to face, and all at once. They know nothing of the Akassa, or the High Rocks, or the Far High Hills. They know nothing of our people. To face that all at once would be too much to ask of nearly anyone, Ned Webb. How can I help you?"

Ned was touched once more by the kindness and understanding of the Sassen. Nimraugh was willing to help Waschini, many of whom, given the chance, would murder any of his kind on the spot without question.

Ned didn't want to return to the village with Nimraugh without preparing his family, so he asked that they meet at the edge of the village near darkfall. Then he prayed for the words to reach his family and assure them of the benevolence of these huge hulking giants whose existence he was about to reveal to them.

The day dragged on, and Ned's anxiety rose. Though he had prayed, he found himself letting his mind take off with images of failure. He thought back to when he and Newell were first introduced to the Sassen. How Oh'Dar had taken their weapons away, knowing their reaction would be of fear, perhaps even terror, and that in this state of mind, they might well have killed Nimraugh and any of the others. But his family was not in the exhausted and agitated state of mind that he and Newell had been in by the time the Sassen appeared. In addition, his family had accepted An'Kru, so perhaps he was misjudging their acceptance of the Sassen.

Ned had told his brother-in-law he was preparing to introduce Nimraugh to them, and Newell would back him despite wishing it could have come later rather than sooner.

"They have barely adjusted to this life here, but we cannot change what is. It's different for you, Ned. You wanted to live this life," Newell said. "You chose this. I'd had enough of it by the time the Chief's people were safely returned to their village. I couldn't wait to get home to Grace, to normalcy, and it's not my choice to be here now. However, I would have been a fool not to have brought my family back here with you. Better to offer them some life—even if it isn't the one I wanted—than to risk any of them perishing in the hard times that you say are to come."

"Not what *I* say are to come," Ned corrected. "It is

what An'Kru has said. And I have no doubt he will talk about it again at the Brotherhood meeting. When you hear him speak of it, it will become as real and as life-changing an experience to you as it is to me and everyone else who heard him speak of it before."

"Well, until then, we have other obstacles to overcome."

"And the first is about to take place in a few hours."

"Hmmph." Newell shook his head. "What does that mean nowadays, hours, minutes? There are no longer increments to the day. Now I understand why Miss Vivian and Ben cherished that mantle clock Grayson brought back for them. How comforting it must have been, like an old friend marking the moments for them."

"And I see it just the opposite, Newell. Each second ticking by, marking the moments one after another? Soldiering time into definable pieces, each flaring into a brief existence, then extinguished forever. The stream of our existence chopped into definable pieces. No flow, no experience of the moment. Just one slice of time after another sectioned off and discarded for the next. And the next. And the next. Not once allowing for the experience of the never-ending now. I do not miss the rigidity of that life, lived according to concepts and schedules, instead of letting life and each day unfold as they would."

"This life has made a poet of you, I think," Newell joked. "Where is the small-town boy who wanted to be an animal doctor? Who toyed with the affections of Alicia Baxter?"

Now it was Ned's turn to laugh. "I never toyed with Alicia Baxter's affections, of that I am sure. As for what happened to that small-town boy you speak of, I count him one of the very fortunate few. One who found the courage and conviction to follow his heart, his calling. One who, at the end of his life, no matter what becomes of him, can look back with peace in his soul because, to the end, he was true to himself and his beliefs."

Newell shrugged, "No man can ask more than that for his life, Ned. That is to be sure."

Evening meal was over, and the sun's rays were nearing the horizon. Ned and Awantia gathered Ned's family together.

"This has been a good day for everyone, I hope?" Ned began.

Nat was the first to answer. "We are learning how to make bows and arrows. Sakinay is teaching us."

Ned stole a glance at Awantia, remembering the difficult time Sakinay had given him in his bow-making lesson, which was about far more than making the bow.

"And how is it going?" he couldn't help but ask.

"I am having trouble learning how to set the feathers properly in the arrow, but Sakinay is very patient," was Nat's answer, to Ned's relief. He should have known Sakinay would never treat a child as he had been treated, and he also knew Sakinay had only been trying to help him stand up for himself, to come into his own as a man among the Brothers.

Over to the side, Ned could see Kele pacing. It seemed Nimraugh was not far away, and Kele's patience in waiting for the spectacular reveal was wearing thin.

"Remember the other night, after we met An'Kru, Newell was telling you about someone who spoke with Oh'Dar when Newell and I were helping Chief Kotori's people get back home?"

"He said he was really big and hairy with dark brown eyes," Nat volunteered.

"Yes. His name was Nimraugh, and he is one of the other kinds of people who live here among the Brothers, called the Sassen. When you meet him, remember how your father and I told you the Sassen are gentle and kind."

"Are we going to meet him? Oh, when, when?" Luke was nearly bouncing out of his seat.

Ned looked at his sister and his mother. Newell had promised to speak to them and let them know it would happen tonight. He couldn't tell what they were feeling, but regardless, his first concern was still for his father. At the moment, he regretted not talking to his father first. It now seemed a huge omission, but it was too late. Kele would not be able to contain his excitement much longer, and it was just a matter of moments before he gave away Nimraugh's presence.

"Very soon. He's the same one your father talked about. Nimraugh. He is here to meet you." Ned glanced over to where Kele was standing. Following his motion, the others looked in the same direction.

"That's just Kele," Luke scowled.

"I know," Ned laughed. "But Nimraugh is with him, trust me. Nimraugh and his people are seldom ever seen unless they want to be. Remember, he is our friend."

Kele was no longer pacing; he was hopping up and down and pointing.

"Wait here," Ned said. He rose and walked over to Kele. Then he turned back to face his family and beckoned for Nimraugh to come out from the tree line.

No words could describe the look on the faces of Ned's family when Nimraugh stepped into sight. Even though Ned and Newell had warned them all about the Sassen's appearance, their instinctive reactions kicked in.

Newell had assured the women there was

nothing to fear, but Grace immediately pushed her children behind her and, in turn, stood behind her husband. Nora joined her, adding to the barrier between the giant figure and the children.

Matthew had another reaction. Despite his debilitating condition, he raced out, closing the distance between his family and Ned.

"Get away from him! Get away!" Matthew gestured wildly, trying to get Ned and Kele to move.

"Papa, it's alright." Ned stepped forward to meet his father and grabbed him by both arms. "It's alright, I promise. He isn't going to hurt anyone."

"What— What—"

"He is Nimraugh, the one I have been talking about." Ned's voice was raised, drawing others from the village to come closer. "Yes, I know he is frightening. He is huge and hairy and looks dangerous, but he is not. Father, stop reacting and look with your heart and soul, not your fears. If he wanted to hurt us, he would have already."

Seeing the Sassen standing next to Kele, many of the Brothers broke out in smiles and words of welcome. "Oh'Mah! Oh'Mah has made himself known to us!"

Awantia now stepped forward to where Ned was still holding Matthew at bay.

"He will not harm you. He will not harm any of us," she said in a soothing voice. "Ned's father, as Ned has told you, Nimraugh is our friend and our protector. He and his people are a blessing to us and to all of Etera."

As if on cue, Kele crawled up into Nimraugh's arms and was quickly perched on the behemoth's shoulders as he had been so many times.

"Me!" young Tommy called out, dashing forward.

"No!" Matthew broke away from Ned and ran back to scoop up his grandson. He clutched the boy to him.

Chief Kotori stepped out of the crowd that had gathered. "Oh'Mah has blessed us with his presence. He is a reminder of the watchful love and care of the Great Spirit."

The Chief walked over to where Matthew was still protectively holding Tommy.

"These people are our friends. Though you react as any man who would give his life to protect his family, it is not necessary. Of all the people of Etera, of all the creatures we share her with, Oh'Mah is the one who should concern you the least. Put your grandson down. Rejoice with us at the blessing that one of the Sassen has made himself visible to us."

Newell went to Matthew and gently removed his hands from Tommy. "It is alright, Matthew. I promise. I know the Sassen, remember? I have met them before, and this fellow in particular. I understand your reaction, believe me, I had the same, but try to calm down and see the truth of the situation, not just your fears."

Matthew's grasp on his grandson relaxed, and Newell was able to take Tommy from him.

"Go to your mother," Newell said.

"But, but," Tommy objected, pointing at Nimraugh.

"Now, I said."

And Tommy scuttled back to his mother's side, his head hanging with disappointment.

Ned could see the tension in his father's frame. "Papa, I am sorry. I should have prepared you properly."

"You tried, son. You tried. Another conversation wouldn't have mattered, trust me." Matthew's tone was conciliatory, to Ned's great relief. "So why are we meeting him, this Nimraugh person?"

As if the challenges of the moment had not been enough, now Ned had to explain that he intended to deliver his family into the midst of an entire community of these creatures. And the Akassa would also be present.

"The Sassen are part of the Brotherhood I spoke of. The Brothers, the Sassen, and the Akassa. An'Kru is one of the Akassa, though he is not typical. He is something more. But when you meet them, you will see they look very much like An'Kru. Far more like us and the Brothers than the Sassen here do."

"Where do they come from?"

Ned was relieved to see his father's thinking was

returning, which meant the bottomless well of fear that had taken him over was subsiding.

"If you are asking where they live, they live here in the forest as the Brothers do. If you're asking how they came to exist, I am not sure. That is a question for someone else. Perhaps Grayson."

"So what happens now?" Matthew asked.

"Before long, we will all travel with Chief Kotori and many of his people to where the Akassa live. There you will meet their Leader, his wife, and many other Akassa. Other tribes of the Brothers will also be there, and, of course, more of Nimraugh's people, the Sassen. We are being called together so An'Kru can address us again and prepare us for what is about to happen."

"I am afraid to ask what that is," Matthew's voice was low.

"The end of the world as we have known it, and, I believe, the beginning of a world that could be everything we had ever hoped it would be."

CHAPTER 18

They came in over several days from every Akassa community and all the neighboring communities of the Brothers. The weather was warm, and the work of the Sassen to prepare outdoor shelters had been well worth it. Many came bringing food, knowing the People's stores could not sustain as many as would be there. The air was tinged with excitement and something else. Something that felt like anticipation but was laced with a thread of trepidation. The word had been carried to every person, whether Sassen, Akassa, or Brother. Huge changes were coming, changes that would require a great commitment from every living soul to help reach the Waschini and turn them from their destructive ways.

The journey from Chief Kotori's village was a long one, though made easier in part by the Webbs' wagons. Children were carried or walked with their parents but also took turns riding on the back of the wagons. Everyone who had felt called to go with Chief Kotori was allowed to go, and the other Chiefs had taken the same approach. So they traveled from all directions to a single destination, the High Rocks —Kthama.

Grace had mixed feelings about returning to Kthama. This time, she would be able to experience all that had been blocked from her awareness when she and Ned came to find Miss Vivian and Ben. But Miss Vivian and Ben were not going to be there, so her anticipation was mixed with sadness. There was more. She was not going back as herself or even Ned's sister; she had children to be concerned about. Despite the excitement over what was happening, she worried it might be overwhelming. Ned had answered every question her boys came up with, questions she'd also had, and, no doubt, the same as her parents had. About how many Akassa there were. And how many Sassen. Were they separated within their own cave systems, or did they live together? Did they marry? What did they eat? Did they wear clothing? Ned had tirelessly answered every question, but when the time came, only the experience itself would answer those questions they did not know to ask.

They had been told the Sassen would accompany them on the journey, that they were always around, though unseen. And the more Grace and the rest were able to accept that the Sassen were peaceful, the more comforting the thought of their presence became. Grace started to understand the reverence in which the Brothers held the Sassen and the gratitude they felt.

Though, previously, she had not seen the approach to the High Rocks, she knew they were getting closer by the increased talk among her fellow travelers. She warned herself not to get so caught up in her own reactions that she forgot about what her children might be experiencing. That last night, the exercise from traveling meant her three sons slept deeply; otherwise, they would no doubt have stayed up all night still speculating about what might happen.

As far as she could tell, her father had recovered from the introduction to Nimraugh, and though she did not know it for a fact, she suspected Newell had been helping her father in secret. Newell was the bridge between the two worlds, the one of their past and the one that they had to learn to live in now. He had experienced the Akassa and Sassen worlds, and his level-headed approach reached her father, where Ned's emotional pleas could not. Grace figured that, though not the same age, Newell's business success also resonated with her father. He was the closest thing to a peer that her father had.

Ned was traveling ahead but turned back just in front of them. "We are nearing the main path up to Kthama. We will have to leave the wagons someplace close by and travel the rest of the way on foot. It is a long way, so please be careful. If you are tired, we should wait here until everyone is up to it. There are no railings, and in some places, there is a long drop-off to one side. You must concentrate on the steps directly in front of you." Ned's words filled Grace with alarm.

Just then, one of the Sassen appeared as if out of nowhere. She said something, looking directly at Grace as if talking to her.

Ned spoke up, "This is Ensata. Newell and I know her. She was with the group that helped us rescue Chief Kotori's people, and she warmed our shelter during the snowstorm. I told you about her."

He grasped Grace's arm and turned her to face him. "She's just explained that she and others are here to help people up the path. She can carry your sons. All three of them. She is offering to get your children safely to Kthama, and she is more than able, Grace. I promise."

Grace could almost feel Ned's gaze on her, waiting for her to say something. But she was filled with conflict. Did she dare trust her precious children to this—person?

It was then that Grace realized just how much of a toll this had taken on her, after all. She had done her best to be strong for her mother and her children, but now, after too long without enough rest and emotionally at the end of her resources, she feared she was going to break down. And she did not want her children to see her like that.

She managed to speak, "Thank you. Yes. Thank you." She turned to Nat, Luke, and Tommy behind her, her husband bringing up the rear. "Go with— This is Ensata. Go with her. She will carry you safely the rest of the way." Grace watched as Nat took his youngest brother, Tommy, by the hand, and the three of them walked ahead of her.

She heard the female Sassen say something, and then Ned said, "Nat, she's going to pick you up first, then she's going to put you, Tommy, on Nat's lap. Then she'll pick up Luke, alright?" Within a few moments, her three sons were cradled in the female Sassen's arms. They looked so small, but it was reassuring to Grace as it was clear that the Sassen was well able to do as she had offered. With Ruby safe in Newell's embrace, Grace almost relaxed.

"It's alright now. See?" Nora said. "They are all safe. Come on, we can do it. And think how good it will feel to sleep tonight."

Grace didn't know what that would be like, but she didn't care. The way she felt right now, she could sleep on solid rock.

Up everyone went, doing as Ned said and concentrating on each step they took. Not made for a human stride, the stepping stones that did exist were further apart than was comfortable.

This was no time to sightsee; the goal was to reach the top safely.

"We're almost there," Grace heard her brother say. She could feel her husband right behind her, occasionally putting a hand on her hip as if to steady her. It was all she could do to keep her eyes on the climb, but she could hear her sons laughing, so she knew they were alright.

"Don't look up," Grace heard Ned say, "but the entrance is only a short way to go, and it will level out here in just a few steps."

Grace felt the incline ease, and then finally, they were there.

"We made it," Ned said.

Grace looked up to see the gaping entrance of the community of the High Rocks, Kthama. Though it was partially hidden by vines that had grown down, it was mammoth. Then she turned to find her sons and daughter.

"We're right here, Mama," Nat called out. "We're fine!"

As Nora took Ruby from Newell's arms, Grace started to sway. Her husband's firm hands caught her.

"Steady now, steady." Newell brought her up

solidly against him. "It's alright, we made it. We'll get something to eat and then ask to be taken to wherever we are to sleep."

Grace put her hand to her face, trying discreetly to wipe away the tears of exhaustion she could no longer hold back. "But it's still early. Still daylight."

Her husband's laughter warmed her heart, "What are you, one of our children? Whining because it is too light out to go to bed? You're exhausted, and rest is what you need. It's what we all need—your mother, your father, our children. All of us."

She nodded against his chest, taking comfort from his hard strength, and only pulled away when she heard a familiar voice.

"Grace! Ned!" It was Grayson.

Within a few moments, they were all greeting him, their reunion made sweeter at seeing someone they recognized. Then Ruby was placed back in her arms.

"I am Acise; do you remember me?" It was Grayson's wife.

"Yes, yes, I do. Of course. I am just so tired, but thank you so much."

"We are staying here at the High Rocks for the assembly. We have had permanent quarters here for some time," Acise explained.

As the Brothers filed past Grace and her family, she collected herself enough to look around. And up.

Her gaze began at the wide expanse of the rock

floor over to where it met one of the walls, then followed the wall up to an impossible height. Moisture dripped from huge stalactites hanging overhead. She involuntarily cringed as an image of one of them coming crashing down upon them flashed through her mind. Voices returned her attention to the others in the entrance with her, and then she saw them. The people they called the Akassa.

Grayson must have been watching her and saw her startle at the sight of those who had just entered and quickly interjected, "This is the home of the Akassa. These are the people who raised me. They are my family. My father is the Leader, Acaraho, and my mother is the Healer, Adia. You are all welcome here."

Acise spoke up, "There is time for you to meet them and the others and take in the rest of the wonders of this place, but for now, what you need is nourishment and rest. Oh'Dar?"

"My wife is right. I will find out where you are to stay and take you there myself. Do not worry about what you brought with you in the wagons or about the horses. I will make sure your things are brought to your quarters and the wagon and horses taken to Chief Is'Taqa's village to be cared for there."

Grace watched Grayson walk over to a group of people and return after some words were exchanged.

He motioned for them to follow, and they walked after him across the wide expanse of Kthama's entrance and into a large tunnel. It was dark, but there was enough light to see where they were going. Memories flooded Grace's mind—the feel of the floor under her feet, the smell of the rock walls, the humidity on her skin. Her excitement at the thought of seeing Ben and Miss Vivian, twinges of fear at being so helpless under the control of people she could not see or understand.

Oh'Dar stopped and gestured toward a doorway. A wooden door made up of branches tied together somehow had been propped open. Grace waited for her father to go in first and followed him.

She watched him look around, taking in the large size of the room. Sunlight streamed in from some opening overhead. There were bowls, woven baskets, and what were probably water containers hanging overhead. She realized they had been hung low enough to be easily reached. They were of manageable sizes, which meant they had been specially prepared for their coming. She moved her head and neck to release the tension and began to relax. Her brother was right; they were welcome here.

"There are two other rooms all the same, right next to each other. Use them as you wish. If you need more room, please let me know, and we'll see what we can do."

"This is more than adequate," her father answered. "We are grateful."

Luke was pulling on Nora's sleeve, "Can we stay

with you and Papa? Like we did in the wagons?" He turned to Grace, "Please, Mama?"

"If your grandparents agree, yes, but remember they are older than you are, and they need more rest than you do. You must promise to be quiet when they are sleeping and not rush them to wake up."

"We'll be fine," Nora said. "This way, you and Newell and Ruby can have some peace and quiet. Well, some, at least."

Remembering the numbers streaming toward Kthama, they decided they could get by with two rooms, leaving the third one free for someone else.

A large female appeared at the door. Grace could tell she was older by the lines on her face.

"I am Mapiya," the female said.

Grace smiled at hearing the Akassa speak English and relaxed some more.

"I will bring you a variety of things to eat shortly." She pointed overhead. "There is water in these baskets. There is a small cove at the back," she pointed, "for your personal care. While you are here, if you decide you prefer to eat in your rooms instead of with everyone else in the common eating area, we will all understand. You can tell me later what you decide."

"I suggest you rest now," Oh'Dar said. "This is enough for one day, and tomorrow will bring more excitement and more adjustments."

Grace didn't ask what he meant as she doubted

she would understand, anyway. Things here had to be experienced for themselves. All the effort Ned had made had still not truly prepared them for what the reality was of being here. She had known something was being kept from her and Ned when they were first brought there so many years ago now, but she had not guessed at this. Never this. Giant people and huge hair-covered creatures who spoke and had families and laws and a culture? It was real.

Acaraho and the others had been right. The High Rocks could not hold all those who came. Many of the People were busy welcoming the arrivals and answering questions, escorting some to where they would be staying, and directing others. A celebratory feeling set in as new friendships flickered into possibility, and old acquaintances were renewed. Thoughts of what was ahead were pushed away as quickly as they surfaced. Whatever was coming would be given its due, but for now, there were happy moments to be relished and memories to be made.

For the time being, Oh'Dar and his family had moved into their quarters within Kthama. Though Oh'Dar had been present at his grandparents' deaths and had seen their ease at passing from this realm to the next, he could not bring himself to walk by the door of their quarters, which remained sealed off at his request. In sharp contrast was the peace his three children felt over Ben and Miss Vivian's passing. He and Acise had spoken of it many times, attributing it to their visit to the Corridor with An'Kru. For their sakes, he was glad. But An'Kru's reassurance that I'Layah, Tsonakwa, and Ashova were well able to do what would in the future be required of them had not quelled his or Acise's anxiety about what that might be.

With Ned and his family settled, Oh'Dar went to get help offloading the wagons. He knew Noshoba would care for the horses, so once the supplies were being carried into Kthama, Oh'Dar and Acise each drove one of the wagons back to the village.

Chief Is'Taqa and his family would be attending the Brotherhood meeting. The majority of his people had met An'Kru when he came to ask Chief Is'Taqa to go to the rebel camp, Zuenerth. They had heard his speech then, and many also wanted to attend.

Once the wagons were stowed away and the horses taken care of, Chief Is'Taqa and his people traveled with Oh'Dar and Acise back to the High Rocks.

Finally, the watchers reported no newcomers on their way; now they had only to wait for An'Kru's appearance, and then they would call everyone to the prepared site outside to hear his address.

The adult Webbs were content to spend as much of their time in their quarters as they could.

"Mama, don't you want to see all the different people who are here?" Nat coaxed. "There are so many of the Brothers and the Sassen. Most of them seem to be sleeping outside."

"Oh'Dar said his sons would take you and Luke around," Newell said. "But you must stay close to them. No wandering off."

"Newell," Grace interrupted, concerned.

"Grace, either they'll be fine or they won't; we can't protect them forever. Look at where we are, in an underground cave system with whole communities of people unlike any we've seen before, all of which are strong enough to kill any of us without a second thought, should they wish to. Grayson's children have been raised here, and if there was any threat to ours, he would not have offered to let Tsonakwa and Ashova take charge of them."

Grace shook her head, "I don't want to argue in front of the boys." Then she said to Nat and Luke, "Do as your father said. Only don't do anything dangerous. And don't wander off too far. And do whatever Tsonakwa tells you to."

"He's hardly older than me," Nat objected.

"He has lived here much of his life," Grace said a little harshly. "You listen to him, or you don't go. It's that simple."

"Fine," Nat answered.

Grace had said Tommy was not old enough to go, and his face was now reflecting his disappointment.

The tension was broken by the appearance of Tson-akwa and Ashova in the doorway.

"Are you ready to go?" Tsonakwa asked, looking first at Nat and then at Luke.

The four children filed out and down the passageway.

Matthew passed them as he was coming in. "Where are they off to?"

"A tour of Kthama, I believe," Nora answered.

"And you let them go by themselves?" Matthew stared at Grace and then at Newell.

"They're as safe here as anywhere," Newell said. "You all forget I lived not only among the Brothers as we are doing now but also among the Akassa and the Sassen. Maybe not for a long time, but long enough to lose my anxiety about them and their intentions. You will in time, too."

"I suppose," Matthew said. "Well, I guess if you trust your boys to go off alone, then I will have to trust your judgment."

"They're not alone, Papa," Grace said. "Grayson's children grew up here and won't let anything happen to our boys."

Matthew nodded and sat down. "I wonder how long before the meeting takes place."

"Take advantage of the break, Matthew," Nora said. "It's just as long a trip back as it was to get here."

CHAPTER 19

"Where is An'Kru?" Acaraho thought out loud.

"The waiting is hard," said Adia, "especially since everyone is here. But he will come; we know he will."

Acaraho got up from where he had been sitting next to her. "It is not like I want it to be over with; I fear we will never see our son again."

Adia also rose and went over to her mate, "I know. My heart is breaking too."

At that moment, a now-familiar light appeared in the corner of their quarters, followed by An'Kru's presence.

"We were just talking about you," Acaraho said as both he and Adia went over to greet their son.

"I know, Father. It is nearly time to assemble. Let all of the High Rocks and Kht'shWea be emptied; let us prepare to put in motion the last chance for those with evil in their hearts."

Every slope, every valley was filled. Never before had there been a coming together of such numbers as these. The usual conversation was stilled as if there was nothing else to conjecture. It was now finally time to find out whether what they had speculated about would happen. The youngsters all seemed subdued as if even they knew something momentous was about to take place.

An'Kru took his place at the highest point. A warm, sweet spring breeze carried the fragrance of the late spring blooms, and, high overhead, eagles rode the air currents. Life, as they had known it on Etera, would continue for a short while longer.

Closest to the front were Acaraho and his Circle of Counsel, Haan and his, and the six female Sassen Guardians. Nootau, Iella, and their son were stationed there, too, with Urilla Wuti. The Webbs and Oh'Dar and his family were standing toward the front. The other Leaders and their families were spread out through the rest of the assembly among their community members, and some of the older people sat on the soft green spring grasses.

Finally, An'Kru spoke. "I have returned, and the appointed time is nearly upon us."

To everyone's surprise, his voice carried clearly over the vast numbers assembled.

"Too long has evil preyed on the weak, helpless, and trusting. Too long have Etera's resources been squandered, poisoned, and hoarded by this evil. It is time for evil to be revealed for what it is, for masks to fall. For I have come not to bring unity to Etera, but division."

An'Kru raised his right hand high. In it was the crystal from the 'Tor Leader's staff. "This crystal was given to Wrollonan'Tor many thousands and thousands of years ago. Wrollonan'Tor gave it to Moc'Tor, who stored it safely in the 'Tor Leader's staff until the time would come when it was needed. That time is now."

An'Kru turned as the six male Sassen Guardians who had gone with Pan to Lulnomia walked up to join their mates, the six female Sassen Guardians.

Haan could not stop himself. "The Twelve? But, An'Kru, we were told the Twelve could never be together in your presence."

"When I was an offspring, that was true, for I did not have the ability to control the power that is manifested by us being together, and it would have alerted the rebels to my existence. But I am grown, and I am strong enough to harness the energy that now circulates between us and also down into the depths of the vortex beneath Kthama. It is through us that the path home to the Great Spirit will be opened to those who have lost their way."

"When the power of the vortex was released at the opening of Kthama Minor, the Sassen Guardians, as well as I, unborn, still in my mother's water cradle, were transformed at a very basic level. The tremendous release of the Aezaiteran life force transformed even the smallest pieces of our beings. The twelve Sassen you see here are pure. Perfect. Their blood has been cleared of all impurities. Every element of each of them was re-created, down to parts so small as to be invisible. This also means they can pair as they wish, and so can their offspring."

Urilla Wuti looked around to catch Khon'Tor's eye. Their conversation at the last High Council meeting had haunted her ever since that meeting— the question of whether the People were to breed with the Sassen or the Waschini or to disappear from the face of Etera. Now the Promised One was speaking of something related to their pairing problem.

"Within a few days," An'Kru continued, "I will release the power of the vortex but at a level many, many times stronger than when Kthama Minor was opened. And this same power, which transformed me and the Twelve, will affect everyone with the Aezaitera in their veins. The same perfection the Aezaitera created in me and the Twelve will also be bestowed upon all the Akassa and all the Sassen."

"You will be able to pair among yourselves without concern," An'Kru continued. "And for a time longer than you can imagine, your bodies, to the very smallest parts, will be as pure as is possible. But I caution you; in time, the negativity of this realm will cause defects to seep back into your bloodlines, so do not return to the mistakes of The Fathers-Of-Us-All and pair indiscriminately."

Khon'Tor and Hatos'Mok were pushing through the crowd to reach Urilla Wuti.

"Did you hear that?" Hatos'Mok exclaimed. "Our prayers are being answered. The People, the Sassen, will not perish from Etera!"

An'Kru paused for a few moments while those assembled murmured among themselves. The hardest of what he had to tell them was to come, and he wanted their full attention.

"In contrast to the creation of this perfection in many of you, the release of the vortex's power will cause great destruction across the face of Etera. And this must happen for all the reasons I explained before. The Waschini and their kind are close to where their destructive will can give rise to far-reaching action. If not stopped, in time, they will develop terrible weapons of destruction. Weapons that can destroy life on an unimaginable scale, even making Etera herself uninhabitable.

"So our battle to save Etera takes place in both the spiritual and physical realms. The hard shell of their arrogance—the arrogance of those who court evil in their hearts, who prey on the helpless and trusting—must be broken. They must be brought low, into a place of humility, and we must pray the Brothers will be able to reach them, to set them back on the path to their reunion with the Great Spirit."

An'Kru fell silent as if a great sadness was rising within him.

"The hope of Etera lies in the Brothers, just as it did in Moc'Tor's time. And yet, what if even this fails? What if not all of them step away from their selfish and arrogant ways? And what of the good and the kind? Those who already walk the Great Spirit's path. What of them? What peace can there be for them if they are always vulnerable to the evil others would do. Therefore, for justice to be served, a line must be drawn. For all those who wish to turn from their evil ways, ample time will be given to do so. But the day may come when no amount of evil will be tolerated on Etera."

"What does that mean?" Newell whispered to Matthew, who only shrugged in reply.

"When the Six join with me to harness the vortex below the High Rocks, the perfection and power present in my physical form will be fused with the structure of this crystal. As a result, the crystal will be transformed, similar to the way in which the granite stones in the meadow not far from here were transformed when the Sassen Guardians were created.

This crystal will be synchronized with the pure vibration of the Aezaitera that flows within my body. And, within it will rest the power to remove from Etera all that does not resonate with its vibration.

"What does that mean?" An'Kru spoke aloud the question in the minds of each one there. "If the Brothers' efforts fail, the time may come that those who refuse to change from their path of evil must be removed from Etera. At that time, the Sassen Guardians, together with the help of the Generator Stones, will have the ability to use this crystal to eliminate all evil from Etera. But that would require all twelve Sassen Guardians.

"Do not ask what will become of the evil ones; instead, pray it will never come to this end. But make no mistake, while the Great Spirit is not willing that any perish, neither will evil be permitted to prey forever on those who are seeking him."

An'Kru was standing alone on the crest, facing the listeners, so only he saw the color drain from Newell's face and tension creep into his shoulders. And how he unconsciously shook his head in disagreement with what An'Kru was saying.

"The time is drawing near. Return to your homes or take shelter among friends, but do so quickly. When night turns to day and the winds rise and the waters surge and the ground shakes and it seems the very stars will fall from the sky, you will know the moment is upon you. Until then, prepare and pray."

The crowd seemed stunned as An'Kru turned and walked out of sight. Overwhelmed by the different emotions his speech had stirred in them, all were lost in their own thoughts.

The huge crowd broke up silently.

Adia turned to Acaraho. "Our son. Our son is going to perish. It is as E'ranale told me in the Corridor; he has come to make a way for all to return to the Great Spirit. But this chance they will be given will come at great cost. And only with this cost being paid can the path be opened for them to find their way home. I knew what she meant when she said it, but I did not want to face it."

"What do we do now?" Nora asked. "It sounds as if everything is going to be destroyed. Will we be safe with the Brothers?"

"Safer than mixed in with the others of our kind," Ned added a little too quickly. "These people here have lived in harmony with each other and nature for thousands of years. They do not hoard and squander. They do not waste, leaving insufficient for the next person. I was never ashamed of my own kind until I came to live here and saw the contrast so clearly. I pray this is successful, for I do not want any to lose their lives. But I understand everything An'Kru was saying, and if it comes to the worst for our kind, then I could accept it."

"Really?" Newell frowned. "You agree that everyone who doesn't join in this prescribed way back to—wherever—should be destroyed? Wiped off the face of the planet? And how is that justice?"

"What would you do, Newell?" Ned stepped closer. "What if a student at school was bullying little Ruby? What if no matter what you did, no matter how many times you talked to the other child's parents, the bullying continued. How long would you let it go on, putting your daughter's well-being and happiness at risk? What is the justice in that? I think you very well would do the same thing An'Kru is proposing; either remove her or remove the threat. Seems perfectly fair to me."

Matthew stepped between the two men. "Everyone, calm down, please. We were tired before, now we are even more drained—and now this? The destruction of all we knew of our prior lives?"

"This isn't the life I wanted for my children—" Newell started again, but Ned cut him off.

"Are we going to go through this again?"

"No, we're not. I understand, Ned. I am just thinking out loud, and you didn't let me finish. No, this isn't the life I wanted for my children, but it is better than no life at all. If it is going to get as bad back home as it sounds, then being here is the only choice we have, and I am grateful to you for giving it to us. But that doesn't mean the idea of vast multitudes of people being whisked into oblivion by the unleashed vibration of some magic crystal handed down eons ago makes me happy."

Ned tugged the hair on the top of his head. "I'm sorry, Newell. Father is right; we are all too tired for any conversation of this type. Think about what you want to do and let me know. Whatever you both decide, I'll stand with you. If you want to stay here until this is all over, among these people here, that is fine. If you want to go back to Chief Kotori's village and weather it out there, I'll take you back."

Then he took Awantia's hand and led her away.

Ned turned to his life-walker. "You didn't say anything."

"What could I possibly add to what the Promised One said? But I will do as you wish, my love, as my place is wherever you decide to be. If you wish to remain here, we will remain here. It is as you said."

Three weeks later, all krell broke loose.

CHAPTER 20

An'Kru and the six male Sassen Guardians stood in the meadow above Kthama. One by one, each of the Sassen Guardians took his place in front of a Generator stone. With the crystal in his right hand, An'Kru walked into the middle of the circle they had formed. As he had instructed them, they began the ancient prayers, those used to invoke the Rah-hora. After a while, An'Kru lifted the crystal high overhead and, at the same time, reached with his essence down into the molten core of Etera, directly connecting with the Aezaiteran force that was waiting for his call.

A force like that which had created Etera herself screamed up from below, borne on a blinding white light. Night became day, and the ground began to shake and roll. Every creature sought shelter. High winds picked up all around Etera as the magnetic streams deep within her began shifting. Flexing. It was as if the Great Spirit had taken in a mighty breath, pulling them together. All the people of Etera felt the effects of the power at play. Leaves blew everywhere, and branches and even trees were tossed around as easily as a youngster might toss a ball. Elsewhere, the Waschini buildings creaked and wobbled before splintering apart and collapsing. Families ran out into the dark-now-daylight just in time to see nearly everything around them turned to rubble.

Along Etera's shorelines, the waters receded, exposing great expanses of land never before seen. Mountain tops crumbled, and boulders crashed down, taking other rocks and debris with them.

Whatever force had breathed in the magnetic web, then released it. And another wave of destruction rolled across Etera. The receding waters gathered into giant waves which looked nearly to touch the clouds above, returning to shore with devastating effects. Many ships were tossed along the shoreline, others were carried far out to sea. Docks were destroyed, shipments of goods scattered everywhere, their crates broken open.

The white light bursting forth from the vortex below Kthama burned even brighter and then quickly collapsed back on itself, vanishing once more into the bowels of Etera. The winds died, and darkness returned. The six Sassen swore later that they had heard words spoken just beyond the cacophony and carried away by the winds, *"Kah-Sol 'Rin."*

It is done.

Having been forewarned, the people of the Brotherhood calmly waited it out. For the most part, the Sassen and the Akassa had returned to their communities. Some of the Brothers had taken shelter at the Akassa cave systems nearest them, while others returned to their own villages. They had all taken An'Kru's assurances and nursed them, keeping them alive deep within their hearts. Whereas many would forever see this as a time of destruction and chaos, the Brothers, the People, and the Sassen saw it for what it was—a time of hope for all Etera's people.

Within their living quarters in Kthama, Adia felt her heart fill with peace. Her son An'Kru walked Etera no more, but he had fulfilled what he was born to do, and she knew she would see him again. She knew this life was just a passageway, a first step in the many levels of return to the one who loved them most of all. Each step of her journey had led her to this place of peace. And now, surprisingly, her happiness knew no limits.

What would she do now? Just what she had said she would do so many, many years ago when asked the same thing by the then Second Chief Is'Taqa. She would do as she had always done. She would live her life and find joy and happiness wherever she could. And she would help others also to do so. And she would become the teacher her mother had equipped her to become.

As Pan was walking with young An'Kru through the halls of Lulnomia to the living quarters he and Nootau shared, a great peace passed over her. Somehow she knew her father had been freed from the vortex and was now reunited with her mother, E'ranale. Tears filled her eyes.

Little An'Kru looked up at Pan and asked, "Did you feel that?"

"I did," she smiled, looking down at her young charge, the hope of Etera.

"What happened?" he asked further.

"What had to, An'Kru. What had to. Come, now, time for bed. Tomorrow we must continue your training."

A few days later, after the excitement had died down and the task of clearing the debris from around the High Rocks was complete, Adia and

Acaraho went out for a walk. They followed a bend and stopped.

"An'Kru?" Adia squeaked out. "I had not thought of this, that you have returned? But your body was destroyed? Is this possible?"

"I thought you would be overjoyed to see me," An'Kru laughed. "Not perplexed at how it could be possible."

"Well, I am!" Acaraho came out of his wonderment and embraced his son. "And so is your mother; she is just very confused."

"I do not understand," Adia said.

"It is not something to understand, Mother. It is something to accept."

"Oh, my heart is filled with joy; it is, it is!" And she ran forward to embrace her son. "Have you come to stay with us? To help us move forward into what awaits?"

"No. I have done what I came here to do. I only came back this one last time to bring a gift."

"A gift for us? You are alive. What better gift could there possibly be to give us?" Acaraho asked.

"Not both of you, Father. You. I came to bring you a gift."

In the next moment, Acaraho was standing with Adia in a place far more beautiful than he could have imagined. By Adia's descriptions, he knew it must be the Corridor. It was as she had said; everything— even down to the air he was breathing—was alive and filled with joy. He struggled to find words to think about what he was experiencing.

"It is just like home, only more— Everything," he said.

"That is because what you know as life on Etera is but a pale reflection of your true home," An'Kru explained. "As if looking at yourself in the still waters or the polished stone of Etera's living quarter's walls. Only you did not know that until I brought you here to experience how much more there is to life than you have known it to be. But, even more than that, there is something else I want to give you."

An'Kru gestured to the left. A couple stood as if waiting to speak with him.

"Are these—? Are you—?" Acaraho was overwhelmed.

The two stepped closer.

The female spoke first. "Acaraho, yes, we are your parents. We have come to help you find peace about your past. We know you found a way to push it far down within you and rise to excellence in spite of what happened. But it is time for the questions to be answered, and only we can do that for you."

"Your mother and I were deeply in love," Acaraho's father said with a loving glance at his mate. "There was not a moment I did not want to be with her. I would have done anything for her; she had only to ask. But as it was, your mother had an independent streak. Still does. And she insisted on spearfishing no matter the weather. It was on a particularly cold winter morning that she insisted on trying her luck."

His mother continued the story. "It was foolish. I was so bent on having fish for dinner that I did not take precautions. As a result, I slipped on the river-bank and fell into the icy waters. Your father saw me go in, and he immediately went in to save me. But the waters were too turbulent and too cold, and we both perished. Oh, how it broke our hearts to leave you, Acaraho."

"You were left alone on the snowy riverbank," continued his father. "Unattended. It was a miracle you did not drown or freeze to death. But you did not. And soon, others found you. It was a terrible tragedy. Yes, there were relatives who wanted to raise you, but after much heart-wrenching discussion, it was decided you would be better off being raised in another community. One where the tragedy would not haunt you. One that would not cast a shadow of despair over your entire life. So you were taken to the High Rocks and raised by your cousin Awan's family."

Acaraho nodded. "You are right. It would have scarred me to grow up with such grief. I have seen what my beloved Adia has borne, her mother having died after giving birth. You were wise to spare me that. It was better I did not know what happened until now."

"You were too young to remember. At least, we prayed you were."

"I do not remember any of it. I have only a faint memory of being outside and being cold and someone finding me. I stored away nothing else about it."

"This, this is healing." Acaraho turned to An'Kru. "Thank you for bringing me here. Thank you for answering my lingering questions about my mysterious start in life."

"You are more than welcome, Father," An'Kru said. "But far more than the experience of this place and of hearing your parents' story, I hope what you take with you is that love never dies. We never die. Just as love goes on, so our lives go on. Our bodies carry us on our journey for a while, but eventually, they have served their purpose, and our true essence moves on. Just as you see here. Our true home is not on Etera or even here in the Corridor. And as wonderful as it is here, there are even greater joys and deeper beauties to be experienced as we continue on our path back to the arms of the Great Spirit."

EPILOGUE

The winds died down, the tumult passed, and the Six knew An'Kru was no more. Thord looked into the center of their circle to see the crystal lying there. He stepped over and stared at it. Phenomenally beautiful but radiating ice cold as it shone and coursed with power. Mist rose up from where it lay in the warm grass.

But now what? Would those who had strayed from connection with the Great Spirit humble themselves and be willing to learn a new way of living from the Brothers? One of gratitude and helping others? Great struggles lay ahead of them all, but far more was at stake than a new way of living. The Brothers would do their best to reach them, but in the end, it would be each soul's personal decision whether to choose the path toward the Great Spirit.

If not, the crystal would be there, waiting.

An'Kru's words echoed in Thord's mind. *We should pray it never happens that you must use it.*

AN INTERVIEW WITH THE CHARACTERS, WHO WERE SITTING AROUND WAITING TO SPEAK WITH ME.

Newell: I take back everything I said at the end of Series One, Book Thirteen.

LR: What was it you said?

Newell: I said that whatever was coming next, it couldn't be any more alarming than what we just went through. I was wrong.

Ned: Yes, and I remember, Leigh, you had a peculiar smile on your face when he said that. And then you said we never know what is around the corner. Well, that was certainly true.

LR: Who would have thought that not only both of you but also your families would now be living safely among the People?

Newell, whose voice trailed off: I suppose. That they're safe, that is—

LR: What's wrong, Newell? Still unsure about life among the Akassa?

Newell: Oh, I believe I will adjust to that, as will my family. But listening to what An'Kru said before he unleashed the power of the vortex, the future is very uncertain.

LR: The future is always uncertain. It is only our need to believe it is predictable which keeps us from facing that fact.

(Newell gave me a look that told me I wasn't really helping.)

Oh'Dar: I can't help but look back from where this all started. Look how much we have all been through.

Adia: You especially, my beloved son. How brave you were to leave the only home you had ever known to try to find your Waschini blood. And look what has come of it; a true Brotherhood has been formed, one that includes all of us. The People, the Sassen, the Brothers, and the Waschini.

Oh'Dar: It was my grandparents who were brave. Yes, I left my life at Kthama, but in the end, I had the luxury of going back and forth between my two lives. With no hope of ever going back, they gave up the only life they knew to come here.

Acise, leaning in and taking Oh'Dar's hands in hers: I know how much you miss them.

Oh'Dar: My head knows they are still alive in the Corridor, reunited with everyone they loved and lost, but my heart aches not to have them still here with me. Here with us.

Acaraho: Yes, you will see them again, son. I know this for a fact.

Eitel: So what happens next, Leigh?

Before speaking, I couldn't hold back a sigh: The question I keep getting is, how long will Series Three be? At present, this will be the last book for a while. I know, I know; I keep saying that, and then I keep writing! But this is a good place to pause it, and if I didn't write any more in the story, I think it can rest at this point and be a satisfactory ending place.

Eitel: But Paldar'Krah and I have just been paired. We want offling to raise! There is still so much to happen!

LR: That will always be true, Eitel. There will always be the question of *What If*. What if Louis is able to find Oh'Dar? Will Louis finally take revenge on him? Will the wayward listen to the Brothers and find their way back to the path home? I am sure Oh'Dar, Acise, and others wonder what prompted An'Kru to take I'Layah, Tsonakwa, and Ashoka to the Corridor. What can their future hold that would lead him to do that? What about the crystal, perfected when the vortex fused An'Kru's life force within it? Will it ever have to be used? Ahhhh, the answers to those questions and more may be a story for another time. But for now, I need to switch gears.

Ned: What does that mean — to *switch gears*?

LR: That's a phrase from my time. It means to go in another direction. You see, when I first decided to self-publish, I had a book nearly written. But when I talked to the publishing coach I was working with, he convinced me to go with another idea I had. I had a nearly completed book at hand, but he convinced me to go with my utterly different concept. One for which I hadn't even put pen to paper and which, of course, turned out to be *The Etera Chronicles*.

So during all this time, the book I wrote so many years ago has been sitting, waiting for me to come back to it. I believe that book's time is now. I hope the readers of The Etera Chronicles will come along on that journey with me.

Adia: I understand, Leigh. We are in a good place, really. There is hope for Etera. The Brothers have been saved from being decimated by the Waschini. Almost all the rebels from Zuenerth have been reunited with the other Mothoc at Lulnomia. Eitel was rescued. Nootau and Iella have their son to raise. Khon'Tor and Tehya are safe and sound and have their family, too.

Nora: Wait, though. I don't understand. What happens to us while Leigh decides whether or not to bring us back to life?

LR: Oh, Nora, you and the others will live on in the hearts of all the readers. You will continue to have adventures of your own in their imaginations and in mine. Nothing created can ever really be destroyed. If I continue the story, it will merely be like calling actors back to the stage!

Nora: I understand that; I've seen a play before!

I was glad to see a smile on her face.

Khon'Tor had been quiet until now.

Khon'Tor: When I look back, I see how my path changed me in ways I needed to be changed. I would not have the wonderful life I have now if I had not been through the hard times I created for myself.

The hard times open our eyes to our mistakes. They show us where we have lost our way, and then faith helps us find our way back.

LR: What about you, Pan? How are you feeling?

Pan: It has been a hard road, as Khon'Tor said. But here I am now, reunited with my beloved and my brother, Dak'Tor. And most of the Mothoc. What a dream come true; I could not have seen it coming.

Dak'Tor: I always wondered how far your abilities extended, Pan. So you don't know everything? What about Wrollonan'Tor?

Pan: No. Guardians are not all-powerful. We are not all-knowing. Those abilities belong only to the One-Who-Is-Three. But I agree with you, Adia; this is a good resting point. I have peace in my soul. An'Kru's sacrifice freed my father from the vortex, and he and my mother were reunited in the Corridor. I felt it. It was the most intense release of love, relief, gratitude, and sheer joy I've ever felt.

Iella spoke up: If no one else is going to ask it, I will. What will happen with An'Kru now? He is still at Lulnomia with you, Pan, still a young offspring.

Pan: I will continue his training. He will grow up at Lulnomia with Nootau. But what happens after that, I do not know.

Iella: What do you mean you do not know? He will grow up, and he will come back and bring Nootau home to me, open the vortex, and we will pick up our lives and go on as we are now.

LR: Oh boy. We're down the rabbit hole now.

Pan: Leigh is right. You see, the future An'Kru came back in time to stop will now never happen. The Brothers will *not* be all but annihilated. The Waschini and their like will, hopefully, *not* develop weapons capable of destroying Etera. The rebel Mothoc will *not* now continue with their determination to destroy the Akassa and Sassen. So, there will be no need for An'Kru to return here to us in what would be the past. There will be no catastrophes to prevent.

Adia: So you are saying—are you saying An'Kru will not have to come back as he did and sacrifice himself? He could continue living in the future that is now yet to happen?

Pan: It is possible. He still lives at Lulnomia. He will continue to grow and develop, but there will be no need to open the vortex, sacrifice himself to free my father, and fuse his Aezaitera to the crystal's structure. It has already been done. *Kah–Sol 'Rin.*

Matthew: Stop, please; I can't follow this. I'd rather leave it all here. Let us wait and see what happens if you decide to write more stories about us, Leigh. Please?

I couldn't help but chuckle. We've been on a long journey together, you, me, and our readers. All starting with the question *What If?*

What if...I could write an engaging story filled with characters readers could relate to, care about, and even hate. Characters like you, with whom the reader would be able to suffer through the hard times in life's valleys and rejoice in the victorious mountain-top experiences life also brings. Who can take the readers along with them on your path, let them feel for you, with you.

But I meant *The Etera Chronicles* to be more than an entertaining story.

I intended for your stories to help our readers when they are perhaps lonely, afraid, overwhelmed, discouraged, or at the end of their rope. I intended for them to help with looking for answers when there seem to be none. To help when nothing about life seems to make sense—during the moments of *What is the point of all this? Doesn't anyone care?* To help others when they are reaching for faith that seems out of reach.

I wrote *The Etera Chronicles* to share some of the ideas that helped me by weaving them into the interesting tale of a young Healer's search for the same things we all hold dear. **Love, belonging, justice, faith,** and **truth**.

At some point, I'll be gone, and my hope is that *The Etera Chronicles* and all of us will live on in the minds of our readers.

And someday in the future, someone will experience your struggles, triumphs, valleys, and mountaintops and think, "Gosh, *that story helped me*."

PLEASE READ

Dear Readers,

I believe Book Two: *Bloodlines* was a little tough on some of you. I am sorry for that. I am hoping *Intervention* has healed any distress I inflicted. I was taught that people read for the emotional experience, to feel something, but I guess that for some people, I overshot the mark on that one. I hope I have made it up to you in *Intervention*.

I want you to know that I didn't write the events at the end of *Bloodlines* to traumatize you, and I didn't put them in simply for the sake of drama. There is a message I wanted to relay, and I hope that when you read the beginning of *Intervention,* you understood why I wrote what I wrote. There was always what I hoped was a comforting intention and message behind it.

What is Your *Why*?

Whatever we do, if it takes any effort at all, we have to have a driving reason for doing it. Our *Why*. For some non-fiction authors, it is about writing a book related to their primary business, a way to reach their customers or clients to promote their area of expertise.

For some, it is the creative process itself. Others have a memoir they want to share or someone they want to honor. I wanted to help people who were perhaps having a hard time getting through this thing we call life. Some people have very tragic circumstances, huge wounds they bear. But for many of us, the difficulties we have weathered are not front-page-worthy. They are easy to dismiss as, *well, buck up, buttercup; that's just life*. But it doesn't mean that whatever hurts we suffered didn't take their toll on us and that we don't have the right to receive help and heal from them. It's not a contest. Just because one person's experiences seem harder than another's doesn't dismiss the truth of our pain and struggle. Not all problems in life barrel over us like a tsunami. A constant drip of water can cause great damage over time.

As an Introvert, I lived in my inner world. A world of "*What If?*" It was my sanctuary, my safe place. During those hard childhood days, I would console myself with the thought that in a few hours, I would be back home safe in my bed; in my imaginary world of "*What If?*".

I made many mistakes growing up, and as an adult, I still do. I'm still learning. I hope learning isn't over until life is. I hope we are on a lifelong search for meaning and answers. But the point is that my questioning of why things are and why things happen as they do brought ideas that felt like answers, and that helped me. The answers didn't take all the problems away, but they helped me keep going. Much as I was comforted as a child by my knowledge that once I got through the day, I would be safe in my bed, and nothing could hurt me, making it possible to keep moving forward.

To Keep Moving Forward...

That's it, isn't it? To keep moving forward. But to what? Or where? Or to *Whom*? Having read the Etera Chronicles, I think you know very well what my answer is.

Blessings —
    Leigh

ACKNOWLEDGMENTS

To my loved ones, my friends, and all my dear readers, thank you.

Made in the USA
Las Vegas, NV
20 February 2024

86028828R00225